D1525065

Ah Q AND OTHERS

魯迅選集 *Ah* Q AND OTHERS

SELECTED STORIES OF *Lusin*

TRANSLATED BY CHI-CHEN WANG

GREENWOOD PRESS, PUBLISHERS
WESTPORT, CONNECTICUT

TO MY BROTHER CHI-KUEH

born 1907 and killed in the bombing of Chungking
in the spring of 1940, just as a new Road to Life opened
up before him with its promise of the freedom and independence to which he was stranger all his life, I
dedicate these translations of Lusin whom we both
admired above all other Chinese writers, ancient and
modern, and who did more than any one else to clear
the Road to Life of the weeds of tradition and of the
traps and pitfalls that man-eating men set for the
young, the unwary, and the helpless.

Introduction

TO the average American who gets his ideas about China from the movies and detective stories, China means Charlie Chan, Fu Manchu, and other nameless but equally familiar figures, it means chop suey, and Chinatown shop fronts covered with picturesque but meaningless hieroglyphics. Upon this fantastic hodgepodge of inventions and half-truths, sympathetic writers have in recent years superimposed a sentimental montage of a land where peace and tradition reign, where every earth-turning peasant is unobtrusively a philosopher. Now, sympathetic and flattering as this picture is, it has brought China no nearer to the American people and made China no more real. The fact is that there is no short cut to mutual respect and understanding between peoples any more than there is between individuals, the claims of the experts in how to perpetuate the honeymoon and how to win friends to the contrary notwithstanding.

One of the best ways of arriving at a real understanding of a country is undoubtedly through its literature, the richest, the most revealing and the most imperishable of national heritages. In these stories of Lusin, acclaimed the greatest of modern Chinese writers in his own country, the reader will be able to get glimpses of China through the eyes of one of its keenest and most original minds. Here he will find none of the considered sympathetic treatment at the bottom of which often lurks condescension; he will encounter no *apologia* that is invariably the earmark of Ah Q-ism and a sense of inferiority. Lusin was not constrained to be polite because he wrote primarily for a Chinese audience; he was not constrained to gloss over or to explain away China's sore spots or disguise her weaknesses because he had faith in China and was conscious of her strength.

The reader will find here not only the plainest speaking yet to come out of China, but some of the very plainest speaking anywhere since Swift hurled upon us the epithet of Yahoo and pronounced us the most despicable and unteachable of all God's creatures. Above all, he will find in Lusin, *for the first time in all Chinese history,* a full embodiment and expression of that quality of indignation and that spirit of revolt which we usually associate with the European temperament and without which it is impossible to achieve freedom and progress. At first glance it may seem far-fetched to link Lusin's indignation with the magnificent struggle for freedom that China has been carrying on against Japan. Nevertheless, just as the spirit of acceptance and resignation which until recently dominated China was responsible for her submission to the rule of alien dynasties in the past, so is the new spirit of indignation and revolt which found its fullest expression in Lusin responsible for her determination to carry on her battle for freedom.

Lusin was, indeed, the spiritual offspring of the West, though he had no first-hand contact with Western civilization. It was the spirit of revolt in Western literature that encouraged his rebel heart to speak out. It was the realistic and psychological fiction of the West that brought home to him that fiction could be made an instrument of social criticism and reform. It was, finally, by contrast with the Western temperament that he was able to see the weakness in the Chinese character and to apply to it the outspoken criticism it had so long needed. In him the modern spirit first matured in a Chinese mind and through him and others like him became the dominant spirit of the Chinese nation. In Lusin that spirit manifested itself in a revolt against and denunciation of "man-eating men"; in the Chinese people as a whole it manifested itself in the conception of nationalism. He represented the first real break from traditionalism that any Chinese has been able to achieve.

These stories of Lusin will not, therefore, interest those who think of China as a dead civilization with only a past to recommend it; they will interest even less those to whom China represents an idea and a perfection either because they happen to be enchanted with the grandeur and symmetry of the palace architecture of Peking or because they so thoroughly enjoyed what to them was the Chinese way of life during their stay in that land of idle and yet happy masters and of toiling and even happier coolies and servants. They may even shock and displease those Occidentals and Chinese who make it their profession to tell the Western world what a wonderful country China is (or was, if they happen to be those who pine for the olden times) and what a happy people the Chinese are in spite of their squalor and disease.

These translations are addressed, rather, to those whose interest in humanity goes deeper than its outward trappings and who are tired of the unreal and impersonal representations of life that the average admirer of China finds so charming in traditional Chinese literature and art. To them these stories of modern China will come like a breath of fresh air that sweeps across a putrid swamp, cleansing and revitalizing its atmosphere, and they will welcome Lusin as a symbol of China's awakening and as a promise that China will play its part, for better or for worse, in the unceasing drama of humanity.

Lusin's real name was Chou Shu-jen.[1] He was born on September 25, 1881, in Shao-hsing (the "city of S——" in several of his stories), Chekiang province. At the time, China was very much as it had always been, self-satisfied and unwilling to learn in spite of the shocking revelations of the country's weakness in the debacles of Opium War in 1841 and the Anglo-French occupation of Peking in 1860. Attempts at reform along Western lines were sporadic and half-hearted: for example, in 1876 China sent abroad the first group of students to study Western methods of war and technology; at home, that same year, she reclaimed and destroyed a product of Western engineering—the country's first railroad, a ten-mile stretch between Shanghai and Woosung that had been built by British concessionaires. Throughout these years the country as a whole was as complacent as if nothing had happened; the Chinese took comfort in the Ah Q-ish delusion that though China was defeated in war she was nevertheless superior to the barbarians from the West and that in the end the superiority of her civilization would enable her to prevail by her famous process of assimilation.

Lusin belonged, therefore, to the older generation. During his early years, his family was well-to-do and he was prepared for the examinations as were most young men in similar circumstances. Family reverses, however, made it necessary for him to seek admission into one of those much despised

[1] Lusin is also given as Lu Hsin or Lu Hsün. The last is the correct rendering as far as the Wade system of transliteration is concerned, but the first is more pronounceable for English readers and was the author's own choice. For a more detailed account of Lusin's life see Wang, "Lusin: a Chronological Record," in *China Institute Bulletin*, Jan., 1939.

"foreign" schools established by the government. These schools were not only free of tuition but also provided students with room and board and a small amount of spending money. In 1898 Lusin entered the Naval Academy-at Nanking and later the College of Railway and Mines in the same city. Here for the first time he came into contact with Western learning. He was particularly excited by Yen Fu's translation of Huxley's *Evolution and Ethics* which appeared in 1898. Early in 1902 he went to Japan on a government scholarship, and after studying the Japanese language in a preparatory school in Tokyo, entered the Sendai Medical College in 1904. But he did not finish his medical course. The apathy of the Chinese in general toward the Russo-Japanese War (which was fought, it will be recalled, on Chinese soil) disgusted him and made him realize that it was just as important to stir a people out of its mental and spiritual lethargy as to cure its physical ills. He decided to give up the study of medicine and to devote his life to literature, which was, he was convinced, the best means of awakening the Chinese people.

His own preference had always been, as a matter of fact, literary matters. He was an omnivorous reader even as a child and had the industrious habit of the Chinese scholar of copying out extensive passages from the books he read, sometimes entire works that were not easily available or which he could not afford. After his arrival in Japan he devoted all his spare moments to reading Japanese translations of important European works, especially history, philosophy, and literature.

But he was, unfortunately, too far ahead of his time. His generation as a whole were still under the delusion that a new political window dressing was all that was necessary for the salvation of China, just as the generation before had labored under the delusion that China was superior to the West in everything but methods of warfare.

The students at Tokyo in those days were mostly interested in subjects that led to profitable jobs when they went back to China—in politics, law, police administration, and more rarely science and technology. They could not see why Lusin chose to follow so useless a pursuit as literature. His efforts to launch in Tokyo a literary magazine to be known as _New Life_ ended in failure and his essays calling attention to the spiritual aspects of Western civilization went unnoticed.

Undoubtedly, however, these essays will be regarded as the most important documents in the history of the intellectual revolution in China. For here we have the first indication of a Chinese appreciation of the spiritual aspects of European civilization. The first essay was an exposition of the philosophy of Haeckel; the second a survey of the history of Western science. The third is perhaps the most important, because it furnishes a clue to Lusin's fundamental intellectual skepticism and sets forth at the same time Lusin's fundamental belief in the fostering and development of individual genius. Having outlined China's complacency in the past, due to her cultural isolation, and her rude awakening after defeat in the hands of the foreign powers, he goes on to point out that materialism, industrial development, and political democracy—panaceas recommended by reformers of the time— were by no means the ultimate or the currently accepted philosophies of the West, but only phases in its historical development. Since civilization is built upon the past, he argues, it is always in a state of flux and always subject to change and improvement. The materialistic character of nineteenth-century civilization in the West represented, he tells us, an extreme reaction to the life-denying tendencies of the Middle Ages which began with modern science, just as the rule of the majority was an extreme reaction toward the doctrine of the divine right of kings. These reactions, he declares, had gone too far, as reactions have a way of doing and must be rectified and remedied. In the course of his exposition he cites extensively Nietzsche, Schopenhauer, Ibsen, Stirner and other rebel spirits of the nineteenth century and cautioned the Chinese not to follow too blindly the superficial aspects of Western civilization.

In the fourth essay Lusin surveys at some length what he calls the power of Mara poetry, after the Hindu god of destruction and rebellion. Here we find, of course, the classic exposition of the spirit of man in terms of Apollonian conservatism and Dionysian rebellion, popularized a generation back by Nietzsche and his followers. Here we find also his admonition to his fellow country men that the way to raise the prestige of their country was by new achievements, not by boasting about its past.

These essays were published in obscure student magazines. Not only did they meet with no response at the time, it is doubtful that more than a handful of people have read them to this day, though they were included with others in *Tomb*, published in 1926. For one thing they were not only in the old literary style but also in a rather archaic literary style; but the real reason is that even to this day they represent a dissenting minority view.

Thus it was in a disillusioned mood that he went back to China in 1909. He taught for a while at Hangchow and then at his native city Shao-hsing. His experience as a teacher could not have been a happy one as reflected in "A Hermit at Large." The achievement of the political revolution of 1911

only depressed him further, for he found, as did the villagers
of Wei in "Our Story of Ah Q," that things were much the
same as they had always been except in name. The worst of it
was that his experience in Tokyo and Shao-hsing had made
him aware of his own limitations and convinced him that he
was not one of those born leaders "at whose call people
gathered like clouds."

In 1912 he accepted a post as counsellor in the Ministry of
Education in the Provisional Government at Nanking and
went to Peking in the same year when the seat of the government was transferred to the latter city. There in a secluded
room in the Guild House of his native Chekiang he sought
escape and forgetfulness in China's past. The Chinese scholar
in him asserted itself and for the next five or six years he
occupied himself in reading and literary research and in
collecting and transcribing rubbings of ancient monuments.
Lusin was always modest and self-deprecatory about these
literary efforts, though his achievements were considerable
and included the first and so far still the best history of Chinese fiction. He called this preoccupation his own form of
opium smoking.

In 1918, however, he was awakened out of his "opium
dreams" and dragged from seclusion by his friend Ch'ien
Hsuan-t'ung, who was actively associated with Hu Shih and
Ch'en Tu-hsiu on the *New Youth* which launched the literary revolution. Lusin's mood and the skepticism with
which he viewed the prospects of the movement can best be
told in his own words.

"Supposing [he is speaking to Ch'ien] there is an iron chamber
which has absolutely no window or door and is impossible to
break down. Supposing there are many people fast asleep in it who
are gradually being suffocated to death. Since they will pass from

sleep to death, they will not experience the fear and agony of approaching death. But you people start shouting; you rouse the few who are not sound asleep, only to make them suffer the agony of death. Do you think you are doing them a kindness?"

"But if a few should wake up [Ch'ien replied], you cannot say there is absolutely no hope of breaking down the iron chamber."

He was right. Although I had my own ideas about the prospects of the future, I had no right to dash to pieces the hopes of more sanguine spirits. I must not try to convince them that they were wrong, since they were happier in thinking they were right. Therefore, I ended by promising to write something for them.

The first piece he wrote for the *New Youth* was "The Diary of a Madman" which may be regarded as the overture and finale of all his writings. In it he branded the whole of Chinese history as a record of man-eating though it is apparently and ostensibly a history of the triumph of "benevolence and righteousness." He pronounced his everlasting curse upon man-eating men and insisted that the fact that "it has always been so" does not mean that "it is as it should be." He would not resign himself to the various forms of man-eating and accept them as "necessary evils" inherent in "human nature" (the most damnable admission of our impotence and defeatism). He refused to change the subject, as the wiser men in China and everywhere do, and talk about more pleasant things, such "eternal values" or the "moonlight and breezes" of traditional Chinese literature.

But Lusin was neither a reformer with pet schemes nor an opportunist leader riding the "wave" of his time. He had too much intellectual honesty for the one and too much moral integrity for the other. He was primarily a humanitarian to whom everything seems pale and unimportant in the face of hunger and starvation, and all talk about first principles and eternal values idle and heartless in the face of man's inhumanity to man. It was because of this fundamental humanism in him that he took to his "opium smoking" in his despair, for in the last analysis the drunkard is a better man, morally, than those who try to justify the sorry parts that they have to play in society. It was this humanism, too, that made him, once he found an opportunity to command an audience, the ruthless critic dedicated to the unpleasant but necessary task of reminding us of our man-eating past and our man-eating tendencies of the present, and the relentless iconoclast who devoted his life to the destruction of old superstitions and ancient hypocrisies that tend to perpetuate the institution of man-eating. He never made any attempt to formulate and express his own beliefs regarding man's ultimate future. When pressed to do so, he invariably gave the laconic answer that he was only interested in the immediate objectives that must be achieved before everything else. These are, he said, (1) the right to life, (2) the right to food and shelter, and (3) the right to the unlimited development of the individual. "Everything that stands in the way of these three objectives," he declared, "must be trampled under foot and stamped out, whether it be ancient faiths or modern fads." The only elaboration that he would make on these three objectives was that by life he did not mean mere existence, by food and shelter he did not mean unnecessary luxuries, and by the free development of the individual he did not mean unwarranted licence.

If we bear these three touchstones constantly in mind as Lusin did, all the apparent inconsistencies in his writings will disappear and we shall understand his apparent quarrelsomeness. We'll understand why he quarreled with the "new gentry"—well-fed and well-washed students who returned from England and America with their "gentlemanly" ideas of moderation and compromise—as well as with the old gentry—men who had seen better times and would preserve the "national essence"; why he directed his scorn and irony against the art-for-art's-sakers as much as he did against the old "moonlight and breezes" school, though the former wrote in the new *pai hua* medium; why he made impartial fun of new slogans and ancient shibboleths; and why, finally, he joined the ranks of the Leftist writers himself when the only hope of progress and national salvation seemed to lie in that direction.

The most consistent object of Lusin's well-directed blows was naturally the national essence or heritage of the old gentry. In volume after volume of his notes and comments he exposed one by one what the reactionaries really mean by their precious national heritage. He was better qualified to expose the so-called "national medicine," the "national art of self-defense" (the hocus-pocus of the Boxers that precipitated the allied expedition of 1900), and "national learning" (which found sanction and inspiration in European "Sinology")—he was better qualified for this task than anyone else not only because of the "sharpness" of his pen, but also because he was himself a Chinese scholar without a peer and knew what he was talking about better than most of the reactionaries who made so much of their Chinese learning.

What is this national essence? [Lusin asks.] On the face of it it must mean something that one nation alone possesses, something which no other country can boast of, something, in other words, peculiar to the nation in question. But something that is peculiar may not necessarily be good. The question is, why should it be preserved.

For instance, a man who has a wart on his face or a boil on his forehead is different from one not so afflicted, and his wart or boil may be regarded as his "essence." But to my mind it is better for him to do away with this kind of peculiarity and be like others.

If you say that our national essence is both peculiar and good, then why is it that conditions are as terrible as they are, causing the new school to shake their heads and the old school to heave long sighs?

If you say that conditions are what they are because we have not been able to preserve our national essence, because we have been contaminated by the West, then things ought to have been different before the foreigners came, when the entire country was permeated with this national essence. Why is it, then, that we have had such periods of chaos and disaster as the Spring and Autumn period, the age of the Warring States, and of the Sixteen Kingdoms, that caused the ancients also to heave long sighs?

A friend of mine has once said: "Before we can be expected to preserve our national essence, our national essence must have qualities that will preserve us."

One of the trump cards that advocators of the national heritage have often played (and still play) is that China's national heritage must be good since even foreigners are interested in it. They point to the European Sinologists, for instance, in support of the revival of textual criticism and archaeological research. Lusin's retort was that it was one thing to study antiquities but another thing to "preserve" them.

There are some foreigners [he says] who want China to remain forever a huge curio for their enjoyment and delectation. This is, of course, detestable, but not so strange, for they are, after all, foreigners. What I can't understand is that there should be Chinese who, not satisfied with remaining curios themselves, want to encourage youths and infants to remain curios for the enjoyment or delectation of the foreigners. I wonder what sorts of hearts they have! . . . The advocates of the preservation of ancient ways must be familiar with ancient books. Surely they cannot condemn as bestial "Lin Hui, who threw aside a jade worth a thousand pieces of gold in order to rescue an infant." If not, then what do they say to abandoning the infants in order to rescue a piece of jade?

Nor would Lusin accept as valid evidence of the superiority of the Chinese national essence the testimony of foreign visitors who find the "Chinese way of life" so delightful because to them it means an infinite amount of leisure, interminable banquets, and an endless flow of languid and meaningless observations on what they call life and the art of living. To Lusin such banquets in the midst of famine and starvation are feasts of the man-eating men, as damnable as the actual cases of cannibalism reported with shocking frequency from the worst famine areas. "Only those foreigners who are qualified to attend such man-eating banquets and who nevertheless curse present conditions in China are men of feeling, men that we should admire," he declared, and not those who relish them.

Nor did he share the views of the Bertrand Russell school of visitors, which have become very popular of late, who, impressed by the apparent good humor of their sweating ricksha coolies and sedan bearers, call China an "artist nation" and attribute to the Chinese people that quality of "instinctive happiness" which makes it possible for them to lead a "life full of enjoyment" in spite of their squalor and misery. Lusin's retort to this was that "if the sedan carriers are not so smiling and contented in their attitude toward those who ride in sedan chairs, China would not be what it is today." Like Hu Shih, Lusin does not see anything spiritual in famine and disease and misery. As Hu Shih has eloquently argued in the symposium *Whither Mankind*, the civilization that substitutes the machine and the automobile for human labor is infinitely more spiritual than civilizations that still use men as beasts of burden.

It was this docile and smiling acceptance that made it impossible for the Chinese masses to be anything more than slaves. That they were as a matter of fact willing slaves, Lusin pointed out again and again; they were only unhappy during periods of war and dynastic change when it was not clear whose slaves they were, when they were slaughtered first by one set and then another set of masters. It was this spirit of resignation that we find reflected in the famous lines:

> I'd rather be a dog in time of peace and security
> Than a man in days of war and separation.

The Bertrand Russell school of "instinctive happiness" might not have been shopping for a subject race when they praised the Chinese for that quality, but that is how it has worked out in practice.

Effective and important as are these notes and comments in which Lusin gave expression to his indignations and protests, he will probably be remembered for his short stories. These notes and comments were for the most part running commentaries on the contemporary scene, prompted by things he had seen or heard or read in the daily press. A great deal of this material would require extensive notes by the future generation of Sinologists before it is intelligible.

Of his stories, "Our Story of Ah Q" will stand out not only as his most important work but also as the most important single contribution to Chinese literature since the literary revolution, for in this story Lusin succeeded in translating his diagnosis of China's fundamental weakness in terms that everyone can understand. Briefly, Ah Q is the personification of two of the most despicable traits in human nature: the tendency to rationalize things to our own supposed advantage and the cowardly habit of turning upon those weaker than ourselves after we have been abused by those stronger than we are. "When a man of courage is outraged," he writes elsewhere, "he draws his sword against an oppressor stronger than he. When a coward is outraged, he draws his sword against a man weaker than he. Among a race of hopeless cowards, there must be heroes who specialize in browbeating children." This is Ah Q's way of trying to be brave when he first picked on Wang the Beard, and then on little Don when he found that he could not even afford to be brave even with Wang. But Ah Q excels especially in his ability to turn defeat into victory by such processes of rationalization as imaging himself a poor father who has been beaten by an unfilial son. He is a "philosopher" too in his placid acceptance of his fate. When arrested and thrust behind the grilled door of his prison cell and later forced to sign a confession that he could not read, he only reflected "philosophically" that "in a man's life there must be times when he would be seized and thrust behind grilled doors and be required to make a circle on a sheet of paper." When he finally realized that he was going to be executed, his only reaction, equally "philosophical," was that "it was in the nature of things that some people should be unlucky enough to have their heads cut off."

Ah Q is the only character out of contemporary Chinese fiction that has passed into contemporary Chinese thought. Such expressions as "That's Ah Q-ism," "That's Ah Q logic," "Don't be so Ah Q like," and "He is the perfect image of Ah Q" have become part of the living speech. Ah Q has become the symbol of everything that is undesirable and contemptible in the Chinese character and a watch word to put people on their guard.

In 1926 Lusin left Peking, which had become the stronghold of reaction and where he was in danger of being arrested as a Bolshevik, and went to lecture at the University of Amoy at the invitation of Lin Yutang, then dean of the College of Letters in that institution. He did not find the atmosphere there congenial and went to Canton, "the home of the Revolution," early in the following year, only to discover that he had either to follow the line laid down by the faction in power at the moment or get out. He got out, and went to Shanghai, where he lived until his death on October 19, 1936.

The year 1927 was a crucial one for China. It will be recalled that it was the year in which the triumph of the Nationalist Revolution was followed by the triumph of the conservative element in the Kuomintang over the more liberal element within the party and the split between the Kuomintang and the Communists. Lusin witnessed the bloody purge at Canton and was constrained to write:

Revolution, counter-revolution, non-revolution.

The revolutionaries are executed by the counter-revolutionaries and the counter-revolutionaries by the revolutionaries. The non-revolutionaries are sometimes taken for revolutionaries and executed by the counter-revolutionaries, sometimes taken for counter-revolutionaries and executed by the revolutionaries, and sometimes executed by either the revolutionaries or the counter-revolutionaries for no apparent reason at all.

He felt that the masses had again been betrayed just as they were betrayed after the 1911 revolution, which made no change in their slave status except to make them into "slaves of ex-slaves."

Following the victory of the reactionary forces, free speech was totally suppressed, all opposition forces were branded as Communists or counter-revolutionaries and were ruthlessly persecuted and "purged." Revulsion at these events drove Lusin farther and farther to the Left. In 1930 he joined the League of Left Wing Writers and soon came to be known as the foremost revolutionary writer of China in Leftist circles both in Europe and America. Articles by and about him appeared, for instance, in the *New Masses* and *China Today*. (It was in the latter magazine, incidentally, that Ah Q was first introduced to the American reading public.) Since his death he has been, ironically, deified by the Communist literati as their patron saint; the principal cultural institution at Yenan, capital of the Chinese Communists, is named after him. But Lusin was a revolutionary only in the sense that all great writers of the past of any vitality and influence were revolutionaries. No one familiar with his writings— even though the extent of his familiarity does not go beyond the present collection—could conceive of him as a revolutionary in the orthodox Stalinist, or even the Marxist, sense.

Lusin had only a very modest conception of his role as a writer. He regarded his own utterances as "cheers from the sidelines," always making certain, to be sure, that he was in the right cheering section as measured according to the three principles that he had laid down for himself. He never thought of himself as an "artist" or his short stories as "art."

I have nothing that cries to be said [he confesses in "How I Came to Write Our Story of Ah Q"], nothing that needs to be written. But I have one bad habit. It is that I sometimes cannot help cheering from the sidelines in order to make things merrier. I am like a tired ox. I know that I am not much good for anything, but there is no harm in trying to make the best use of a useless thing, and so when the Changs want me to plough a piece of land, it's all right with me; when the Lis want me to take a turn at the mill, it's all right with me, too. I am willing to give in without protest even when the Chaos want me to stand in front of their shop with a sign stuck on my back saying: "We sell high-grade pasteurized milk from our own fat cows," that is, so long as their milk is safe and uncontaminated, although I know very well that I am terribly lean and that I am a bull at that and have no milk. For I can appreciate the fact that business must go on. But I won't stand for it if they try to work me too hard, for I have to have time to breathe and to look for grass to eat. It won't do either if they try to make me their exclusive property and shut me up in their cowshed, for I may want to help some one else who has grain to be ground. If they should go so far as to want to cut me up and sell me for meat, it certainly won't do for reasons too obvious to go into.

In conclusion let us quote the last article of Lusin's "testament," written in jest shortly before his death. It will make explicit what I have already implied in the foregoing pages—his deep hatred of all forms of hypocrisy.

"You must under no circumstances have anything to do with those who profess opposition to revenge and advocate forgiveness, even as they are engaged in the act of doing harm and injury to other people's eyes and teeth."

Translating from the Chinese is a difficult task at best. Lusin offers special difficulties as the humor and the effectiveness of his style depends so much upon the ironical twists and turns that he gives to classical allusions and contemporary slogans. It is hoped that the present translator has succeeded in conveying some of these effects here and there, though he realizes only too well that to render Lusin effectively into English requires greater resources than he has at his command.

BIBLIOGRAPHICAL NOTE

Lusin's published writings may be divided into four groups. There are five titles in the first group, consisting of the two collections of short stories from which the present selections are made, one volume of old legends in modern dress, one of reminiscences and one of "prose poems" and other miscellaneous material. The second group contains fourteen volumes consisting mostly of his notes and comments, and two volumes of his letters. In the third group are found his studies in Chinese literature, consisting of seven titles, including his *History of Chinese Fiction*. Thirty-two volumes of translations make up the last group; they consist mostly of Russian fiction, with occasional stories by Balkan authors and of essays and other prose miscellanies. Most of the translations are made from Japanese versions, though in many cases Lusin consulted the original versions. The European authors represented in his translations included the following: Artzibashev, Andreyev, Chekhov, Eroshenko, Pio Baroja' (*Idilios Vascos*), Fadayev, Gogol (*Dead Souls*), Gorky, Lunacharsky (art and criticism), Panteleev, Plekhanov (on art), Yakovlev (*October*) and others. The twenty volumes of his *Collected Works* were published in 1937. With but two exceptions, these contain all of his writings previously published, and also a few items not previously published. The present selection constitutes more than two thirds of Lusin's original fiction as far as bulk is concerned, though it contains less than half in number of stories.

Some of Lusin's stories are included in Edgar Snow's *Living China* (London, 1936) and Kyn Yn Yu's *The Tragedy of Ah Qui* (London and New York, 1931). Snow's volume contains five stories and two typical miscellaneous pieces by Lusin, together with a biographical note by Snow himself and a survey of contemporary Chinese literature by Nym Wales. Kyn's volume first appeared in French in 1929 and contains three stories by Lusin. Of the translations included in the present volume, "The Divorce" and "The Widow" appear also in Snow's anthology, while "Ah Q" and "My Native Heath" are also found in Kyn's selection.

For the convenience of those who wish to read more of Lusin, the following translations are suggested: "Medicine," "A Little Incident," "Kung I-chi" (Snow, in *Living China*); "Kung I-chi" (Kyn, in *The Tragedy of Ah Qui*); "The Dawn" (Wang, in *The Far Eastern Magazine*, New York, March, 1940); "Warning to the Populace," "Professor Kao," "A Happy Family" (Wang, in *The China Journal*, Shanghai, June, July, August, 1940, respectively); "Dragon Boat Festival" (anonymously translated, in *People's Tribune*, Shanghai, March 1, 1936); and "Looking Back to the Past" (Feng Yu-sing, in *T'ien Hsia Monthly*, Shanghai, February, 1938).

CHI-CHEN WANG

Columbia University
April 15, 1941

Contents

Ah Q and others

My Native Heath

IT WAS bitter cold as I set forth, after an absence of more than twenty years, on a visit to my native heath[1] over two thousand *li* away.

It was in the deep of winter, and as I neared my destination, the sky became overcast and a cold wind began to moan through the boat. Looking through the cracks in the mat covering, I saw a few dismal and forlorn villages scattered over the landscape under a pale yellow sky, without any signs of life, and I could not help but experience a feeling of sadness.

Ah, this could not be the countryside that had been constantly in my thoughts for the past twenty years!

The country that I remembered was entirely different and so much better than this. But when I tried to recall its particular beauty and describe its special merits, I could think of none, and I realized that it was, after all, about as I now beheld it. My native heath, I explained to myself, must have been like this always. It might not have made any progress, but there was nothing particularly sad about it; it appeared so to me only because of the state of my own feelings, which was not exactly cheerful on the occasion of this visit.

[1] Though heath may sound more Scottish than English, there is no better equivalent for the Chinese term *ku-hsiang* (literally, "old country"), which can be town or country and indicates an indefinite region or district rather than any specific place.

It was, in fact, a farewell visit. We had previously sold, by consent of all those concerned, the old house in which our family had lived for several generations and had agreed to turn the house over to the new owners before the first of the year. It was necessary for us to bid farewell to the old house and the familiar countryside and to settle down in another part of the country, where I made my living.

I arrived at our house the following day, early in the morning. The broken blades of dry grass that grew between the roof tiles rustled in the wind and explained better than words could why the old house had to change owners. It was very quiet, as ours was the last branch of the family to move away. My mother met me at the gate of our own compound, soon joined by my eight-year-old nephew Hung-erh, who came out running.

My mother was happy to see me, but I could detect that there was a trace of sadness in her, too. She told me to sit down and rest and have some tea and not to talk about the matter of moving till later. As Hung-erh had never seen me before, he stood and watched me intently from a distance.

In the end we came to the matter of moving. I said that I had rented a house and bought a few pieces of furniture and that we must sell all our old furniture and buy more with the proceeds. My mother approved of my arrangements. It was going to be a fairly simple matter as most of the packing had been done already and some of the larger pieces of furniture had been sold. The only difficulty was in getting the buyers to pay.

"After you have rested a few days and visited our relatives, we shall be able to start," mother said.

"Yes," I answered.

"By the way, every time Yun-t'u comes to our house, he

always asks about you. He wants very much to see you. I sent a message telling him the probable date of your arrival. He will be here soon."

A scene full of novelty and mystery suddenly flashed across my mind: a full moon, golden and yellow, hung in the sky, and below, against the emerald green of an endless expanse of watermelon plants on a sandy beach by the sea, stood a boy eleven or twelve years old, a silver ring around his neck and a steel pitchfork in his hand. He was aiming at a "ch'a" with his fork, but as he struck with all his might, the "ch'a" ducked and scuttled off between his legs.

The boy was Yun-t'u. I was about the same age when I first met him, almost thirty years ago. My father was still living then, and our family was in good circumstances. I was, in other words, a *shao-yeh*, a young master. It was our turn to take charge of a particularly important ancestral sacrifice which came around only once in more than thirty years and was, therefore, an even more important occasion for us than for the rest of the clan. The offerings made before the ancestral portraits in the first month were rich and varied, the sacrificial vessels elaborate, and the participants many. It was necessary to keep a careful watch over the sacrificial vessels to guard against theft. As the work was too much for our *mang-yueh*, he asked father's permission to send for his son Yun-t'u to take charge of the sacrificial vessels. (In our part of the country there were three kinds of help: those who hired themselves out by the year were known as *chang-nien* or all-year; those who hired themselves out by the day were known as *tuan-kung* or short-labor; while those who worked their own land and only hired themselves out during the New Year and other festivals or during rent time were known as *mang-yueh* or busy-month.)

I was very glad that father gave his consent, for I had heard of Yun-t'u and knew that he was of my own age. He was named Yun-t'u because he was born in an intercallary (*yun*) month and lacked, according to the system of correspondences of the astrologers, the element of earth (*t'u*) in his horoscope. He knew how to set up a trap to catch birds.

I began to look forward to the coming of the New Year as it meant that Yun-t'u would come, too. Finally the end of the year approached and one day mother told me that Yun-t'u had come. I ran to see him and found him in the kitchen. He had a ruddy face and wore a felt scalp cap, and a silver ring around his neck. It was evident that his father loved him very much, was afraid that he might not live long, and had, after making a vow before the gods, put this ring around his neck to hold him. Yun-t'u was very shy with grown-ups but not with me, and would talk freely with me when there was no one else around. In a few hours we had become fast friends.

I don't know what we talked about then; I only remember that Yun-t'u was very happy and told me that he had seen, since he came to the city, many things which he had never seen before.

The following day I wanted him to show me how to catch birds, but he said: "We cannot do it now. We have to wait until after the snow. Back home I sweep off a spot in the snow and set up a big basket with a stick and scatter some grain under the basket. When the birds come to eat the grain I pull the string tied to the stick and the basket falls and catches the birds underneath. I catch all kinds of birds: wild fowls, wood pigeons, blue-backs, and so on."

And so I hoped it would snow.

Yun-t'u also said to me: "It is now too cold, but you come

to our place in the summer. In the daytime we'll go to the seashore to pick shells. We have all kinds of shells, red ones and green ones, devil's-terrors and Kuanyin's-hands. In the evening you can go with my father and me to watch the watermelon patch."

"To guard against thieves?"

"No. We do not consider it stealing if a passer-by is thirsty and helps himself to a melon. We watch for badgers, hedgehogs, and especially the 'ch'a.' You can hear them gnawing on the melons in the moonlight, crunch, crunch. Then you get hold of your fork and walk up lightly ——"

I did not know what a "ch'a" was—I don't know to this day—but for some reason or other I imagined it to be something like a small puppy, only more fierce.

"Don't they bite?"

"But you have your fork. When you get close and see it, you strike it with your fork. The beast is very quick. It will rush toward you and run off between your legs. Its fur is as slippery as oil."

I never knew that there were such new and marvelous things in the world: that there were shells of so many colors on the seashore and that watermelons could have a more exciting experience than being displayed in fruit shops.

"When the tide is in, there are lots and lots of jumping fish. They all have two legs like young frogs."

Ah, Yun-t'u knew about an infinite number of strange things which none of my usual playmates knew anything about. They knew absolutely nothing, for when Yun-t'u was playing on the seashore, they, like myself, could only see a four-cornered sky above the walls of the courtyard.

Unfortunately the first month came to an end and Yun-t'u had to go home. I cried, and Yun-t'u also hid in the kitchen and cried and refused to go, but in the end he was taken away by his father. Later he sent me by his father a package of sea shells and a few pretty feathers. I, too, sent things to him once or twice, but I had not seen him since.

So when my mother spoke of him, my childhood memories were revived in a lightning flash and my native heath again assumed the beauty that my memories had always clothed it with.

"That's excellent!" I said. "How—how is he?"

"Well, his circumstances are not very happy," my mother answered. As she looked toward the yard, she cried, "There are those people again. They come here under the pretext of buying furniture but they are apt to help themselves to things when no one is looking. I must go and keep an eye on them."

She got up and went out. There were women's voices outside. I called Hung-erh to me and talked with him: I asked him whether he could write, whether he would like to go away.

"Shall we ride in a train?"

"Yes, we'll ride in a train."

"How about boats?"

"We'll take a boat first."

"Ha! So this is he! and what a beard he has grown!" A sharp, raucous voice suddenly broke in.

I looked up, startled, and saw before me a woman of around fifty years with high cheekbones and thin lips, her arms akimbo. She wore no skirt and her feet stuck out like a pair of compasses such as draftsmen use.

I looked puzzled.

"Don't you know who I am? I used to hold you in my arms!"

I was more puzzled than ever. Fortunately my mother came in then and said, "He has been away so many years he has forgotten everything." Then turning to me she added, "You ought to remember her. This is Sister Yang from across the way . . . they have a bean-curd shop."

Yes, I remembered now. Out of my childhood memories I recalled the image of a Sister Yang seated all day long in the bean-curd shop across the street. She was nicknamed "Bean Curd Hsi Shih."[2] But she powdered her face then and her cheekbones were not so high, her lips not so thin, and, because she was seated all day long, I had no recollection of her compasslike feet. She was young and attractive then, and it was said that her shop flourished for that reason. However, my child mind was not susceptible to a young woman's charms and she had made no impression on me. Compasses was very indignant and her face assumed a jeering expression at my lapse, which to her must have seemed as unforgivable as a Frenchman's not knowing Napoleon or an American's not knowing Washington.

"So you have forgotten who I am! Well, this is what you call the forgetfulness of the great."

"It is no such thing—I—I," I stood up, stammering with embarrassment.

"Then let me tell you something, Brother Hsun. You are now rich and have no use for this dilapidated furniture. The pieces are too heavy and clumsy to take with you. Give them to me. We are poor and can use those things."

"I am not rich. I have to sell these things in order to . . ."

"What's that you say? You have been appointed a Daotai and yet you say you are not rich. You have three concubines

[2] Hsi Shih was the Helen of Chinese antiquity.

and go about in a huge sedan with eight carriers, and you tell me that you are not rich. *Heng,* you can't fool me!"

I realized that there was no use arguing with her and so kept still.

"*Aiya, Aiya!* Truly the more money you have the more you would not let even a hair go, and the more you would not even let a hair go the more money you would have!" Compasses grumbled as she turned around and indignantly walked away, helping herself to my mother's gloves, tucking them under her coat.

After this my relatives and kinsmen in the neighborhood came to call on me. In my spare moments I packed. Thus three or four days went by.

One afternoon as I was drinking tea after lunch I heard footsteps coming from outside. I glanced around and, discovering to my surprise who it was, I got up and hastened to meet him.

It was Yun-t'u. Although I knew it was he the minute I saw him, yet it was not the Yun-t'u of my memories. He was now almost twice as tall as when I last saw him; his ruddy, round face had become an ashen yellow, furrowed with wrinkles; his eyes were like those of his father, with the thick, red lids common to people who live near the sea and are constantly exposed to the sea breeze. He wore an old scalp cap and a light cotton padded coat and shivered with cold. He held a paper package and a long pipe in his hands, hands no longer plump and ruddy as I remembered them but coarse, clumsy, and cracked like the bark of a pine tree.

I was deeply moved but I did not know what to say.

"Ah, Brother Yun-t'u—so you have at last come," I said clumsily. There were many things that I wanted to say to him, things that swelled up within me—wild fowl, jumping fish, sea shells, "ch'a"—but they seemed to be blocked by something, so that they whirled around in my brain and could not find expression.

He stood before me with an expression of mixed joy and sadness. His lips moved but no sound came. When he did manage to speak it was formal and respectful: "Your Honor . . ."

I must have shuddered as I realized what a heavy, sorrowful wall had come between us. I found nothing to say.

"Come, Shui-sheng, and kowtow to His Honor," he said to a boy that he dragged out from behind him. The child was the image of Yun-t'u twenty years ago, except that he was thinner and more sallow and had no silver ring about his neck. "He is my fifth, has never been away from home and so he is very shy."

My mother and Hung-erh now came down, probably having heard the visitors.

"*Lao-tai-tai,*" Yun-t'u said, "I received your message and I was very happy to hear that His Honor had come back."

"But why so formal?" my mother protested. "Didn't you use to call one another brother? Do as before, call him Brother Hsun."

"*Aiya,* how kind you are! But that won't do. It might have been all right then. I was only a boy and did not know any better." Yun-t'u again tried to induce his son to come forward and greet my mother, but the boy hid closely behind his back.

"Is that Shui-sheng? Isn't he the fifth one? With so many strangers around no wonder he is shy. Let him go with Hung-erh," mother said.

At this Hung-erh went up to Shui-sheng and the latter readily went with him. Mother bade Yun-t'u sit down, which he did after some hesitation. He leaned his long pipe against the table and handed the paper package to me, saying, "We have nothing fresh in the winter. These dried green beans are from our own land. I hope Your Honor . . ."

I asked him about his circumstances, which he told me with many a headshaking.

"It is very bad. My sixth is now old enough to help, but there is never enough food to feed them all. Moreover, times are not peaceful—everywhere money, money, and always new and irregular taxes—harvests bad. When we do harvest something and try to sell it, we hardly get enough to pay the various taxes imposed all along the way. If we don't try to sell, then it only rots away on our hands . . ."

He kept on shaking his head. His face, though deeply furrowed, was expressionless as a stone image. He felt his hardships bitterly, but was unable to express them. After a few moments of silence he took up his pipe and smoked.

My mother questioned him and found that he had a great deal to do at home and had to go back the following day. As he had not yet had lunch, mother told him to go into the kitchen and fry some rice for himself. After he went out, mother and I sighed at the man's lot: too many sons, famine, oppressive taxes, soldiers, bandits, officials, the gentry— all these contributed to make the burden heavy for the poor peasant, crushing him and draining the life out of him until he was scarcely more than a wooden image. Mother said we should give him everything that we could neither use nor find a buyer for.

In the afternoon he picked out some things that he could use: two long tables, four chairs, a set consisting of an incense burner and candlesticks, a scale. He asked us to give him all the rice-straw ash. (We use rice straws for fuel and

the ash for fertilizer.) He was to come for them with a boat
before we started off on our journey.

In the evening we had another chat, about nothing in
particular. He went away with Shui-sheng the following
morning.

Nine days later we left our old home. Yun-t'u came early
in the morning. He did not bring Shui-sheng with him but
brought a five-year-old girl to watch the boat. We were
busy all day and had little chance to talk. There were many
guests, some had come to see us off, others to fetch things,
still others both to see us off and to fetch things. When we
finally embarked toward evening, the old house was cleared
of everything that was of any possible use.

Our boat went slowly on, leaving behind the darkening
green hills on either bank. Hung-erh, who had been watching the obscure landscape with me from a window, suddenly said to me, "Uncle, when are we coming back?"

"Coming back? But why should you be thinking of coming back when we have just started?"

"But Shui-sheng has asked me to visit him at his home,"
the boy said reflectively with his black eyes wide open.

Both mother and I were touched by the boy's remark and
our conversation again turned to Yun-t'u. She said that
Sister Yang had been coming to our house every day since
we began to pack. Two days before we started she discovered
some dishes and bowls in the ash pile, which she insisted
had been hidden there by Yun-t'u so that he could take them
away with him when he came to get the ash. Sister Yang was
very pleased with herself for her discovery, and on the
strength of it she helped herself to our "dog's-exasperation."
(A contrivance used for feeding chickens in our native place.
It consists of a wooden cage over a trough containing feed.

The chickens can stick their necks through the bars to get at the feed while the dogs can only stare through them in exasperation. Hence the name.) As she made off with it, Mother said she never suspected that Sister Yang was capable of running so fast, with her small bound feet and high heels.

I felt no regret as our old house and native hills and streams dropped behind us. I only had an oppressive sense of being surrounded and isolated from the world by invisible walls and a feeling of sadness because the image of my little hero with a silver ring around his neck in the water-melon patch had suddenly become blurred and indistinct, whereas, before, it had been so sharp and clear.

Both mother and Hung-erh had fallen asleep.

As I lay in my corner and listened to the sound of water lapping against the boat, I knew that we were on our way. What a barrier had come between Yun-t'u and myself! There was, fortunately, no such barrier between the younger generation as yet (was not Hung-erh thinking about Shui-sheng and asking about him?) and I hoped that no such barrier would ever come between them. However, I did not want them to live, as a price for their continued companion-ship, the bitter and rootless life that I lived; I did not want them to live the bitter and wretched life that Yun-t'u lived; I did not want them to live the bitter and shameless life that others lived. They must have a new kind of life, a life that we of the older generation had not known.

As I realized what I was doing, I suddenly became afraid. I had laughed to myself when Yun-t'u asked for the incense burner and candlesticks and had pitied him because he could not for a moment forget his superstitions. But what was this so-called hope of mine if not also an idol fashioned with our own hands? The only difference between us was that his wishes and hopes were concerned with more immediate things while mine were concerned with the more remote.

In the darkness the green watermelon patch again appeared before my eyes and above it a golden moon hung in a deep blue sky. Perhaps, I thought to myself, hope is not absolute, not something of which we can say that it does or does not exist, but something very much like the roads that travelers make across the face of the earth where there were none before.

The Cake of Soap

MRS. SSU-MING, with her eight-year-old daughter
Hsiu-erh, was making paper ingots in the slanting sunlight
when she suddenly heard the thump, thump of slow and
heavy footsteps of someone wearing cloth-soled shoes. Although she recognized the step of Ssu-ming, she did not stop
to look up but went on with her work. When the footsteps
drew close and stopped right by her side, however, she could
not help looking up, and when she did so she found Ssu-ming
engaged in reaching down into the pocket of his long robe
underneath a horse jacket.

With a great deal of difficulty he finally succeeded in
extricating his hand from his pocket and handed a small,
oblong package, palm green in color, to Mrs. Ssu. As soon
as she took the package in her hand she smelled an exotic
fragrance which was something, and yet not quite, like the
fragrance of olives; on the palm-green paper wrapping there
was a golden seal and some elaborate patterns. Hsiu-erh
jumped up to her and asked to see it but Mrs. Ssu pushed
her away.

"Been to town?" she asked, as she examined the package.

"Mm, mm," he answered, also looking at the package.

The palm-green package was then opened, revealing another layer of thin paper, also palm green; and it was not
until this thin paper was removed that the object itself was
exposed. It was firm and smooth, also palm green in color,

with a pattern impressed upon it. The exotic fragrance which smelled something but not quite like the fragrance of olives became stronger.

"Oh, what fine soap," Mrs. Ssu said, as she held the palm-green object up to her nose, as delicately as if she were holding an infant, and sniffed at it.

"Mm, mm, you can use that from now on . . ."

As he said this, she noticed, his eyes were fixed on her neck. Her face felt warm from the cheeks down. She had always felt a roughness whenever she happened to touch her neck, especially behind the ears, and she had realized that it was due to an accumulation of ancient dirt. She had not paid the slightest attention to it, but now under his gaze and before the cake of exotic-smelling soap, she could not prevent the warmth in the face. Moreover, the warm feeling spread and soon reached to her ears. She made up her mind then that she was going to give herself a good scrubbing with that soap after supper.

"There are spots where mere *tsao-chia* soap won't do any good," she said to herself.

"Ma, give that to me," Hsiu-erh said, reaching out for the palm-green paper. Chao-erh, the younger daughter who had been playing out in the yard, also came running in. Mrs. Ssu pushed them aside, wrapped the soap as before, first in the thin paper and then the palm-green paper, and, reaching up, put it on the topmost shelf on the washstand. She gave it a final caressing glance and then turned back to her work.

"Hsueh-cheng!" Ssu-ming suddenly called, as if he had just remembered something, and sat down in a high-backed chair opposite his wife.

"Hsueh-cheng!" she also called.

She put down her paper ingots and listened but there was

no answer. She felt apologetic when she saw her husband waiting impatiently with his head turned upward, and she called again at the top of her shrill voice, resorting this time to the boy's more familiar milk name.

This produced immediate results. The clap, clap of leather soles neared, and soon Chuan-erh stood before them wearing a short coat, his fat round face glistening with perspiration.

"What were you doing? Can't you hear your *dieh* calling?" she scolded.

"I was practicing *pa-kua-ch'üan*," he said and turning to Ssu-ming he stood respectfully and waited inquiringly.

"Hsueh-cheng, I want to ask you this: what is the meaning of *o-du-foo*?"

"*O-du-foo?* . . . Does that not mean 'a ferocious woman'?"

"Nonsense! Stupid!" Ssu-ming suddenly burst out angrily. "Do you mean to suggest that I am a woman?"

Hsueh-cheng was scared by the outburst; he withdrew two steps and stood more respectfully erect than before. Though he had secretly felt that his father's gait resembled that of the actors of old men's parts, he had never thought him as having any effeminate traits. But he was certain that he had given the wrong answer.

"Do you think that I am so stupid as not to know that *o-du-foo* means a ferocious woman and have to ask you about it? This is not Chinese but foreign language, let me tell you. What does it mean? Do you understand it?"

"I . . . I do not understand it," Hsueh-cheng became more and more scared.

"*Huh,* I have spent a lot of money in sending you to school and you tell me that you don't understand even this? So this is what they call 'emphasis on both ear and mouth'? The speaker of those foreign words was only about fourteen or fifteen years old, younger than yourself, and yet he was able to chatter glibly away, while you do not even understand it. Shame on you! Now go and look it up for me!"

Hsueh-cheng answered with a throaty "yes" and backed out respectfully.

"The students are getting more and more impossible every day," Ssu-ming said indignantly after a while. "Even as far back as the Kuang Hsu period, I was one of the most outspoken advocates of modern education. But I never, never thought that schools would come to this: it is emancipation this and freedom that, but they never learn anything. I have spent lots of money on Hsueh-cheng, and it has all been spent in vain. It was with considerable difficulty that I got him into one of these schools where both Chinese and Western learning are given equal attention. You would think that he ought to learn something there, wouldn't you? And yet after a year he cannot even understand *o-du-foo*. They must be still teaching them by rote. What sort of school do you call this? What have they turned out? I say they should be closed up, every one of them!"

"You are right, you can't do better than to close all of them," Mrs. Ssu said sympathetically, still engaged in making paper ingots.

"We don't need to send Hsiu-erh and Chao-erh to school. 'What's the use of sending girls to school?' Great Uncle Nine used to say, and how I attacked him for his opposition to girls' schools! But now I am inclined to think the old people are right after all. Just think, isn't it bad enough to have women parading about the streets, without their bobbing their hair? There is nothing I hate more than girl students with bobbed hair. In my opinion soldiers and bandits are

more forgivable than they, for it is they that have corrupted
and subverted morality. They should be punished . . ."

"That's right. It is bad enough to have men cut their hair
off like monks without the women trying to imitate the
nuns."

"Hsueh-cheng!"

The boy had at that moment come in with a small, thick
volume with gilt edges, which he held up to Ssu-ming and
said pointing to some page: "This looks like it, this one
here."

Ssu-ming took the book, which he knew to be a dictionary,
but the print was very small and the lines ran sidewise. He
took it over to the window and squinted at the line which
Hsueh-cheng had pointed to and read: " 'The name of a
coöperative society founded in the eighteenth century.' Mm,
that's not it—How do you pronounce this?" he asked, pointing to the foreign words.

"O-do-fo-lo-ssu."[1]

"No, no, that's not it," Ssu-ming became angry again. "Let
me tell you that it is a bad word, a curse word, something
applied to one like myself. Do you understand now? Go and
try to find it!"

Hsueh-cheng looked at him but did not move.

"What sort of riddle is this? You must explain it more
clearly so that he can look it up," Mrs. Ssu interceded, taking
pity upon Hsueh-cheng's helplessness and showing some dissatisfaction at her husband's behavior.

"It happened while I was buying the soap at Kuang Yun
Hsiang's," Ssu-ming responded, turning to her. "There were
three students besides myself in the shop. From their point
of view I was, of course, somewhat troublesome. I looked

[1] Odd Fellows.

at six or seven different kinds without taking any as they
were all over forty cents. I finally decided to take some
medium-priced variety and bought the green piece over there
at twenty-four cents. The clerk was one of those snobs that
toady to the rich, with his eyes growing upward on his forehead, and he assumed a doggish snout soon enough. In the
meantime the students were winking at one another and
jabbering in the foreign devil's language. Later I wanted
to open up the package and take a look before I paid, but
the snob not only would not let me do it but became un-
reasonable and said a lot of unnecessary and unpleasant
things, at which the students chimed in with their jabber and
laughter. That particular sentence came from the youngest
of them. He was looking at me when he said it and all the
others laughed. It is clear that it is bad language." Then
turning to Hsueh-cheng he said "You'll have to look for it
under the category of 'bad language'!"

Hsueh-cheng answered with another throaty "yes" and
withdrew respectfully.

"They are always yelling and yelling about the 'new
culture' but what has the 'new culture' brought them to?"
Ssu-ming went on, his eyes fixed on the roof. "Now there is
no longer any morality among the students, no morality
among society in general. If nothing is done about it China
will certainly vanish from the earth. Just think how terrible
that would be . . ."

"What's that?" his wife said, indifferently.

"I have in mind," he said seriously, "a filial maid.
There were two beggars on the street, one of them a girl,
about eighteen or nineteen—not a very suitable age to be
begging on the street, I must say, but that was what she was
doing. She was with a woman about sixty or seventy, white

haired and blind, and they sat under the eaves of a cloth shop begging for alms. People all say that she was a filial maid, the old woman being her grandmother. Whenever she got anything she gave it to her grandmother and willingly went hungry herself. But did anyone give anything to such a filial maid?" he asked with his eyes turned on her as if testing her.

She did not answer but kept her eyes on him as if waiting, in turn, for him to explain what happened.

"*Heng,* none," he answered the question himself finally. "I watched them for a long time and in all that time only one person gave her a small copper, while the rest looked on them as objects for their amusement. Moreover, a ruffian went so far as to say to his companion thus: 'Ah-fa, do not overlook this piece of goods just because it happens to be dirty. All you have to do is to buy two cakes of soap and *k-chee, k-chee,* give her a thorough scrubbing and she will be as nice a piece of goods as you'll ever find.' Now just consider what sort of world this has become!"

"*Heng,*" she said looking down at her work and then asked casually after a long while, "Did you give her anything?"

"I? No. I couldn't very well give her just a copper or two. She was no ordinary beggar. At least . . ."

But she got up slowly without waiting for him to finish his sentence and went to the kitchen. Dusk was falling thick and it was supper time.

Ssu-ming also got up and went out into the yard. It was lighter outside than in the room. Hsueh-cheng was practicing *pa-kua-ch'üan* at a corner near the wall in accordance with the admonition that he should utilize the space where day and night met for this particular purpose since there was not light enough to read but enough to exercise by. Ssu-ming nodded slightly in approval and began to pace back and forth with his arms crossed behind him. Presently the only potted plant—a ten-thousand-year green—became lost in the darkness, a few stars twinkled through the fleecy clouds, and night began its reign. Ssu-ming became more vigorous and acted as if he was about to do great things, to declare war against the corrupt students and the evil influences of society. The braver and more vigorous he felt, the longer grew his strides and the louder sounded his footsteps, until the hens and chickens, which had been roosting peacefully in their cages, became frightened and started to cluck and twit.

The appearance of lamplight in the hall served as a beacon summoning the family to supper and all flocked to the table placed in the center of the room. At the head of the table was Ssu-ming, who was fat and round faced like Hsueh-cheng but had a thin moustache. Sitting alone on one side of the table and seen through the cloud of vapor from the hot soup, he looked very much like the god of wealth across the altar in his temple. On the left sat Mrs. Ssu and Chao-erh; on the right Hsueh-cheng and Hsiu-erh. The chopsticks clattered on the dishes and bowls like raindrops, and made supper a very lively affair, though no one spoke.

Chao-erh upset her bowl, spilling its contents over half the table. Ssu-ming glared at her with a fixed stare and did not relent until she was about to cry. Thereupon he turned to pick up a piece of tender vegetable which he had previously spotted in the communal bowl. But it had disappeared. He looked around the table and caught Hsueh-cheng in the act of stuffing the prized morsel into his wide-open mouth. There was nothing for him to do but to content himself with a chopstickful of vegetable leaves.

"Hsueh-cheng," he said looking at him, "have you found out the word yet?"

"What word?—Oh, that? No, not yet."

"*Heng,* just look at him. He has learned nothing but eat and eat! It would be better if you learned something from the filial maid, who, though she is only a beggar, gives everything to her grandmother and willingly goes hungry herself. But, of course, you students know nothing of these things. You have no fears and beliefs; you'll turn out exactly like that ruffian . . ."

"I did think of a word, but I don't know whether it is right or not. What he said was perhaps 'o-erh-de-foo-erh.' "[2]

"Yes, yes, that's it, that's exactly it. But the way he said it sounded more like *o-du-foo.* Now what does it mean? You are of the same tribe as they and you ought to know."

"It means—I am afraid that I don't know what it means."

"Nonsense! You are concealing it from me. You are all bad eggs!"

"Even 'Heaven would not strike one who is eating.' What has come over you today that you act like this, 'striking the chicks and cursing the dogs' even at the supper table? What can you expect from them when they are only children?" Mrs. Ssu suddenly remonstrated.

"What's that?" Ssu-ming was about to continue his tirade, but he took a look at his wife and thought better of it, for her cheeks were puffed out, her color changed, her triangular eyes flashing an ugly light. He said instead, "Nothing has come over me. I am only trying to impress Hsueh-cheng that he must try to learn some good traits."

"How can he learn since he cannot read your mind?" She was angrier than ever. "If he could read what's in your mind,

[2] Old fool.

he would have long ago lit the lantern, sought out the filial
maid and brought her to you. Fortunately you have already
bought a cake of soap for her. All you have to do now is
to buy another cake and . . ."

"Nonsense! that's what the ruffian said."

"I am not sure of that. All you have to do is buy another
cake and *k-chee, k-chee,* give her a good scrubbing, and set
her up on an altar and peace will reign in the world again."

"What are you talking about? What has that got to do
with it? It was only because I happened to remember that
you did not have any soap . . ."

"That has everything to do with it. You have specially
bought that for the filial maid. You go and give her, *k-chee,
k-chee,* a good scrubbing yourself. I am not worthy of it, I
don't want it, I don't want anything that was intended for
the filial maid."

"Now what are you talking about? You women . . . ,"
Ssu-ming parried, his face covered with a greasy sweat, just
like Hsueh-cheng's after he had finished his *pa-kua-ch'üan*
exercises, although it might have been due to the heat of
the rice.

"What's wrong with us women? We women are much
better than you men. You men are either cursing eighteen-
or nineteen-year-old girl students or praising eighteen- or
nineteen-year-old beggar girls. You haven't a decent thought
in your heads. *K-chee, k-chee!* Shameless wretches!"

"Did I not say that it was a ruffian who said that? Have
I . . ."

"Brother Ssu!" a loud voice sounded in the darkness
outside.

"Is that you, Brother Tao? I'll be with you directly." Ssu-
ming recognized the voice of Ho Tao-tung, known for his

loudness, and welcomed him as if he were a messenger bringing an unexpected reprieve. "Hsueh-cheng, light a lamp right away and show Uncle Ho to the study!"

Hsueh-cheng lit a candle and led Tao-tung into a side room to the west, followed by another guest by the name of Pu Wei-yuan.

"Pardon me for not going out to meet you, pardon me, pardon me," Ssu-ming came out and said, raising his clasped hands in greeting and still chewing his last mouthful of rice. "Would you deign to have a bite with us?"

"We have already selfishly preceded you," Wei-yuan said, also shaking his own clasped hands before him. "We have come to disturb you at night because we want to discuss with you the themes for the literary contest of the Ethical Literary Society, for don't you realize that it is a 'seventh' day tomorrow?"

"Oh, is today the sixteenth already?" Ssu-ming exclaimed.

"See how stupid of us!" Tao-tung shouted.

"Then we must send the themes to the newspaper office tonight and make sure that they get into tomorrow's edition."

"I have already drafted a theme for the essay contest. Take a look at it and see if it is all right," Tao-tung said, as he fished out a strip of paper from the carry-all improvised with a handkerchief and handed it over to Ssu-ming. The latter took it over to the candle light, unfolded the strip of paper and read slowly the following:

> A proposed petition to be sent by the citizens of the entire Nation to His Excellency the President requesting him to promulgate a mandate commanding the study of the Confucian Canon and the Canonization of the mother of Mencius as a means of saving

the declining morals and preserving the National essence.

"Excellent, excellent," Ssu-ming said. "But is it not too long?"

"It does not matter!" Tao-tung said loudly. "I have counted it over and found that we do not have to pay anything over our reserved space. But how about the theme for the verse contest?"

"The verse contest?" Ssu-ming was suddenly reverential in manner. "I have one that I would like to suggest. It is: 'Ballad of the Filial Maid.' It happens to be a true incident and we ought to give it a wider acknowledgment. Today as I was walking on the street . . ."

"That will not do," Wei-yuan interrupted, shaking his hand in disapproval. "I have seen her myself. She must be a stranger in these parts, for I could not understand her and she could not understand me. I don't know where she comes from. Everyone said that she is a filial maid, but when I asked her whether she could write poetry, she shook her head. It would be much better if she could write poetry."

"Loyalty and filial piety are cardinal virtues and we must overlook the inability to write verse . . ."

"Nay, it is not so, that is in no wise true," Wei-yuan said with affectation, as he shook his hand vigorously and going up to Ssu-ming. "It would be much more interesting if she could write poetry."

"We'll use this theme," Ssu-ming said, brushing aside his objection. "We'll add an explanatory note and have it printed in the newspaper. In the first place this will give her some deserved acknowledgment; in the second place it will furnish an opportunity to give the public a few shots of a much-needed needle of criticism. What has the world come to? I watched the two women a long time but I did not see anyone give any money. Does that not show that people have no heart any more?"

"But Brother Ssu," Wei-yuan again objected, "you are now 'cursing a bald head in front a monk.' I was one of those who did not give anything. It happened that I did not have any money with me."

"Don't be so sensitive, Brother Wei. Of course it is another question with you. Let me finish: a big crowd gathered before them, but no one showed any respect. Instead they made fun of them. There were two ruffians who behaved especially badly. One of them said, 'Ah-fa, go and buy two cakes of soap and *k-chee, k-chee,* give her a good scrubbing. She'll be very good then.' Just imagine . . ."

"Ha, ha, ha! Two cakes of soap!" Tao-tung suddenly burst out in his loud guffaw, which vibrated in every one's ear. "You buy—ha, ha, ha-a . . ."

"Brother Tao, Brother Tao, please do not shout like that," Ssu-ming was frightened and spoke hastily.

"*K-chee, k-chee,* ha, ha, ha-a . . ."

"Brother Tao," Ssu-ming said seriously, "why do you insist on joking when we have business to discuss? Listen, we'll use these two themes and send them to the paper right away and make sure that they get in tomorrow's edition. I'll have to impose this errand on you two gentlemen."

"We'll be glad to do it, of course," Wei-yuan said eagerly.

"Ah, ah, a good scrubbing, *k-chee* . . . he, he . . ."

"Brother Tao!" Ssu-ming said with annoyance.

This quieted Tao-tung at last. Then they drafted the conditions of the contest. After Wei-yuan had copied everything out on letter paper, he went off to the newspaper office with Tao-tung. Ssu-ming escorted them to the gate with the candle and as he approached the hall on his way back he began to feel uncomfortable again, though he ended up by stepping inside after a moment's hesitation. The first thing to come under his observation as he entered the hall was the package of soap in green wrappers in the center of the table. The golden seal glittered in the lamplight and the delicate patterns could be seen.

Hsiu-erh and Chao-erh were playing, squatted on the ground in front of the table, while Hsueh-cheng was looking up words in the dictionary on the right side of the table. Farthest away from the lamp Mrs. Ssu sat on the high-backed chair in the dimness, her face immobile and expressionless and her eyes staring vacantly at nothingness.

"*K-chee, k-chee,* shameless wretches . . ."

This seemed to have come from Hsui-erh, but when Ssu-ming looked back he only saw Chao-erh scratching her face with her two little hands.

Aware that the atmosphere was none too favorable, he extinguished his candle and strolled out again into the yard, where he began to pace back and forth. The minute he forgot himself, the hens and chicks would begin to cluck and twit, whereupon he would make his steps lighter and walk farther away from the chicken cage. After a long time the lamp in the central room was shifted to the bedroom. Moonlight covered the ground like a sheet of seamless white muslin, while overhead the jade disc of the full moon shone between white clouds and showed not the slightest imperfection.

He was a little sad and felt himself a lonely man, as forgotten and neglected as the filial maid. He did not go to bed until very late that night.

But the services of the soap were enlisted early the following morning. He got up later than usual that day and found his wife bent over the washstand scrubbing her neck. The soap lather rose in billows behind her ears, as foamy as water bubbles that form over the mouth of huge crabs. The difference between this and ordinary *tsao-chia* was as great as the difference that exists between heaven and earth. From then on there was always an exotic fragrance about the person of Mrs. Ssu which was something and yet not quite like the fragrance of olives. It was not until almost half a year later that she began to have a different odor, which, according to those who noticed it, smelled of sandalwood.

The Divorce

"AH, AH, Uncle Mu! Happy New Year! *Fa-tsai, fa-tsai!*"[1]

"*Ni-how*, Pa-san! Happy New Year!"

"Ai, ai, Happy New Year! Ai-ku also here?"

"Ah, ah, Uncle Mu . . ."

A chorus of voices thus greeted Chuang Mu-san and his daughter Ai-ku as they stepped on the passenger boat at Mu Lien Bridge. Some of the passengers raised their clasped hands in salutation, while others made room on the plank along the side of the boat. Chuang Mu-san greeted them all as he sat down, leaning his long pipe against the side of the boat. Ai-ku sat to his left and her sicklelike feet formed the character eight[2] with the more open side facing Pa-san.

"Are you going to the city, Uncle Mu?" asked one with a crab-shell face.

"Not to the city," Uncle Mu answered with a worried look—though one could not be sure of the worry, so wrinkled was his brown-sugar colored face. "I am going Pang-chuang for a little while."

The boat was silent and all eyes were fixed on them.

"Is it still about Ai-ku's affair?" Pa-san asked after a long while.

"Still about her . . . How sick of it I am! It has been

---

[1] May you become rich.

[2] Like a "V" but open at both ends.

going on now for all of three years, always fighting, making up, nothing ever settled . . ."

"Is it going to be at His Honor Wei's house again?"

"Yes, still at his house. He has acted as peacemaker several times for them, but I never agreed to the terms. But that does not matter much. This time they are entertaining relatives at the New Year, even His Honor Seven from the city is going to be there."

"His Honor Seven?" Pa-san's eyes popped wide open. "Is he taking a hand in the matter too? That is . . . But last year we really gave them a good example of what we are capable of, when we topped it all by tearing up their stove. That made us about even. Moreover, Ai-ku will hardly find it comfortable there after all that has happened." After saying this, he looked down at the bottom of the boat.

"It is not that I am anxious to go back to them, Pa-san-ko!" Ai-ku said, raising her head angrily. "I am doing this to spite them. The little beast cannot throw me aside for that little widow. I'll show them that he cannot get away with it so easily. The old beast always sides with his son and he wants to get rid of me, too. It won't be easy, I tell you. What if His Honor Seven is taking a hand? Do you mean to say that he would not talk human speech, simply because he has become a sworn brother of the magistrate? He'll know better than merely to say that it is better to break up. I should like to tell him what I've suffered in the last few years and see what he has to say."

Pa-san was silenced by this outburst of eloquence. The boat was quiet except for the splashing of water against the bow. Chuang Mu-san took his pipe and filled it. A fat man seated next to Pa-san and diagonally across from Mu-san took from his pocket a set of flint and steel, lighted the tinder, and held it to the bowl.

"Thank you, thank you," Mu-san said, nodding.

"Although this is our first meeting, I've known Uncle Mu's name for a long time," the fat man said deferentially. "Yes, who in these three-six-eighteen[3] villages by the sea does not know all about the affair? We all know that that Shih family's son is carrying on with a widow. When Uncle Mu and his six sons went to their house and tore up their stove last year, was there any one who did not say that it served them right? You, sir, are one who can walk through the tallest gates and into the biggest houses with the greatest ease and confidence. You need have no fear of them!"

"Uncle, you are surely an understanding one," Ai-ku said, pleased, "though I do not know who you are."

"My name is Wang Te-kuei," the fat man said eagerly.

Ai-ku continued, "It just won't do to cast me aside. I do not care whether it is His Honor Seven or His Honor Eight. I'll keep them going until their home is destroyed and their people dead! Didn't His Honor Wei beg me four times to give them peace? Father got dizzy from counting the money they had to pay . . ."

"Keep quiet, your mother's ——!" Mu-san muttered to his daughter.

"I was told that the Shihs presented His Honor Wei with a complete banquet[4] at the last year-end," said the man with the crab-shell face.

"That doesn't make any difference," said Wang Te-kuei.

[3] Read 3 × 6 = 18. A common formula used partly for euphony and partly from habit.

[4] A banquet is often ordered and delivered to some one's house as a present.

"A banquet cannot make one blind to all justice. If a banquet can do that, then what about a banquet in foreign style?[5] These scholars are understanding men and they make it a point to help those who have justice on their side. For instance, if a crowd of men should pick on one man, the scholars would come out and stand up for him. They wouldn't care whether they got any wine to drink or not. Last year-end His Honor Jung came back from Peking. He has seen the world; he is different from us country people. And he said that the best of the lot in that house is Kuang *tai-tai*, she is so independent."

"Passengers for Wang's Cove ashore!" shouted the boatman, as the boat slowed down.

"I'm getting off!" The fat man quickly grabbed his pipe and jumped ashore. "Excuse me, excuse me," he said to the people in the boat.

The boat resumed its forward movement in the new silence and the splashing of water became quite audible again. Pa-san began to doze and his mouth dropped open in the direction of the sicklelike feet. Two old women in the front part of the cabin started to murmur the names of the Buddhas, counting them off on their prayer beads. They glanced at Ai-ku, and then looked, nodded and tilted their mouths at each other.

Ai-ku's eyes were fixed on the ceiling of mat which covered the boat, probably rehearsing how she was going to plague her in-laws until "their home was destroyed and their people dead," until both the "old beast" and the "little beast" did not know what to do or where to turn. She did not think much of His Honor Wei—she had seen him twice

[5] A dinner in European style is known as *ta-ts'an* or "great feast" and is considered the last word in luxury and fashion.

before—he was nothing but a short man with a round face and a round head. In her own village there were several people like him, except that they were darker and more sunburned.

Chuang Mu-san's pipe had been smoked down to the bottom and the fire made a sizzling noise as he continued to puff at it. He knew that Pang-chuang was right next to Wang's Cove: in fact it was already possible to see the Kuei-hsing Tower at the entrance to the former village. He had been to Pang-chuang several times before to see those unspeakable people and His Honor Wei. He remembered how his daughter had come back crying, how detestable his son-in-law was, how he had plagued them and got even with them. Reviewing the details of his previous raids and incursions, he remembered how he used to smile the cold smile of confidence as he planned what he would do this time; but on the present occasion he did not smile: for into the familiar pattern of his calculations the fat figure of His Honor Seven had suddenly intruded itself, making it impossible to imagine what might happen.

The boat continued its way in silence. The sound of the invocation of the Buddhas became louder. Otherwise all was quiet, as if to help Mu-san and Ai-ku with their thoughts.

"Uncle Mu, this is where you get off. We are at Pang-chuang."

Mu-san woke from his reflections to find that they were now in front of the Kuei-hsing Tower.

He jumped ashore, followed by Ai-ku, passed by under the tower and walked in the direction of His Honor Wei's house, which was reached after passing about twenty or thirty houses and making a turn at the end. There were four boats moored in a row in front of the house.

They entered the gate with black doors and were ushered into the gatekeeper's room. Outside under the archway there were tables already filled with boatmen and hired men. Ai-ku was not quite brazen enough to look at them closely but a brief glance told her that the "old beast" and the "little beast" were not among them. By the time the New Year pudding soup was brought out, she became more uneasy than ever, without knowing why. "Is it possible that he won't talk human speech, simply because he has become a sworn brother of the magistrate?" she said to herself in an effort to bolster up her courage. "Yes, scholars are understanding men. I'll explain everything to His Honor Seven. I'll begin with the time when I was married into their house at the age of fifteen . . ."

When she finished her pudding soup she surmised that the moment was near. Soon she and her father were following a hired man and making their way toward the inner compound. They passed through the great hall, turned a corner, and stepped into the reception hall.

She did not have time to look carefully at all the things in the room or the people in it, but she was impressed by the shiny, purple-blue satin horse jackets that so many of them wore. She was sure that the man who caught her eyes first was His Honor Seven. Although he also was round faced and round headed, he was nevertheless much heavier and more impressive than His Honor Wei. His huge face carried two thin, slitlike eyes and a thin moustache. His head was close shaven and both his scalp and face were pink and shiny. Ai-ku marveled at it, but she found an explanation immediately: he must have smeared himself with pork fat.

"This is known as an 'anus-stopper,' something which the

ancients inserted into the anus of the dead at encoffining
time," His Honor Seven was saying as he held up a mottled
stone object. He rubbed it a couple of times against the side
of his nose and continued, "Too bad it is comparatively new.
But it is worth buying. At the latest, Han. Look at this, it is
known as 'quick silver impregnate' . . ."

Several heads were immediately bent over the mysterious
phenomenon. His Honor Wei's head was, naturally, among
these, but there were also the heads of several young masters,
whom Ai-ku had not noticed as their presence had been
overwhelmed by more luminous personages.

She did not comprehend the last remark, but she had
neither the curiosity nor the courage to seek enlightenment.
Therefore, she took the opportunity to steal a look around
the room and behold! there close to the wall at one side of
the door stood the "old beast" and the "little beast." Though
it was only a glance, she could see clearly that both seemed
older and more weary than when she saw them last, about
a half year ago.

The crowd around the "quick silver impregnate" broke
up. His Honor Wei took the "anus-stopper" and sat down.
Then turning to Chuang Mu-san he said, while fondling the
extraordinary object:

"Just you two?"

"Yes."

"Didn't any of your sons come with you?"

"They didn't have time."

"I did not mean to disturb you at New Year time. But—
it is still about that matter . . . I think you have done
enough. Has it not gone on for more than two years now?
It is my opinion that it is better to reconcile enmities than

to contract them. Since Ai-ku cannot get along with her
husband and is not liked by her parents-in-law, it is best
to do what I had suggested before: separate. But my prestige
is not great enough and I have not been able to persuade
you. Now His Honor Seven is a most just and understanding man, as you well know. Now His Honor also thinks the
same, the same as I do. However, His Honor says that both
sides should retreat a step. Let the Shihs pay ten dollars more,
he says. That makes ninety dollars!"

As Chuang Mu-san said nothing, he continued: "Ninety
dollars! You'll never get that much even if you take the
case all the way up to the Emperor himself, and he an uncle
of yours. But our honorable Seven is a generous man: no
one else would offer you so much."

The honorable Seven fixed his eyes on Chuang Mu-san
and nodded.

Ai-ku realized that the situation was getting critical. She
was peeved at her father's silence, her father who ordinarily
inspired no small degree of awe in the inhabitants along the
seashore. She felt that his timidity was unnecessary. Though
she did not understand much of what the honorable Seven
said, yet she felt that he was to all appearances a gentle and
kindly man and that there was nothing in him to be afraid
of, as she had first imagined.

"Your Honor is a scholar and an understanding man, a
most understanding man," she said, as she gathered courage.
"Not like us country people. I have a grievance for which
I have not been able to get redress and I want to tell it to
Your Honor. Ever since I was married into their house I
have always bowed my head in and bowed my head out,
and I have never done anything lacking in propriety. But

they all picked on me, every one of them! Year before last when a weasel killed a cock, did they not accuse me of not having securely fastened the chicken coop? Whereas it was that good for nothing mangy dog which pushed the door open to steal the feed! Without trying to find out which was white and which was black, the little beast there gave me a slap in the face . . ."

His Honor cast a look at her at this point.

"I knew why. There was a reason. It cannot escape Your Honor's all-seeing eyes, for Your Honor is a scholar and understanding man who sees everything. It was because he had been bewitched by that promiscuous whore and wanted to drive me out. But my marriage was contracted with the three teas and six gifts, and I was brought over in a regular bridal sedan! I am not so easy to get rid of. I swear I'll show them what I can do, I am not afraid of lawsuits. If I cannot get justice from the district, there is still the prefect . . ."

"His Honor knows all these things," His Honor Wei raised his head and added, "Ai-ku, let me tell you that you won't get much satisfaction if you will not listen to reason. You are always so wayward. See how understanding your father is, so unlike you and your brothers. Yes, you can appeal the case to the prefect, but do you suppose the prefect would fail to consult His Honor Seven about it? When it comes to that, everything will be done strictly according to law and then you . . ."

"Then I'll stake my life against them, I'll willingly die to bring ruin and death to them!"

"But it is not a question of staking your life against any one," His Honor Seven said slowly, at last. "You are still very young. You must learn that one should always try to be gentle, for 'Gentleness brings wealth.' That is something you'll never get by law. According to law, you'll have to go when your parents-in-law say 'Go!' Not only does this hold at the prefect's yamen, it is exactly the same in Shanghai, in Peking. It is the same even in foreign lands, as that young gentleman there who has just returned from a foreign school in Peking will tell you. If you don't believe it you can ask him yourself." Thereupon he turned to a young master with a pointed chin and said, "Am I not right?"

"It is exactly so," answered the young master with the pointed chin, drawing himself up reverently.

Ai-ku felt entirely alone. Her father would not say a word, her brothers had not even dared to come, His Honor Wei had always sided with *them*, the honorable Seven seemed doubtful, and the young master with the pointed chin did nothing but echo back what was expected of him. But in spite of her confusion and helplessness, she made a final effort.

"How is it that even Your Honor . . . ," Her eyes were full of fear and despair as she went on. "Yes, I know that we are only simple people, we know nothing. I can only blame my father for his ignorance of the ways of the world. I'll let the old beast and the little beast do what they like with me; they know the ways of the world, they know how to crawl through dog holes and how to fawn upon people . . ."

"Please note, Your Honor," the "little beast" who had been standing in silence behind her, suddenly broke in, "please note that even before Your Honor she behaves like this. When she was at our house, truly she would not even let the six domestic beasts in peace. As Your Honor notices, she calls my father 'old beast' and me 'little beast,' or 'bastard' for variation."

"Which son of a hundred-thousand-men whore ever called you a bastard?" Ai-ku turned around and protested loudly. Then turning to the honorable Seven again she continued, "There is something else that I want to say before everyone present. He never had a kind word for me. Whenever he opened his mouth, it was 'offspring of a cheap womb' by way of introduction, and 'your mother's this and that' by way of conclusion. Since he took up with that whore, he has even included my ancestors in his foul words. Judge for me, Your Honor, could any . . ."

At this point she stopped abruptly with a shudder, for His Honor suddenly turned up his eyes, threw back his round face, and at the same time released a loud echoing sound from underneath the moustache covering his mouth.

"Lai-a-a!"[6] called His Honor.

Her heart stopped for a moment and then started pounding, for it seemed to her that all was over, that the situation had suddenly changed. She felt as if she had slipped and fallen into the water and she felt, moreover, that it was all her own fault.

At once a man wearing a blue robe and a black vest came in and stood like a wooden stick before His Honor, hands hanging stiffly at his sides. In the entire room "even birds stood still." His Honor's mouth moved but no one caught what he said. The man, however, had caught it. It was evidently an order, an order that seemed to have penetrated to his marrow, for he jerked his body a couple of times—one could almost see his hair standing on end—and answered simultaneously, "Yes."

[6] "Come." Used by masters of many servants and affected by others who do not have so many to summon an attendant.

He walked backwards two or three steps and then turned and went out.

Ai-ku knew that something extraordinary was about to happen, something quite impossible to predict, something quite impossible to forestall. She realized, too, that His Honor was indeed august, that she had entirely misinterpreted his character and that she had been, therefore, entirely too impertinent and blunt. She regretted deeply and was constrained to say, "Of course I have been from the beginning only waiting for Your Honor's command . . ."

Although her voice was as light as gossamer, to His Honor Wei, however, it was, in the midst of the silence, like a clap of thunder. He jumped up.

"Now you are talking! His Honor Seven is most just and Ai-ku most understanding," he flattered. Then he turned to Chuang Mu-san, saying, "Old Mu, of course you'll have no objections since she herself has accepted the terms. I suppose you have brought your red and green papers, as I asked you to do. Then let us all bring the papers out . . ."

Ai-ku looked at her father and found him taking something out of his pocket. At the same time the wooden-stick-like man also came in and handed His Honor Seven a black, flat object that looked something like a small turtle. Ai-ku was afraid that the situation might again change and quickly turned to see what her father was doing. He had already opened up a blue cloth bag on the tea table and had taken out the silver dollars.

His Honor Seven now pulled off the head of the small turtle and poured something from the turtle's body into the palm of his hand. The sticklike man relieved him of the flat object. Then His Honor rubbed a finger of the other hand

in his palm and held it up to his nose and sniffed, whereupon his nostrils and upper lips assumed the color of burned
yellow. His nose wrinkled up as if he was about to sneeze.
Chuang Mu-san was now counting the money. His Honor
Wei took part of the uncounted pile and handed it to the
"old beast." He also exchanged their papers for them, giving
back to each party their part of the marriage contract, saying,
"Now take good care of them, both of you. And old Mu, be
sure to count carefully, for money is no laughing matter."

"Ah-cheoooo!" Ai-ku knew from the noise that His Honor
had just sneezed, yet she could not resist the urge to turn
around. She saw that his mouth was open, his nose still
wrinkled up. He was rubbing the side of his nose with an
object which he held between two fingers of one hand: it was
"something which the ancients inserted into the anus of the
dead at encoffining time."

At last Chuang Mu-san finished counting his money. He
put the marriage papers safely away. The tension was gone.
Every one relaxed and an atmosphere of peace and harmony
reigned in the room.

"Good! The thing is at last satisfactorily finished," His
Honor Wei said, noticing that both sides showed a desire to
take their leave. "And, er, there isn't anything else, is there?
I congratulate you for having brought the thing to an end.
Are you going? Don't go yet, wait until you have had a New
Year cup with us: it is an occasion that comes only once a
year."

"We won't have any now. Wait till next year," Ai-ku
replied.

"Thank you, Your Honor. We won't have any now. We
have business to attend to," said Chuang Mu-san, the "old

beast," and the "little beast," together, as they withdrew respectfully.

"Oh, what? Not going to have any?" His Honor Wei said, looking at Ai-ku, the last one to go out.

"No, not this time. Thank you, Your Honor."

Reunion in a Restaurant

AFTER making a visit to my native home during a journey to the southeast, I found myself in the city of S——, where I had once taught school for a year. It was only thirty *li* from my native village and could be reached in less than half a day by boat. The atmosphere was bleak and dismal after the late winter snow, and inertia and a desire to revisit once familiar scenes caused me to put up at the Lo Ssu Hotel, which had been built since my earlier stay in S——. I went around to call upon some of my old colleagues that I thought might still be in the city, but none of them was to be found, having gone I knew not where. Passing by the school, I found its name and features changed and unfamiliar. The city was not large; in less than two hours I had exhausted the interest that it held for me, and I began to feel that this visit had been ill-considered and unnecessary.

The hotel rent did not include food, which had to be specially arranged for and was insipid and tasted like mud. From the window there was nothing to see but a spotted and dirty wall covered with dead moss; above, the sky was leaden, a grayish white without relief. A light snow was beginning to fall. As I had not eaten much at the midday meal and had nothing to amuse myself with, I very naturally thought of a restaurant that I used to go to, known as the One Stone Lodge. It was not far from the hotel. So I locked my room and went out on the street and walked in the direction of the restaurant. Really I was more interested in escaping from the dismal hotel room than in food and drink.

The One Stone Lodge was still there, the dark and narrow shop front and the old worn signs were the same, but no one in the restaurant, from the manager to the waiter, was familiar to me. I had become a stranger at the One Stone Lodge. Nevertheless, I ended by climbing the familiar steps at a corner of the shop and went into the small second-story room. Little had been changed. There were still just five tables as before; the paper in the latticed window at the back, however, had been replaced with glass.

"One pot of Shao-hsing. Relishes? Ten pieces of fried bean curd with plenty of hot pepper sauce," I said to the waiter who followed me up the stairs, as I walked toward the back window and sat down at a table. As the room was empty, I selected the best seat so that I could command a view of the deserted garden, which did not, I think, belong to the restaurant. I had looked upon it many times before, sometimes also when snow was falling. But, now, as I looked at it with eyes that had become accustomed to the climate of the North, the garden presented a very remarkable sight: the old plum trees were covered with blossoms in spite of the snow, as if unmindful of the winter; near the ruined pavilion a camellia displayed among its thick, dark-green foliage some red flowers bright and startling as flames in the snow, angry and proud as if disdainful of the wanderer that had chosen to travel in distant parts. I suddenly realized how moist and soft was the snow here, how the flakes clung to things, how brilliant and crystalline they were, and how unlike the snow in the North, which was dry as powder, filling the air like mist when driven by the wind.

"Sir, here is your wine," the waiter said wearily, setting down the cup, chopsticks, wine pot, and dishes.

I turned to the table, arranged the things, and poured some wine. The North was not my native place, and yet here in the South, also, I was looked upon as a stranger. No matter how dry and powdery the snow flies over there, or how soft and clinging it is here, it was none of my concern. I felt sad and melancholy, but I took a draught of wine with pleasure. It tasted excellent and the fried bean curd was nicely cooked. It was a pity that the pepper sauce was very weak; the people of the city of S—— did not know what hot things were.

I suppose it must have been because it was early in the afternoon that the restaurant was so quiet and so unlike a restaurant in atmosphere. I had already finished three cups of wine, but the other four tables were still vacant. Looking at the deserted garden, I felt my loneliness and desolation increase, though I did not wish for the intrusion of other patrons either. When I heard an occasional footstep on the stairs I could not help feeling a little resentful, and was relieved to see that it was only the waiter. I drank two more cups of wine.

Footsteps sounded on the stairs again. "It must surely be some customer this time," I thought, for the steps were much slower than the waiter's. When I thought that he must have reached the top of the stairs, I looked up very reluctantly at this chance companion of the wine shop, and then stood up with surprise. I did not expect to meet here a friend—if he still allowed me to call him friend. For the man who came up was without a doubt a former schoolmate of mine and a colleague in my teaching days. Though his features had changed somewhat, I had no difficulty in recognizing him. His movements, however, were noticeably slower than they used to be, quite unlike the animated, clever, and shrewd Lu Wei-fu that I used to know.

"Ah, Wei-fu, is it you? I never would have thought of meeting you here."

"Ah, ah, is it you? Neither would I."

I invited him to sit down at my table, which he did after some hesitation. My first delight and surprise gave place to a feeling of sadness and depression. Looking at him more closely, I found that his hair and beard were still bushy and unruly, but his pale, long face had become thin and lined. He seemed very calm and serene, but it might have been weariness. The eyes under his thick, dark brows had lost their luster, though when he looked around the room and saw the deserted garden, they gleamed with a fire familiar to us in our student days.

"It must be ten years now," I said with forced gaiety, "since we last saw each other. Isn't it? I knew that you were at Tsinan but I have been too lazy to write."

"It is the same with all of us. But now I am at Taiyuan; I've been there over two years now, with my mother. When I came to get her, I learned that you had moved away—made a very clean move, I was told."

"What are you doing at Taiyuan?" I asked.

"Teaching, in the family of a fellow provincial."

"And before that?"

"Before that?" he said, lighting the cigarette that he had taken out of his pocket and watching reflectively the curls of smoke. "Nothing but very inconsequential things. It amounts to having done nothing at all."

He asked what I had been doing since we parted, and I told him briefly, after first telling the waiter to bring another cup and pair of chopsticks so that my friend could join me immediately. I then ordered two more pots of wine and more relishes. We did not use to stand on ceremony, but now each insisted that the other should do the honor of ordering. Finally we ordered four dishes from the menu recited by the waiter, without knowing who ordered which—spiced beans, cold meat, more fried bean curd, and smoked fish.

"I realized the futility of it all as soon as I returned," he said, half smiling, one hand holding the cigarette and the other touching the wine cup. "When I was a boy I used to watch flies or bees at rest. When something disturbed them, they would fly away, but after circling around a few times they would return to the same spot. I thought they were very funny and pitiable then. I did not foresee that I too would be flying back to the same place after describing a small circle. And I did not expect that you would be back here too. Couldn't you fly farther than this?"

"I don't know," I said, also half smiling. "But why did you fly back here?"

"Also because of very inconsequential things," he said, emptying his cup and puffing at his cigarette, his eyes somewhat larger for the stimulant. "Yes, very inconsequential. But we can talk about them."

The waiter brought our orders, which filled the table, and the room seemed more lively with the tobacco smoke and the hot vapor from the fried bean curd. The snow was falling more thickly outside.

"Maybe you know," he continued, "that I had a little brother, who died when he was three and was buried here. I have forgotten what he looked like, but my mother tells me he was a very lovable child and got along splendidly with me. Even now she weeps when she talks about him. This last spring a cousin of mine wrote that water was beginning to approach his tomb and that unless something was done, it might soon be washed into the river. My mother became anxious when she learned about it—I couldn't keep it from her as she knows how to read—and could hardly sleep for several nights. But what could I do? I had neither time nor money for the trip. I could not do a thing at the time.

"It was put off until now. The New Year vacation gave me the opportunity to come back South and rebury his body." He drained another cup and said, looking out the window, "We have no such climate up there—flowers in the snow and temperature above freezing, while snow lies on the ground . . . It was day before yesterday. I bought a small coffin—for I thought that the original one must have rotted away long ago—and some new bedding and cotton batting, and went out to the country with four laborers to attend to the re-interment. I suddenly had an exalted feeling; I wanted to help with the digging; I wanted to see the remains of the little brother who used to get along so splendidly with me. I had never had any experience with such things before. When I arrived at the cemetery, I found that the river was indeed eating into the bank and was now only about two feet from the tomb, which was in a pitiful state, almost level with the ground, as no earth had been heaped upon it for two years. I stood in the snow and, pointing to it, said to the laborers with great resolution, 'Now dig here!' I must have appeared rather foolish. I felt that there was something strangely impressive in my voice, that this was the most important and significant command I had ever given in all my life. But the laborers did not seem to be awed or surprised; they set to work without any emotion. When the chamber was reached, I went over to look, and found, as I expected, that the coffin had almost rotted away. There was only a pile of wood dust and splinters left. With my heart beating violently, I carefully removed the heap of wood so as to get a look at my little brother. But there was nothing—bedding, clothes, bones—nothing! I thought that if these things had all disintegrated, there might at least be some hair left, since I had been told that hair is the most imperishable thing of the human body. I leaned over and searched carefully where his head should have been. There was nothing, not a single hair!"

I suddenly noticed that his eyes had become red but I knew that it was due to the wine rather than to his emotion. He would not eat much, but drank cup after cup, and soon consumed more than a potful. He grew more spirited and his gestures more animated; he was more like the old Lu Wei-fu now. I told the waiter to bring two more pots of wine, and, with cup in hand, turned back to listen silently to his story.

"Really there was no need of reinterment. One could have flattened the ground, sold the coffin, and considered the matter ended. It might seem queer for me to be selling a coffin, but if the price was reasonable enough the shop might have taken it back and I would at least have had some money to buy wine. But that was not what I did. Instead, I collected some earth, wrapped it in the bedding, put the bundle in the coffin, and had it carried to my father's tomb and buried by its side. Because of the brick structure over it, I was busy most of yesterday supervising the workmen. Well, I have at least done what had to be done and I can lie to my mother in order to set her mind at peace. Ah, are you looking at me like that because you are surprised that I am so different from what I used to be? Yes, I also remember the time when we went to the Temple of the City God and pulled off the idol's whiskers; when we used to get so excited over discussions on how to reform and revolutionize China that we came to blows. But now I have become like this. I let things pass, let things slide without getting excited about anything. I myself have sometimes thought that my old friends probably would no longer consider me a friend when they see the way I am. But still this is the way I am now."

He took out another cigarette and lit it.

"I see from your attitude that you still seem to have some hope in me—I am, of course, much more insensible than I used to be, but there are still things that I can notice. This makes me feel grateful but at the same time uncomfortable, for I am afraid that I shall eventually disappoint even those old friends that still entertain kindly feelings towards me and wish me well." He stopped abruptly, puffed at his cigarette and then resumed. "And today, just before I came here, I did another senseless and futile thing, but it was again something that I had wanted to do. When I lived here, my neighbor to the east was Chang-fu the boatman. He had a daughter by the name of Ah[1] Shun. You might have seen her when you used to come to our house, but you probably did not notice her as she was still very little then. She was not pretty when she grew up; her face was thin and plain, shaped like a melon seed, and her complexion was yellow. But her eyes were extraordinarily large, with long lashes; the white of her eyes was as clear as the night sky, the clear sky of the North when there is no wind. Her mother died when she was slightly over ten and the care of her younger brother and

---

[1] "Ah" is a prefix to personal names used chiefly in Southern China; it indicates an even greater degree of familiarity than "lao" (old), its counterpart in Northern China. Some such prefix or suffix (as in the case of "ma" in the name of the maid servant Wu-ma in "Our Story of Ah Q") is necessary in names of one syllable because of the disyllabic tendency of the Chinese language.

sister devolved upon her, and she had to attend to the wants of her father besides. As she was thrifty and managed everything well, the family became more and more substantial. All the neighbors praised her; even Chang-fu often expressed gratification. When I set out for this journey, my mother suddenly remembered her—the memory of old people is really remarkable. She said that Ah Shun had once wanted a red artificial flower made of soft down that she saw someone wear, and had cried all night because she did not get one and was beaten by her father for it. Her eyes were swollen for several days afterward. This particular kind of artificial flower was made in another province, and was not procurable even in the city of S——. How could they get one for her in the country? So my mother asked me to buy a few flowers on my way south and give them to her.

"I did not consider this errand irksome, but was glad of it, for I had a sincere wish to do something for Ah Shun. Year before last when I came back to fetch my mother, Chang-fu happened to be home one day and somehow I found myself engaged in an idle conversation with him. He invited me to have some sweetmeat with him, a kind of buckwheat jelly which he told me was prepared with sugar. You can see that he was not a poor boatman since he could afford to keep sugar in the house, and that he ate well. I could not refuse because of his persistence, so I accepted the invitation but begged him to give me only a small bowl. He said to Ah Shun with a knowing air, 'These scholars cannot eat much, so use a small bowl but put plenty of sugar in it!' When the delicacy was prepared and brought in, the size of the bowl frightened me, though compared with that of Chang-fu mine was indeed a small one. I had never eaten buckwheat jelly before. When I tasted it I did not find it palatable, though it was quite sweet. After a few mouthfuls I was about to stop eating when I caught sight of Ah Shun standing in the far corner of the room. I lost the courage to put down the bowl and chopsticks. The expression on her face was one of fear and hope, fear lest she might not have prepared it properly, and hope that we might enjoy it. I knew that if I left the greater part of the bowl, she would be disappointed and self-reproachful because she had not done better. Thereupon, I made an effort and gulped every bit down, almost as fast as Chang-fu. I learned then what it means to force down food—I remember only one other experience of the sort when as a child I had to take a bowl of brown-sugar syrup mixed with powdered vermifuge. But I did not regret it, for when Ah Shun came to take away the bowls the smile of gratification that she tried so hard to hide more than compensated for my discomfort. So although I did not sleep well that night because of the bloated feeling in my stomach and had some terrible nightmares, I still wished her lifelong happiness, still wished that the world might be changed for the better for her sake. But these thoughts were only the echoes of bygone dreams. I would smile to myself when I thought of them and would soon forget about them.

"I did not know that she had been punished once because of an artificial flower, but when my mother told me about it, I recalled the jelly episode and I became unusually diligent. I searched all over Taiyuan without success. It was not until I got to Tsinan . . ."

There came a rustling sound from outside the window as the snow fell from a camellia tree that had been bent by its weight. The branches straightened out, revealing more completely the shiny luxuriant leaves and the blood-red flowers. The leaden sky was heavier. The birds were chirping plaintively, probably nesting early because the clouds had hastened the twilight and because there was no food to be found on the snow-covered ground.

"It was not until I reached Tsinan," he said, after looking out the window for a while, drinking another cup of wine, and taking a few more puffs at his cigarette, "that I got those flowers. I don't know that they were the same kind of flowers for which she was spanked, but they were made of the same material. I did not know whether she liked deep or light colors, so I bought one of brilliant red and one of pinkish red and brought them here with me.

"This afternoon, immediately after dinner, I went over to see Chang-fu. I stayed over another day just for this. His house was still there, though I seemed to sense a gloom over it, probably because of the state of mind I was in. Chang-fu's son and his second daughter, Ah Chao—both grown up now—were standing at the gate. Ah Chao was not at all like her sister. She was more like a ghost. She fled into the house when she caught sight of me. I questioned the boy and found that Chang-fu was not home. 'And your elder sister?' I asked, finally. Thereupon he glared at me and asked me what I was asking about her for, as if about to pounce on me and eat me up. I stammered some excuses and retreated; I am very diffident and easily discouraged nowadays . . .

"You may not know that I am even more timid about calling on people than I used to be. I know very well that I am an eye-sore—I am an eye-sore even to myself—so why should I deliberately go out of my way to cast a gloom upon others? After some hesitation I went to the firewood shop opposite. The mother of the shopkeeper, Grandma Lao Fa, was still living. She recognized me and asked me to go in and sit down. After we had exchanged greetings, I told her why I had returned to the city of S—— and why I had been looking for Chang-fu. I was surprised when she sighed and said, 'It is a pity that Ah Shun will never have the pleasure of wearing those flowers.'

"Then she told me in great detail what had happened, saying, 'It was about last spring that she began to grow noticeably thinner and paler. Later she began to weep frequently and would not explain the cause when she was asked about it. Sometimes she would cry all night, until it got on Chang-fu's nerves and he scolded her, saying that she must be getting silly as she grew older. In the fall—it was only a cold at first—but she ended up in bed and never got up. A few days before she died she told Chang-fu that for a long time she had been like her mother, suffered women's disorders and sweated at night. She did not want to tell him for fear of causing him anxiety. One evening, his elder uncle Chang-keng came and insisted on borrowing money. This was a frequent occurrence. When Ah Shun would not give it to him, he said, smiling sardonically, "You need not be so proud, your man is not even as good as I am!" Ever since that she was very much worried. She was too bashful to ask questions, so she only cried. Chang-fu tried to console her by telling her how trustworthy and ambitious her man was, but it was too late. Besides, she did not believe it, saying that it didn't matter anymore since she was so ill.'

"Grandma Lao Fa also said, 'It would be a terrible thing indeed if her man was really worse than Chang-keng. What a good-for-nothing he must be if he was not as good as a chicken thief! But when he came to the funeral, I saw him with my own eyes. He was neatly dressed and well featured. He said with tears in his eyes that he had labored hard and saved for half a lifetime to get married, and now his woman had died! One could see that he was really a good man and that Chang-keng had lied. It is very sad indeed that Ah Shun should have believed the lies of a born thief and died for nothing. But then we cannot blame anyone, we can only blame Ah Shun's ill fate.'

"Well, that was that. And I had finished my affairs. But what was I to do with the two flowers I still had with me? Well, I asked Grandma Lao Fa to give them to Ah Chao. I really did not want to give them to her particularly since this Ah Chao ran away from me as if I were a wolf or something worse. But I gave them to her just the same. When I see my mother I shall only tell her that Ah Shun was too happy for words when she got the flowers. What do these things matter anyway? Only to drag along, drag along until after the New Year when I shall begin to teach anew my 'The Master Says' and 'The Book of Poetry Says.'"

"Is that what you teach?" I asked with astonishment.[2]

"Of course. Did you think that I was teaching the ABC's? I had only two pupils at first, one studying the *Book of Poetry* and the other *Mencius*. Recently another one was added, a girl, studying *Precepts for Women*. I do not even teach any arithmetic; not that I don't want to, but because their parents don't."

"I really did not think that you would be teaching such books!"

"That's what their father wants them to read. I am an outsider and it is none of my affair what they read. What do these things matter anyway? One must take things as they come."

His face was red and he seemed a little drunk. But the

[2] The teaching of the Confucian classics was abolished in the primary and secondary schools when the Republic was established.

light had again gone out of his eyes. I sighed softly and could not find anything to say. There were footsteps on the stairs and several customers came in. The first one was a short man with a round bloated face; the second one was tall with a rather prominent red nose; there were others behind them and their steps made the small building tremble. I turned to look at Lu Wei-fu, who had just turned around to look at me. So I called the waiter to reckon the bill.

"Can you manage to live on what you get?" I asked him as we got ready to go.

"I get twenty dollars a month, hardly enough to get along on."

"Then, what are you going to do in the future?"

"The future? I don't know. Think if any of the things we used to dream about ever came out as we wished. I don't know anything about the future. I don't even know about tomorrow."

The waiter brought the bill and gave it to me. Lu Wei-fu was not so ceremonious as when he first came in; he only glanced at me, puffed at his cigarette, and allowed me to pay the bill.

We parted at the door of the restaurant, as the hotel where he stayed lay in the opposite direction from mine. I walked toward my hotel, feeling exhilarated by the cold wind and the snowflakes in my face. Dusk had fallen: the houses and streets were all woven into the texture of a white and restless blanket of snow.

The Story of Hair

WHEN I tore off a sheet from the wall calendar Sunday morning and looked at it, my casual glance became a fixed gaze and I exclaimed to myself, "Ah, October 10! So today is the Double Ten Festival. And yet nothing is marked here!"

Hearing this observation, N——, a senior of mine who happened to be calling, said to me in a displeased tone:

"They are right. Yes, they have forgotten the national holiday, but what of it? You happen to have remembered, but again what of it?"

This N—— was of a perverse temperament; he would get wrought up over things that did not matter and say things that embarrassed people. At such times I usually let him mumble on without putting in a word.

He continued: "I am most amused by the way they celebrate the Double Ten here in Peking. In the morning a policeman knocks on the door and says, 'Hang up the flag!' and you hear the reply, 'Yes, officer, we'll hang up the flag.' A citizen of the Republic emerges from the gate and perfunctorily hangs up a piece of cotton cloth with faded colors. In the evening it is taken down and the gate shut. Sometimes the flag is forgotten and left there until the next morning.

"It is true that they have forgotten to celebrate the national holiday; there is in fact very little for them to celebrate. I, for one, try not to remember, for to remember is to be

reminded of things just before and after the first Double
Ten, things I would rather forget. It is to see once again the
faces of many old friends, some of whom, after years of toil
and struggle, were quietly dispatched with bullets; others
were imprisoned and thrown into the torture chamber; still
others simply disappeared without leaving the slightest trace.

"Scorn, vilification, persecution, and murder were their
lot when they lived; now their tombs, neglected and forgotten, are gradually being leveled by time . . . I have no courage to recall these things. Let us talk about something more
pleasant."

A smile flitted across N——'s face as he said, stroking his
head: "What pleases me most is that since the first Double
Ten I am no longer insulted or laughed at when I go out
on the street. Do you know, my friend, that hair has been
at once the pet and the curse of us Chinese? That innumer-
able people have suffered untold miseries and tortures because of it?

"The ancients of very early times seemed to have attached
little importance to hair. From the point of view of punishment, the most important thing is naturally the head, and
accordingly decapitation was the severest punishment; next
in importance are the reproductive organs, and so castration
and sterilization came to be punishments much dreaded. But
when it comes to cutting off the hair, this was considered of
no consequence; though when one comes to think of it, in-
numerable people must have been insulted and persecuted by
their fellows because of their tell-tale shaven heads.

"Before the Revolution we used to talk about the Ten Days
of Yangchow, the Sack of Kiating, but to tell the truth, that
was only propaganda. In reality, the Chinese opposed the

Manchus not out of patriotism but because they rebelled at having to grow queues.

"Stubborn peasants were put to the sword, ministers from the former dynasty died comfortably in their beds, and the queue became an established institution—but then came the T'ai P'ing Rebellion. My grandmother used to tell me that it was most difficult to be a law-abiding citizen in those days: those who let their hair grow like the Longhairs were executed by the Government troops; those who grew queues like the Manchus were executed by the Longhairs.[1]

"I don't know how many Chinese suffered because of the hair which neither ached nor itched; suffered, were persecuted and destroyed."

N—— looked at the rafters thoughtfully and continued:

"And this unnecessary suffering eventually fell on my head . . . I cut off my queue when I went abroad to study; I had no other reason than that it was less of a bother to be without one. But I immediately became an object of hate to my fellow students, who wound up their queues and concealed them under their hats. The director of the educational mission was wroth and threatened to suspend my scholarship and to have me deported.

"But a few days later the director's own queue was forcibly cut off by a group of students, among whom was Tsou Jung, author of the *Revolutionary Vanguard*. He lost his scholarship because of this, returned to Shanghai and died in a Settlement prison. I suppose you have forgotten about this long ago.

[1] The Manchu queue called for the shaving of a strip of about an inch all around the head, whereas the Chinese style of hair dressing before the Manchu conquest permitted the entire head of hair to grow long.

"A few years later, reduced family circumstances made it necessary for me to get a job, so I returned to China. I got a false queue—it only cost two dollars in those days—as soon as I landed at Shanghai, and went home wearing it. My mother did not say anything, but others studied it suspiciously and grunted when they found it to be false, citing decapitation as my proper punishment. One of my kinsmen considered informing against me, but was deterred by the thought that the treasonable revolutionaries might succeed after all.

"Then deciding that a false queue was not as open and honest as a real shaven head, I discarded it and walked out on the street in a foreign suit.

"Laughter and taunts followed me wherever I went. 'The reckless fool!' 'The fake foreign devil.'

"I discarded my foreign clothes and put on my long robe. But the laughter and taunts grew worse. At the end of my resources, I armed myself with a walking stick and used it vigorously a few times. The taunts ceased gradually, except when I ventured into strange territory where my stick had not yet been brought into play.

"But this expedient depressed me, and even now I recall it with shame. When I was studying in Japan I once read a newspaper item about a certain Dr. Honda who had traveled in China and the Malay States. Now, when this doctor, who spoke neither Chinese nor Malay, was asked how he got along without a knowledge of the native languages, he raised his walking stick and said that that was a language they all understood. I could not get over the feeling of anger and humiliation caused by this for many days. Who'd think that I would resort to it myself? The more ironic that these people did understand the language of the stick!

"In the first year of Hsüan T'ung [1909] I was proctor at

the middle school of my native city. My colleagues avoided me, the authorities set spies on me; I felt as if I lived in an icehouse, as if I were standing on the execution ground; and all for no other reason than that I did not have a queue!

"One day some students came to see me in my room, saying, 'Sir, we want to cut off our queues.'

" 'It won't do!' I said.

" 'Which is better—to have a queue or not to have a queue?'

" 'It is better to be without one . . .'

" 'Then why do you say that it won't do?'

" 'It is not worth it. It is wiser not to cut off your queues. Better wait a little while.'

"They did not say anything to this but they left unconvinced and cut off their queues anyway. It caused a great deal of talk. But I pretended to notice nothing and allowed them to come to class along with those who had queues.

"The disease spread; on the third day six queues were cut off among the students of the Normal School and on that same afternoon the six queueless students were expelled. These six students could not stay in the school and did not dare return home; they suffered like branded criminals until a month or two after the first Double Ten.

"I myself? I also was pardoned. I was only taunted a few times when I came to Peking the winter of the first year of the Republic, but later on the very ones that taunted me had their queues cut off by the police. From then on I was no longer insulted and taunted. But I have not ventured into the more conservative countrysides."

N——'s face softened with an air of satisfaction for a moment, but suddenly it clouded again as he said:

"Now you visionaries are advocating bobbed hair for

women, again trying to cause senseless suffering! Are there not already girls who cannot pass their entrance examinations or are expelled because they have bobbed hair?

"Radical reforms? Where is your weapon? To work one's way through school? But, to do that, where are your factories?

"Better let them grow their hair again and get married and become good daughters-in-law. It is a blessing to forget; if they keep such ideas as equality and freedom in their heads, they will suffer all their lives!

"Let me put to you the question raised by Artzibasheff: You hold out the promise of a golden age to these people's children, but what do you have for these people themselves?

"Ah! before the lashes of nature's whip fall upon the bare back of China, China will remain China; she will not of her own will alter a single hair!

"You people have no poison fangs in your mouths; why must you put the label 'poisonous vipers' on your foreheads to invite destruction by the beggar snake-catchers?"

N——'s talk became more and more confused and difficult to follow, but as soon as he saw that I showed no interest in what he was saying he stood up to get his hat.

"Are you going?" I asked.

"Yes," he replied. "It is going to rain."

Silently I walked with him to the gate. *"Tsai-chien!"* he said, as he put on his hat. "Forgive me for disturbing you. But fortunately tomorrow won't be Double Ten any more and we can forget everything."

Cloud over Luchen

AS THE sun gradually gathered up its yellow rays along the mud banks of the river, the scorched leaves of the tallow trees seemed to recover their breath and a few striped mosquitoes began to buzz underneath the trees. The smoke died out in the chimneys of the peasants' homes facing the river. Women and children sprinkled water on the dusty ground in front of their own houses and set out low tables and benches. It was supper time.

The old folks and the men sat on the low benches and chatted, wielding huge palm fans. The children ran about or squatted under the tallow trees and played with pebbles. The womenfolk carried out *kan-ts'ai* and brown rice, hot and steaming. A pleasure boat went by, carrying a party of literary aesthetes, who, watching the scenes along the banks, were inspired to poetic sentiment about the villagers, uttering, "Unreflecting and without a worry in their heads—this is truly Rural Bliss."

But the sentiments of these literary lights did not exactly accord with the truth, for they could not hear what old Mrs. Nine Pounds was saying. She was at that moment greatly put out by things in general: beating upon the leg of her stool with her frazzled palm fan for emphasis, she was saying,

"I have lived seventy-nine years and I have lived long enough. I do not want to see these signs of family decline.

It is better that I died. In a moment we'll be eating supper, and yet she is eating toasted beans. She'll eat us poor!"

Her great-granddaughter Six Pounds, who was just then coming toward the supper table, thought better of it at the sight of the querulous woman. She ran to the river's edge and hid behind a tallow tree. Then she put out her little head adorned with two hornlike braids and said in a loud voice, "The old Would-Not-Die!"

Though old Mrs. Nine Pounds was of venerable age, she was not very deaf. However, she did not seem to have heard her granddaughter, and continued, "This proves that each generation is worse than the last!"

This village has a peculiar custom. When a baby is born, it is usually weighed and the weight in pounds[1] becomes the milk name[2] of the infant. After old Mrs. Nine Pounds had celebrated her fiftieth birthday she gradually became one of those who mourn for the good old times. When she was young, she said, the weather was not as hot as now, nor were the beans quite as hard. Her perpetual theme was that the world today is all wrong. Moreover, Six Pounds weighed three pounds less at birth than her great-grandfather, and one pound less than her father Seven Pounds. To the old lady these were indisputable proofs of her contention. Therefore she repeated with emphasis, "Truly, each generation is worse than the last!"

Her grand daughter-in-law Sister Seven Pounds came up with the rice basket as this sentiment was repeated and emphasized. She plumped down the basket on the table and said

[1] The Chinese pound or "catty" is generally equal to one and one-third English pounds.

[2] That is, baby name; it is generally discarded when one is old enough to enter school or to marry, though with persons in humble circumstances it may serve to the end of their lives.

in a tone of vexation, "There you go again. When Six Pounds was born was she not actually six pounds and five ounces? Besides, your scales were specially made for you, with eighteen ounces to the pound. If a real sixteen-ounce scale had been used, our Six Pounds would have been over seven pounds. Come to think of it, grandfather and father might not have been actually nine or eight pounds. The scales used might have been only fourteen-ounce scales."

"Each generation worse than the last!"

Before Sister Seven Pounds answered, she suddenly espied her husband coming out of the lane. Thereupon she shifted the direction of her attack and shouted at him, "A fine time for you to be coming home, you dead corpse! Where did you hide off to die? You never care how long people hold up dinner for you, do you?"

Although Seven Pounds lived in the village, he was no ordinary peasant. Three generations, from his grandfather's time to his own, the men of his family had not touched the handle of a hoe. Like many other men of a more progressive nature, Seven Pounds made his living as a boatman. He made a round trip each day, in the morning from Luchen to the city and back to Luchen again by nightfall. Because of this he was well abreast of the times. For instance, he knew that at such and such a place the Thunder God struck dead a centipede monster, or that at such and such a place a maiden gave birth to a yaksha demon; and things of a like nature. He was, therefore, something of a personage in the village. However, in his family supper was still served without benefit of lamplight during the summer months, as was the custom of peasants, and he deserved a scolding for coming home so late.

Seven Pounds approached slowly, his head bowed, and

sat down on a bench. In his hand he held a pipe with a brass
bowl and an ivory mouthpiece and a stem of mottled bamboo
more than six feet long. Six Pounds sneaked out from behind
the tree and sat down beside him, greeting him, "dieh-dieh,"
but Seven Pounds paid no attention to her.

"Each generation worse than the last!" old Mrs. Nine
Pounds said again.

Seven Pounds raised his head slowly and said with a sigh,
"The Emperor has mounted the Dragon Throne."[3]

For a moment Sister Seven Pounds was stupefied by the announcement, but then said with comprehension, "This is
fine, for does it not mean that there will be general pardon
by imperial grace?"

Seven Pounds sighed again and said, "I have no queue."

"Does the Emperor require queues?"

"The Emperor requires queues."

"How do you know?" Sister Seven Pounds asked, somewhat alarmed.

"Every one in the Hsien Heng wine shop says so."

Sister Seven Pounds began to feel that things looked black
indeed for her husband, if they said so at the Hsien Heng
wine shop, the chief source of news for the village. Glancing
at her husband's shaven head, she could not suppress a
mounting anger and resentment against him for having
jeopardized his own safety. She almost hated him. In despair
she filled a bowl with rice and thrust it in front of him and
said, "You had better eat your rice. You will not grow a queue
by pulling a long face!"

Imperceptibly the sun gathered up its last rays and the
river recovered its coolness. The clatter of chopsticks and
bowls echoed all over the open space and beads of sweat

[3] This alludes to the brief restoration of the Manchu dynasty in 1917.

began to form on everyone's back. After finishing her third bowl of rice, Sister Seven Pounds glanced up and her heart began to beat violently when she saw fat, short Mr. Chao the Seventh coming toward them across the single-log bridge. What distressed her most was the fact that Mr. Chao was wearing his long gown of blue cotton cloth.

Mr. Chao was the proprietor of the Mao Yuan wine shop in the neighboring village and the most distinguished personage within a radius of thirty *li*. Because he was something of a scholar, he had about him the air of a man who had seen better days. He owned some ten odd volumes of the *Romance of Three Kingdoms*, with commentaries by Chin Sheng-t'an, and used to sit over them and read aloud word by word. The extent of his erudition was such that he not only knew the names of the Five Tiger Generals but also their derived names.[4] He knew, for instance, that Chao Yun's derived name was Tzu-lung, Chang Fei's was Yi-te and so on. After the Revolution he coiled up his queue on top of his head, like a Taoist priest. He used to say with many a sigh that if Chao Tzu-lung were alive today, the world would not have come to such grief. Sister Seven Pounds had good eyes; she immediately noticed that Mr. Chao had not coiled his hair on top of his head like a Taoist priest but wore it in a queue with the familiar, closely shaven circle around it. From this she concluded that the Emperor must certainly have mounted the Dragon Throne, that wearing the queue was obligatory, and that Seven Pounds' position was most surely of a very precarious character. For Mr. Chao never wore that

---

[4] That is, their *tzu*, usually translated as "style." The connection between the name and the derived name is obvious in the cases of Generals Chao and Chang (as indeed in most cases): the former's name means "cloud," his derived name "Sir dragon"; the latter's name means "to fly," his derived name, "virtue of wings."

long gown of his except on special occasions. In the last three years he had worn it only twice, once when pockmarked Ah Ssu, with whom he once had a quarrel, fell ill, and again when Mr. Lu, who once wrecked his tavern, died. This was the third time and it could only mean that he was celebrating something lucky to himself but unlucky to his enemies.

Sister Seven Pounds remembered that two years earlier her husband had, under the influence of liquor, insulted Mr. Chao by declaring that he was born of a "cheap womb." Therefore she immediately feared for Seven Pounds and she could not still her pounding heart.

As Mr. Chao approached, those who were sitting stood up and said, pointing to their bowls with their chopsticks, "Mr. Seven, please join us!" Mr. Chao nodded and said, "Please go ahead, please go ahead." He went straight to Seven Pounds' table, where he was greeted in the same fashion and returned the same answer. He looked at the fare of rice and steamed *kan-ts'ai*.

"How fragrant your *kan-ts'ai* is! Have you heard?" he asked, standing behind Seven Pounds and opposite Sister Seven Pounds.

"The Emperor has mounted the Dragon Throne," Seven Pounds said.

Sister Seven Pounds watched Mr. Chao's face and said with a placating smile, "Now that the Emperor has mounted the Dragon Throne, when are we going to have the general pardon by imperial grace?"

"General pardon by imperial grace? The general pardon will undoubtedly come in time," Mr. Chao said, and then continued with sudden severity, "But where's Seven Pounds' queue? Yes, the queue is an important matter. Do you know that during the Rebellion of the Longhairs it was a case of 'grow your hair and lose your head or shave your hair and save your head?' "[5]

Seven Pounds and his wife had never had any book learning and so did not quite understand the allusion. But since the learned Mr. Chao said so, the situation must be very grave and unalterable. It was as if the death sentence had been pronounced. Seven Pounds was left speechless with a ringing in his ears.

"Each generation worse than the last," old Mrs. Nine Pounds took the opportunity to voice her grievance to Mr. Chao. "The rebels today only cut off people's queues, making them look like neither monk nor priest. But were the Longhair rebels like this? I have lived seventy-nine years and I have lived long enough. The Longhairs of the old days used whole bolts of red satin to wrap around their heads, with the loose ends hanging down as far as their feet. The Longhair kings used yellow satin, also dangling down to the feet. Yes, yellow satin and red satin, dangling down . . . I have lived long enough; I am seventy-nine years old."

Sister Seven Pounds stood up and murmured to herself, "What are we going to do? All of us, old and young, depend upon him for our living."

Mr. Chao shook his head and said, "That can't be helped. The punishment for not having queues is clearly written in the book. They don't take into account family circumstances."

When she heard that it was clearly written in the book, Sister Seven Pounds gave up all hope. She felt quite helpless and in her helplessness her resentment turned toward Seven Pounds. She pointed at the tip of his nose with her chopsticks and said, "He has brought all this upon himself, the dead corpse! When the rebellion started I told him that he should

[5] See p. 61.

give up poling boats for the time being and should not go into the city. But he insisted on going into the city—on rolling[6] into the city—and when he got there they got hold of him and cut off his queue. Formerly he had a nice, silky, black queue and now he looks like neither monk nor priest. It is all well and good for the jailbird to bring this upon himself, but what have we done? What are we going to do? You walking corpse of a jailbird!"

The villagers had by now hurried through their meal and were gathered around Seven Pounds' table. Conscious of the fact that he was something of a personage, Seven Pounds felt acutely the shame of being scolded by one's wife in public. He raised his head and gently remonstrated, "It is very well for you to say these things now, but, at the time, you . . ."

"You walking corpse of a jailbird!"

Among the onlookers Sister Eighteen was the most kind-hearted. With her two-year-old son in her arms—he was born after the death of her husband—she was standing beside Sister Seven Pounds. She felt sorry for Seven Pounds and tried to put in a word for him, saying, "Sister Seven Pounds, let him be. People are not gods, so who is to foresee what is to come? And did you not say at the time, Sister Seven Pounds, that it was not so bad, after all, to be without a queue? Besides, there has been no official proclamation by his honor the magistrate."

Before she had heard it all, Sister Seven Pounds was already red around the ears. She pointed her chopsticks at Sister Eighteen's nose and said, "What are you talking about, Sister Eighteen? As far as I can see I am the same person now as

[6] To describe some one as "rolling" like an egg, particularly a turtle's egg, or to tell him to "roll away," is very uncomplimentary.

I was then, so how could I have said such a stupid thing? On the contrary, I cried for three days and three nights as everyone knows. Even Six Pounds, the little devil, cried."

Six Pounds had just finished her bowl of rice. She held out her empty bowl and asked for more. Whereupon, Sister Seven Pounds, who was looking for some object for her displeasure, brought down the points of her chopsticks on the child's head right between her hornlike queues and shouted, "Who told you to butt your snout into this, you men-keeping little widow!"

Crash, the empty bowl fell from Six Pounds' hand. It landed on the edge of a brick and a large piece broke off. Seven Pounds jumped to his feet, picked up the broken bowl, pieced it together, and examined it. "Your mother's ——" he shouted and with one slap knocked down Six Pounds, who lay there crying. Old Mrs. Nine Pounds took her hand, helped her up, and led her away, saying "Each generation worse than the last."

Sister Eighteen was also aroused, and said in a loud voice, "Sister Seven Pounds, you are 'pointing at the chicken while really cursing the dog.'"

Mr. Chao had been an onlooker until Sister Eighteen said "besides, there has been no official proclamation by his honor the magistrate." This angered him. Now he stepped forward and said, "'To point at the chicken while really cursing the dog' is a small matter at a time like this. The imperial troops will soon be here. Now you must know that the protector of the imperial equipage this time is Marshall Chang, a descendant of Chang Yi-te of Yen. With his eighteen-foot snake spear, he has the strength of ten thousand warriors.[7] Who can stand up against him?" He grasped his hands into

[7] Formula applied to Chang Fei's famous spear and his prowess.

fists, as if holding an invisible snake spear, and lunged forward toward Sister Eighteen saying, "Can you stand up against him?"

Sister Eighteen, child in arms, was trembling with passion but she was nevertheless frightened to see Mr. Chao, his face full of grease and sweat, his eyes bulging, lunge at her. She did not dare answer, but turned around and walked away. Mr. Chao also walked off. The onlookers blamed Sister Eighteen for bringing this upon herself. They made way for Mr. Chao; several men without queues, who had been trying to rectify the lack by growing one, dodged behind others so as not to be seen by him. Mr. Chao did not try to search them out. He walked through the crowd and, as he turned behind the tallow trees, he repeated, "Can you stand up against him?" He stepped upon the single-log bridge and sauntered off.

The stupefied villagers all admitted to themselves that indeed no one of them was able to stand up against Chang Yi-te and that consequently Seven Pounds must forfeit his life. Since Seven Pounds had committed a crime against His Majesty's laws, he had no business to be so proud and self-satisfied as he related the news he had gathered on his daily trips to the city. Consequently they felt pleased at the fix that Seven Pounds found himself in. They wanted to express themselves on the point, but found they really had nothing to say.

The buzzing grew louder as the mosquitoes flew past the naked backs to hold converse among themselves under the tallow trees. The crowd slowly broke up; one by one the villagers went home, shut their gates and went to bed. Sister Seven Pounds did likewise, grumbling all the while as she gathered up the supper things and took away the table and benches.

Seven Pounds took the broken bowl home and sat upon his doorsill, smoking. But in his worry he forgot to puff at his pipe, and it went out. He knew that the situation was very critical, and he wished to think of some way out, some remedy, but his ideas were vague and disjointed and there was no way to connect them up. "Queue, queue, how about the queue? . . . Eighteen-foot snake spear . . . Each generation worse than the last . . . The Emperor upon his Dragon Throne . . . The broken bowl must be taken to the city to be mended . . . Who can stand up against him? . . . It is clearly written in the book . . . His mother's ——"

The next morning Seven Pounds poled the boat from Luchen to the city and returned in the evening as usual. At supper he told old Mrs. Nine Pounds that he had had the broken bowl mended in the city. The part broken off was very large and required sixteen brass clasps at three *cash* each, a total cost of forty-eight *cash*.

Old Mrs. Nine Pounds was dissatisfied as usual and said, "Each generation worse than the last. I have lived long enough. Three *cash* a clasp! But what sort of clasps are these? In the old days the clasps were different. I have lived seventy-nine years . . ."

From then on, although Seven Pounds went to the city as usual, a certain gloom hung over his household. The villagers avoided him, no longer caring to come to him for news of the city. Sister Seven Pounds had no civil words for him and frequently called him "jailbird."

One evening about ten days later, Seven Pounds returned from the city to find his wife in good spirits. "Did you hear anything in the city?" she asked him.

"I heard nothing."

"Has the Emperor mounted the Dragon Throne?"

"They did not say."

"Didn't anyone at the Hsien Heng tavern say anything about it?"

"No one said anything there either."

"I think the Emperor is not going to mount the Dragon Throne after all. I passed by Mr. Chao's shop today and saw that he was reading his books again. His queue is again coiled up on top of his head and he did not wear his long gown."

"Mm . . ."

"Don't you suppose that the Emperor is not going to mount the Dragon Throne after all?"

"I suppose, perhaps not."

Seven Pounds has long since recovered the respect of the villagers and of his wife and is treated by them with the consideration due to a person of his standing. Now as they are gathered in the open space before their respective gates for their summer meals, they again greet one another with good-natured laughter. Mrs. Nine Pounds celebrated her eighteenth birthday long ago, and is as disgruntled and strong as ever. The two hornlike queues of Six Pounds have now grown into one braid. Although she has just begun to bind her feet, she is still able to help Sister Seven Pounds with the household chores. She is seen hobbling about the open space along the river bank now, the bowl with sixteen brass clasps in her hand.

Our Story of Ah Q

FOR several years now I have been wanting to write "our story" of Ah Q. I am aware that this desire to write about such an insignificant person proves that I am not a man of immortal words, for from time immemorial immortal words have been used only to describe immortal personages, so that in the end it becomes impossible to tell whether the subject is immortalized by the writing or the writing by the subject. I have, nevertheless, undertaken to write about Ah Q, the devil knows why!

But at the very outset of this mortalescent piece, a thousand difficulties confront me. First, the choice of a title. This is a very important matter, for did not Confucius say, "If names are incorrectly defined, it will be impossible to attain truth"? There are all kinds of terms for biographical works: official biography, autobiography, "inner biography" and "outer biography," unofficial biography, family biography, short biography and so on.[1] But none of these seems appropriate for my purpose. Official biography? But this piece does not form part of the biographical section in any of the Dynastic Histories, which include only personages of more conse-

[1] All these terms are two-syllable compounds in the original, with *chuan* (story, record, biography) forming the second syllable. It has been necessary to insert a few transitional phrases in this paragraph as without them it would be difficult to convey facetious effects quite obvious in the original.

quence than Ah Q. Autobiography? But I am certainly not
Ah Q. Though there is nothing official about the so-called
"outer biography," it is usually used when an earlier composition has preëmpted the term "inner biography," another
type of informal writing about the life of an individual.
"Inner biography" will not do either, since Ah Q was de-
cidedly not an immortal; nor is unofficial biography appropriate since it is used in contradistinction to official biography
and as far as I know there has been no Presidential decree
commanding the Institute of National History to write an
official biography of Ah Q. It is true that the great English
writer A. Conan Doyle gave to one of his novels the title of
"The Unofficial Biography of a Gambler"[2] when there is no
official biography of the said gambler in the official history of
England, but such licence is permissible only with great
writers and not with us. Family biography, the next possible
term, is also ruled out, for neither do I know whether Ah Q
and I come from common ancestors nor have I been com-
missioned by his descendants to write his life. Short biography is also unsuitable since there does not exist any long
biography from which it must be distinguished.

This piece may possibly be considered an official biography,
but since it is written in the vulgar language of the street, I
dare not usurp that title. I have, therefore, borrowed the
term "our story" from the stock phrase of humble story-
tellers: "Let us be done with digressions and return to our
story."

My second difficulty is with the established formula for
writing biography, which calls for an opening sentence
something like this: "So and so's derived name is such and

---

[2] The title by which the Chinese version of "Rodney Stone" is
known. Lusin attributed the novel to Dickens.

such; he is a native of such and such a place." The fact is
that I do not know the surname of Ah Q. At one time it appeared to have been Chao, but by the following day it had
become a matter of uncertainty. This was at the time when
the gong-beating messengers brought news that the son of
His Honor Chao had passed his examination. Ah Q had just
drunk two cups of wine and was feeling effusive. He an-
nounced excitedly that it was a great honor for him because
he and His Honor Chao were kinsmen and that he, Ah Q,
was, come to think of it, three generations higher than the
new licentiate in the family tree. This made a great impression on some of the bystanders. But the next day the village
constable summoned Ah Q to His Honor's house. At the
sight of Ah Q, His Honor turned red with fury and thun-
dered:

"Ah Q, you knave! Did you say that I am a kinsman of
yours?"

Ah Q was silent.

This infuriated His Honor still more; he advanced a few
steps, saying, "How dare you blab such nonsense. How could
I have a kinsman like you? Is your surname Chao?"

Ah Q did not open his mouth; he considered a retreat. His
Honor jumped up to him and slapped him in the face.

"How could your name be Chao? You!"

Ah Q did not try to argue that his name was really Chao;
he simply backed out with the constable, nursing his left
cheek. Outside, the constable gave him a lecture and accepted
two hundred *cash* from him for wine money. All those who
heard about this incident agreed that Ah Q had invited the
thrashing by his own impudence, that his surname was
probably not Chao, and that even if it had been, he should
not have been so presumptuous as to talk the way he did.

His family background was never referred to again, and I never did find out just what his surname was.

In the third place, I do not know how Ah Q's name was written. While he was living, everyone called him Ah Quei;[3] but after his death he was promptly forgotten—it is not the lot of such as he to have his name "writ on bamboo and silk." This happens to be the first attempt of the sort and hence is the first to encounter this difficulty. I have often considered whether the *quei* in Ah Quei stands for *quei* meaning *cassia* or for *quei* meaning *honor*. If his derived name had been Yueh-t'ing [moon pavilion], or if he had celebrated his birthday during the month of the harvest moon, then it must have been *quei* meaning *cassia*, which legend associates with the moon. But he did not have any derived name as far as I know, nor did he ever send out invitations for birthday verses. It would be arbitrary to use *quei* meaning *cassia*. Again, if he had had a brother named Fu meaning *wealth*, then his name must have been *quei* meaning *honor*. But he did not have any brother and it would be groundless to write it *quei* meaning *honor*. Other characters with the sound of *quei* cannot possibly fit our requirement as they are all more or less obscure. I once consulted the licentiate, the son of His Honor Chao, but for all his learning he was not able to enlighten me. His conclusion was that the problem could no longer be solved because Ch'en Tu-hsiu's campaign in the magazine *New Youth* for the adoption of the Latin alphabet had destroyed our national culture.

As a last resort I asked a friend of mine back home to consult the official documents bearing on Ah Q's trial. Eight months later, the answer came saying that he could not locate

[3] In Latin letters in the original text.

any document involving anyone whose name approximated *quei*. I do not know whether there was really no record of Ah Q's trial or whether no search had been made, but I do know that I have done everything possible and that it has been of no use. As I am afraid that the national phonetic alphabet is not yet generally known, I have to resort to the use of Latin letters and spell his name Q-u-e-i, according to the system of transliteration current in the English speaking world,[4] and I have abbreviated this to Q. This smacks of blindly following the faddism of the *New Youth*, and I regret it myself, but what can I do since even the esteemed licentiate cannot throw any light on the subject?

The fourth difficulty is Ah Q's native place. If his name had been Chao, we could say that he was a native of T'ien-shui in Lung-hsi, in accordance with the annotations of the *Place Origins of Common Family Names*. Unfortunately, as I have pointed out, we are not sure that this was his patronymic. True, he used to live in Wei village, but he had also lived elsewhere. Even though we disregard such niceties, "a native of the Wei village" somehow does not sound right according to the established usage of historical writing.

The only thing that comforts me is that the character *Ah* is indubitably authentic. There is no stretching the point or reading between the lines about it. As to the rest, it is beyond the capacities of an unlearned person like myself; we can only hope that some day the disciples of the historically minded Hu Shih[5] will take up the problem and throw some light on the various points now in doubt. Only I am afraid

---

[4] The Wade system, standard for the English speaking world, calls for Kuei.

[5] The chief exponent of the Literary Revolution and present Chinese Ambassador at Washington.

that by that time "Our Story of Ah Q" will have long since perished from people's memories.

AH Q'S VICTORIES

Not only were Ah Q's name and origin unknown, but his "life and deeds" were likewise clothed in obscurity. The villagers of Wei were interested in Ah Q only when they needed an extra laborer, only as an object of jibes and practical jokes; no one paid any attention to his life and deeds. Ah Q himself did not throw any light on the subject. When engaged in quarrels he would sometimes allude to his past, saying, "We used to be much better off than you! Who do you think you are?"

Having no home, Ah Q lived in the village temple and worked for people by the day, harvesting wheat, husking rice, punting boats. When his work lasted for a period of time he stayed at his employer's house. So he was remembered only when extra hands were needed; but this was mere labor, not life and deeds. During the slack season, Ah Q himself was completely forgotten, to say nothing of his life and deeds. Once an old man praised him, saying, "What a hard worker Ah Q is!" At that moment Ah Q, stripped to the waist, was standing idle, doing nothing at all. Others were not sure whether the old man was sincere or sarcastic, but Ah Q, not being so precise, was greatly pleased.

Ah Q was very proud and held all the inhabitants of Wei in contempt, even to the extent of sneering at the two students. Now a student might one day pass his examination and become a licentiate. The reason Their Honors Chao and Chien were so esteemed by the villagers was that, besides their wealth, they were fathers of students. But in spirit Ah Q had no special regard for them. "My son would be much better than they," he would assure himself. The few trips that he had undertaken to the city naturally contributed to his pride, though he had no use for city folks either. For instance, to himself and the people of Wei a bench three feet long and three inches wide across the top was a *ch'ang-teng*, yet the city people called it *t'iao-teng*.[6] This was absurd and laughable, he thought. In frying fish, people in Wei used pieces of green onions half an inch in length, but in the city they cut the onion up in fine shreds. This too was absurd and laughable. But what ignorant country louts were the villagers of Wei! They had never seen how fish was fried in the city!

Once much better off, a man of wide experience, hard working—Ah Q would have been a perfect man but for some slight physical flaws. The most humiliating of these were some scars on his head from sores he had had he knew not when. Although these were his own scars Ah Q did not seem to be proud of them, for he avoided the use of the word sores and all its homophones. Later by extension he avoided the words shiny and bright, and still later even candle and lamp were taboo. Whenever these taboos were violated, intentionally or otherwise, Ah Q would become red in the face and would either curse or fight according to whether the offender was slow of words or weak of limb. For some reason or other Ah Q always came out the loser. He gradually changed his tactics and contented himself with an angry glare.

But the idlers of Wei only became more relentless after he adopted this new policy. As soon as they saw him, they would exclaim as though surprised, "Hey! how bright it has become all of a sudden!"

Ah Q glared.

[6] "Long bench" and "a strip of a bench" respectively.

"No wonder! We have a safety lamp hereabouts," someone else would remark, unimpressed by his glare.

"You haven't got it, anyway." This retort, which he finally hit upon, gave him some comfort, as though his scars were no longer shiny evidences of a by-gone affliction but something quite extraordinary, something to be envied.

As the idlers still would not let him alone, a fight usually followed. Ah Q inevitably lost and ended up by being held by the queue while his head was thumped noisily against the wall. This was of course only an outward defeat. After his adversary had gone with the laurels of victory, Ah Q would say to himself, "I have been beaten by my son. What a world we live in today!" and he too would go off satisfied and spiritually victorious.

At first he thought thus only to himself; later he got into the habit of saying it aloud. This method of securing spiritual victory became generally known, so that an idler, holding him by his queue, would say to him:

"Now Ah Q, this is not a case of a son beating his father, but a man beating a beast!"

Protecting his hair with his hands, Ah Q would plead:

"You are beating a worm. I am nothing but a worm. How is that? Now let me go!"

Even after this humiliating admission the idler would not let his victim go without first banging his head half a dozen times against something convenient. Surely Ah Q cannot claim a victory this time, the victor would think as he went away in triumph. But in less than ten seconds Ah Q would also go away in triumph, for he felt that surely he was the most self-deprecatory of men, and is not a superlative—the first or the most of anything—a distinction to be achieved and envied? Is not a *chuang-yuan* only the first in the ranks

of the successful candidates in the triennial examinations?
"So what are you, after all?"

After conquering his enemies by such ingenious means
as these, Ah Q would go to the tavern, drink a few cups of
wine, jest and quarrel a bit, and return, after scoring more
victories, to the temple and would soon fall asleep with a
light heart. If he happened to have any money, he would join
the crowd of gamblers squatted around in a circle, his face
streaming with sweat and his voice heard above every one
else.

"Four hundred *cash* on the Black Dragon!"

"Hey! Here goes!" the dealer would shout as he uncovered
the board, his face also streaming with sweat. "Here goes
Heaven's Gate and Ah Q's money . . . No one seems to like
Human Harmony."

"A hundred on Human Harmony! No, a hundred and
fifty!"

Gradually Ah Q's money would find its way into the
pockets of other perspiring gamblers. Obliged to withdraw
from the inner circle, he would watch from the fringe, shouting and perspiring for the active participants. He could never
tear himself away until the party broke up, when he would
return to the temple with reluctant steps. The next day he
would go to work with swollen eyes.

But "who knows that it is not a blessing for the Tartar to
have lost his horse?" The only occasion on which Ah Q did
win, he came near to tasting defeat. It happened during the
village festival. There was as usual an open air theater and
there were several gambling concessions near the stage. The
gongs and drums sounded very faint in Ah Q's ears, as
though miles away; he could hear only the barking of the
dealer. He won and won, his coppers turning into dimes,

dimes into silver dollars, silver dollars growing into a big pile. He was happy and excited.

"Two dollars on Heaven's Gate!" he shouted.

Suddenly a fight broke out, no one knew who against whom or why. When the commotion subsided and Ah Q crawled to his feet, the gambling concessions and the gamblers had all disappeared. He felt aches here and there, indicating that he must have received a few blows and kicks. People stared at him wonderingly. He went back to the temple with an air of preoccupation and after recovering his wits realized that he no longer had his pile of silver dollars. As most of the gamblers were from other villages, there was nothing that he could do.

A pile of bright, white silver dollars—and his at that—had all disappeared. He could not find any lasting satisfaction in saying to himself that his sons had robbed him, or in calling himself a worm. For the first time he felt something akin to the humiliation of defeat.

But again he turned defeat into victory. He raised his right hand and gave himself two good slaps in the face. This restored his humor, as if one Ah Q had struck another Ah Q, and, after a while, as if Ah Q had struck someone else—although it was his own face that tingled with pain. And so he lay down to sleep as victor, as pleased with himself as ever. And he soon fell asleep.

MORE VICTORIES

Although Ah Q's list of victories was long and impressive, it was not until he was slapped by His Honor Chao that he became famous.

After paying the constable two hundred *cash* he went to his room in the temple and lay down with indignation in his heart. Then he thought, "What a world this is getting to be, a son striking his father." At the thought that His Honor Chao with all his power and prestige was now his son, Ah Q became quite pleased with himself. He got up and went to the tavern singing "The Little Widow at Her Husband's Grave" and feeling quite proud of His Honor Chao now that the latter had become his own son.

The strange thing was that people actually seemed to respect him more. Ah Q liked to think that it was because of the new status that he had conferred upon himself, but this was not the case. If Ah Seven should have a fight with Ah Eight or Li Four with Chang Three, the incident would pass unnoticed in Wei; in order to merit gossip the incident must be in some way connected with a personage such as His Honor Chao. Then by virtue of the fame of the chastizer the chastized would become famous, too. The victim's position was, in other words, analogous to that of the Great Offerings in the Confucian Temple, offerings which, though domestic beasts like other pigs and sheep, become sacred after the Sage has put his chopsticks to them. There was never any question that the fault lay with Ah Q. Wherefore? Because His Honor Chao could not be wrong. Then why was it that people respected him more than formerly? This is a little difficult to explain. Perhaps they were afraid that, even though he was slapped for it, there might be after all something to Ah Q's claim of kinship, and they felt it was better to be on the safe side.

Thus Ah Q basked in this reflected glory for many years.

One spring day as he was walking drunkenly on the street he espied Wang the Beard sitting against a wall in the sun, hunting for fleas in the coat that he had taken off. Ah Q felt an infectious itch. Now Wang was not only bearded but also mangy. Every one called him Mangy Beard Wang, but Ah Q dropped off the word mangy as it reminded him of his by-gone affliction. He held the Beard in great contempt, feeling that the mange was nothing unusual, not like a swarthy, un-sightly beard. Ah Q sat down beside him. If it had been someone else Ah Q might have hesitated, but he was not afraid of the Beard. In fact, he was conferring an honor upon the latter by sitting down beside him.

Ah Q also took off his ragged coat and searched it hope-fully, but, either because it had been recently washed or because of his lack of thoroughness he caught only three or four fleas after a long search. In the meantime the Beard caught one after another, putting them in his mouth and crushing them with a crisp sound between his teeth.

Ah Q felt only disappointment at first, but this feeling soon gave way to indignation. How humiliating that such a worthless fellow as the Beard should have caught so many while he so few! He wished to vindicate himself by finding a big one but after a great deal of trouble he succeeded in finding only a medium-sized one. He put it into his mouth and bit it with determination, but he did not make as much noise as the Beard.

His scars grew red. Throwing his coat on the ground he said, spitting with disgust, "The damned worm!"

"Whom are you cursing, scabby cur?" the Beard said rais-ing his eyes contemptuously.

If the challenge had come from one of the idlers in whose hands he had suffered ignominious defeat, Ah Q, in spite of the distinction that he had recently won and the pride that he took in it, might have been more cautious about taking it up. But he did not feel any need for caution on this occasion; he felt very brave. How dare the hairy face talk to him like that?

"Whoever cares to take it," he said, standing up, his arms akimbo.

"Are your bones itching?" said the Beard, standing up and putting on his coat.

Ah Q thought that the Beard was going to run, so he rushed forward and struck with his fist. But the Beard caught hold of it and gave it a jerk. As Ah Q fell forward, the Beard had him by the queue and was about to bang his head against the wall.

"A gentleman argues with his tongue rather than his fists," Ah Q remonstrated.

The Beard did not seem to care whether he was a gentleman or not. Paying no heed to the remonstrance, he banged Ah Q's head against the wall five times, then gave him a push that sent him sprawling six feet away.

In Ah Q's memory this must have been the greatest humiliation of his life. Heretofore the Beard had been the butt of his scorn, never had he been the object of the Beard's jeers, much less his blows. Could it be true, as rumored on the street, that the Emperor had abolished the examinations, and no longer wanted any licentiates and graduates, so that the Chaos' prestige has been impaired and their kinsman might be treated with impudence?

As Ah Q stood and pondered on this inexplicable event, the eldest son of His Honor Chien, one of Ah Q's foes and abominations, approached from the distance. Young Chien had first gone to the city and entered one of those "foreign" schools and then he had for some reason gone to Japan. Half a year later he came back a different man: his legs had become straight and his queue was gone. His mother cried often and his wife tried to throw herself in the well no less than three times. Later his mother explained that Chien's queue had been cut off by some wicked people after they had made him drunk. "He was to have been appointed a big mandarin," she explained, "but now he must wait until his hair grows again."

Ah Q did not believe the explanations, insisted upon calling Chien a fake foreigner and a traitor, and would curse him under his breath whenever he saw him. What Ah Q hated most was the man's false queue, for surely one could not be said to be a man at all with a false queue, and his wife could not be a virtuous woman since she did not try the well a fourth time.

The fake foreigner drew near.

"Baldhead! Donkey!" Ah Q muttered aloud as his passion and his desire for revenge got the better of him.

The baldhead unexpectedly rushed at him with a yellow varnished stick—which Ah Q called the funeral stick—and instantly Ah Q realized that he was going to receive a thrashing. He tightened his muscles and hunched up his shoulders and waited. He heard a whack and realized that he must have gotten a blow on the head.

"I was speaking of him," Ah Q protested, indicating a boy nearby.

Whack! Whack! Whack!

In Ah Q's memory this must have been the second greatest humiliation of his life. Fortunately the whack-whack seemed to give him a measure of relief, as though ending some suspense for him. Furthermore, forgetfulness, a treasured trait which he had inherited from his ancestors, came to his aid, and enabled him to regain his complacency by the time he reached the tavern.

Just then a little nun from the convent went by. Ah Q had

never let her pass without hurling an insult at her, even when he was quite himself. Now all the resentment that he had felt for his recent defeats and indignities turned against the hapless nun.

"I have been wondering why I have been so unlucky all day, so it's because of you!" he thought.

He went up to her and spat in disgust. The nun walked on without paying the slightest attention to him. Ah Q approached her, thrust out his hand and stroked her clean-shaven head, saying with an idiotic grin, "Baldhead! Hurry home. The monk is waiting for you."

"What has possessed you that you dare to touch me!" the nun said hurrying on, her face flushed.

People in the tavern laughed. Encouraged by the general appreciation, Ah Q pinched her cheek, saying, "Since the monk can touch you, why not I?"

The tavern laughed again. Ah Q became more pleased with himself and gave the nun another pinch for the benefit of the onlookers.

This encounter drove out the memory of Wang the Beard and of the fake foreigner, and avenged all his adversities of the day. He felt more lighthearted than the whack-whack had made him, so lighthearted that he positively floated on air.

"May Ah Q never have any offspring," sounded the pitiful voice of the nun as she hurried off.

"Ha! ha! ha!" laughed Ah Q triumphantly.

"Ha! ha! ha!" echoed the tavern.

THE TRAGEDY OF LOVE

It is said that some conquerors must have foes like tigers and eagles in order to derive any satisfaction from their victories, that foes like lambs or chickens give them no pleasure in conquest. After their conquests are complete and their foes have been either put to the sword or brought under submission, conquerors like these often suffer from loneliness and regret: they find that their conquests have deprived them of worthy foes and outspoken friends and have left them with only abject slaves that chant the familiar refrain of "Your subject trembles and quakes because he knows that he deserves death." Our Ah Q was not afflicted with such flaws in his nature. He was always happy in his victories. Perhaps he was a living proof of the supremacy of the spiritual civilization of the Chinese.

Look at him, he is so pleased and lighthearted that he is positively floating on air!

His latest victory had an unusual effect upon Ah Q. Ordinarily he would begin to snore almost as soon as he lay down, but on this occasion, after floating about the village and finally back to the temple, he could not sleep. His thumb and second finger seemed different, seemed softer and smoother than usual. Had something greasy and smooth on the nun's face stuck to his finger or had his fingers become smooth from their contact with the nun?

"May Ah Q never have any offspring!" He recalled the voice. Yes, he must have a woman, he said to himself; without children there would be no one to make offerings to his spirit after he was dead. Moreover, "Of the three filial impieties, the greatest is to be without heirs." His desire, therefore, was strictly in accordance with the teachings of the sages. Ah Q could not banish these thoughts from his mind and we do not know how long it was before he began to snore.

From this we can see that women are harmful, evil things. Most Chinese men are potential sages but for the corruption of women. The Shang Dynasty perished because of Ta Chi; the Chou Dynasty because of Pao Ssu; the Ch'in Dynasty— although history is silent on this point, we cannot be far wrong if we assume that a woman was also the cause of its fall; and there is no question at all that Tung Cho died because of his passion for Tiao Ch'an.

Ah Q was a moral and upright man; he had always maintained a strict vigilance against contamination by woman, though he had never had any formal instruction in morals. Moreover, he showed a righteous wrath against all heterodoxy—such as that represented by nuns and fake foreigners. It was his firm belief that all nuns have illicit relations with monks, that a woman who is seen on the street must have come out for the express purpose of tempting and corrupting men; that when a man and woman are seen together they must be conspiring to commit adultery. To punish these people, he would glare at them wrathfully, make insinuating remarks, or throw pebbles at them—if he could do so safely.

Who would have thought that at the "age of moral independence"[7] he should succumb to the evil spell of a little nun? His state of mind was far from moral. Women are indeed evil things! If the nun's face had not been so smooth, or if it had been covered with a piece of cloth, Ah Q would not have been bewitched. Five or six years previously he had, standing in the crowd before the country stage, pinched a woman's thigh, but that was through a layer of cloth and the experience did not cause him a sleepless night. This was another proof that nuns and their kind were evil things.

[7] That is, thirty, at which Confucius was said to have achieved this state.

He used to look attentively at the women that must be "out to corrupt men," but none of them smiled at him. He also used to listen attentively to women he chanced to speak with, but none of them ever touched upon the subject of adultery. This was only another hateful trait in women; they all pretend to be virtuous!

One day after supper Ah Q was sitting in the kitchen of His Honor Chao and smoking his pipe, having pounded rice all day. In another house a laborer would have gone home after supper but at His Honor's supper was early. The usual custom in that household was to go to bed immediately after supper so that no lamp need be lit; but there were a few exceptions: first, before His Honor's son passed his examinations he was allowed to read under lamplight; and second, when Ah Q came to pound rice, so that he might continue his work after supper. So Ah Q was still there, smoking his pipe.

Having washed the dishes, Wu-ma, the only maidservant in the house, sat on the bench and gossiped with Ah Q.

"*Tai-tai* has not touched food for two days, because His Honor is thinking of taking a little mistress."

"Women . . . Wu-ma . . . the young widow," Ah Q thought.

"Our *shao nai nai* will give birth to a child in the eighth moon."

"Women . . . ," Ah Q thought.

Ah Q put down his pipe and stood up.

"Our *shao nai nai* . . . ," Wu-ma was continuing.

"I'll sleep with you! I'll sleep with you!" Ah Q suddenly went up to her and knelt before her.

Instantly, silence fell.

"*Ai ya!*" Wu-ma suddenly trembled and rushed out shouting and wailing.

After staring stupidly at the wall for a moment, Ah Q slowly put his hands on the bench and raised himself to his feet, sensing that something was very much amiss. Hastily he stuck his pipe through his sash and started for the milling room. Bang! a heavy blow fell on his head. He turned around and found the licentiate standing before him with a heavy bamboo stick.

"You monster! Have you gone mad?"

The big bamboo stick fell again. Ah Q put up his hands to protect his head and received the blows on his finger joints. He dashed out of the kitchen, receiving another blow on his back.

"*Wang-pa-tan!*" the licentiate hurled after him the favorite epithet of the official world.

Ah Q fled into the milling room and stood there, nursing his aching fingers. *Wang-pa-tan*[8] kept ringing in his ears. This was an epithet which none of the villagers used but was only effected by their betters who hobnobbed with officials; for that reason it impressed him deeply and struck him with awe. He thought no more of women. Curiously enough the rebuke and beating seemed to have had a quieting effect on him and to have purged him of all anxieties. He set to work pounding rice. As he became warmer he stopped and took off his shirt.

Now the commotion without, which had been drowned out by his pounding, reached him. Being addicted to the excitement of crowds, Ah Q left the milling room and turned his steps in the direction of the noise, which led him to the inner court. In the twilight he could make out quite a num-

[8] Literally, turtle egg; son of a prostitute or a cuckold.

ber of people, including *tai-tai* who had not eaten for two days, Sister Taou Seven, and Chao the white-eyed and Chao the watchman, both authentic kin of His Honor Chao.

Shao nai nai was dragging Wu-ma from her room, saying, "Come out here! Don't hide in your room."

"Who does not know of your virtue . . . you must not think of suicide," Sister Taou said to her.

Wu-ma only cried, and murmured words that could not be clearly distinguished.

Ah Q thought, "*Heng*, what is the little widow up to now?" He approached the watchman to seek enlightenment, but caught sight of the licentiate rushing at him with the big bamboo stick and it suddenly came back to him that he had just received a beating and that he had something to do with what he was now watching with such detached interest. He turned around and started for the milling room. The bamboo stick barred the way; he turned again and sneaked out by the back door. Presently he was in the temple.

He sat for a while and began to feel a chill, for though it was spring, it was still cold at night, not suitable weather to go around bare to the waist. He remembered that he had left his shirt at the Chaos. He thought of going back for it, but was afraid of the licentiate's bamboo stick. The constable came in.

"Ah Q, your mother's ——. So you have gone so far as to try to seduce a servant of the Chaos! Have you no fear of the Emperor? You have made it necessary for me to get out of bed, your mother's ——."

And so on and on the constable cursed and lectured him. Ah Q made, of course, no retort. Because he had caused the constable trouble late at night, he had to give him four

hundred *cash* for wine money. As he had no money, he gave
him his felt cap as security. Five conditions were imposed:

1. Ah Q was to go to the Chaos' house to apologize, bringing with him a pair of candles—weighing a pound each—
and a package of incense sticks.

2. Ah Q was to foot the expenses incurred in exorcizing
the evil spirits that might be trying to induce Wu-ma to commit suicide.

3. Ah Q was never to cross Chao's gate again.

4. Ah Q was to be held responsible if anything should
happen to Wu-ma in spite of the exorcism.

5. Ah Q was not to demand his wages and his shirt.

Ah Q, needless to say, agreed to all these conditions, but
he had no money. Fortunately it was spring and as he had no
immediate use for his quilt he pawned it for two thousand
cash and carried out the terms. He actually had a few *cash*
left after he went to the Chaos and kowtowed. However, he
did not redeem his cap but spent the rest of the money all on
drinking. The Chaos did not engage any exorcist but saved
the candles and incense for future occasions when the mistress made offerings to Buddha. Ah Q's shirt was cut up; the
larger pieces were used as diapers for the baby that the young
mistress bore in the eighth moon, the smaller patches went to
make soles for Wu-ma's shoes.

THE PROBLEM OF LIVELIHOOD

That evening, as the sun went down, Ah Q began to feel
that something was definitely wrong with the world. After
a careful analysis he came to the conclusion that it was
because he had nothing on above his waist. He remembered
that he still had his lined shirt. He put it on and lay down.

When he opened his eyes the sun was again shining on the west wall. He sat up, muttering, "Their mothers' ——."

He wandered about the street as usual and soon sensed that there was something else wrong with the world, though this was not quite so poignantly felt as the need for raiment. It appeared that the women of Wei had suddenly become very shy, retreating behind their gates as soon as they saw him coming, so much so that even Sister Tsou, who was almost fifty years old, hid herself with the rest, calling in her eleven-year-old daughter. Ah Q was mystified. "Trying to imitate the young ladies: the harlots!"

What made the world seem amiss more than anything else was a development of some days later. First, the tavern would extend him no more credit; second, the old attendant of the temple mumbled at him, as though wishing to get rid of him; third, for many days, though he could not tell just how many, no one had offered him work. He could abstain from drinking to meet the denial of credit at the tavern; mumble excuses to put off the temple attendant; but when no one offered him work it had the positive effect of making him feel a gnawing hunger, a state of affairs to call forth many a "Their mothers' ——."

He could endure it no longer. He made the rounds of his old employers—excepting the Chaos—and asked about odd jobs. He was received in a different manner from formerly: invariably a male came out with annoyance in his face and waved his hands as though dismissing a beggar—"Nothing here! Go away!"

Ah Q was completely mystified. They used to have a lot of work to be done, he thought, how could they have suddenly ceased to have any work at all? There must be something behind this state of affairs. He made inquiries and

found that they now gave all their work to little Don.[9] Now
this little Don was a poor wretch, skinny and weak, who
occupied in Ah Q's eyes a position even beneath that of the
Beard. And yet this little thing had taken his rice bowl away
from him. Great was Ah Q's indignation. As he walked
fuming with rage, he suddenly raised his hand and sang,
"With my steel whip I shall smite thee!"

A few days later he encountered little Don in front of His
Honor Chien's house. "Foes have a sharp eye for each other,"
so when Ah Q went toward him, little Don stopped.

"Beast!" Ah Q glared at him, foaming at the mouth.

"I am only a worm. Does that suit you better?" little Don
said.

This humility had the effect of further enraging Ah Q. As
he had really no steel whip in his hand, he had to content
himself with throwing himself at little Don and seizing him
by the queue. Little Don, protecting the roots of his hair with
one hand, seized Ah Q's queue with the other, thus forcing
Ah Q to protect his own hair with his free hand. Ah Q used
to consider little Don beneath his notice, but hunger had
weakened him and made him just about a match for little
Don; and so for more than half an hour the two adversaries
were deadlocked and formed a bluish arc against the white
wall, with four hands upon two heads and their bodies bent
low.

"That will do, that will do," some onlookers said, trying
to stop them.

"Bravo! Bravo!" said others, in such a way that it was
difficult to tell whether they were trying to stop the fight,
to applaud it, or to further incite the fighters.

But the combatants paid no heed to them. As Ah Q ad-

[9] The name is so spelled in Latin letters in the original.

vanced three steps, little Don would retreat three. After a brief pause, Ah Q would retreat three steps while little Don advanced, and again there would be a pause. Thus they lumbered back and forth, for about half an hour—there being no clock in the village, it was impossible to tell exactly, perhaps it was twenty minutes—their hair steaming, their foreheads covered with sweat. When Ah Q finally relaxed his hold, little Don immediately relaxed his also. They both stood up straight, backed away and edged out through the crowd.

"Look out next time, your mother's ——," Ah Q said, turning around to give little Don a menacing look.

"Your mother's —— look out next time," Little Don retorted.

Thus this "strife betwixt dragon and tiger" ended without deciding the issue, without, perhaps, giving the onlookers their time's worth, though no one complained or made any comments.

Still no one came to offer him work.

One day it was very warm; the caressing breeze had with it a suggestion of summer. In spite of this, Ah Q felt chilly. This he could bear, but his hunger was more difficult. His quilt, felt cap, and shirt had gone long before; more recently he had sold his padded winter coat. He could not possibly sell the trousers he had on, though they were his; nor would his tattered lined shirt bring anything—it was only good to be given away, or to be cut up and glued together for soles. He dreamed of picking up some money on the street, but such luck persistently eluded him; he fancied coming upon some money in his room, looked sharply as if startled by silver pieces dancing on the floor, but the room was bare and had not even obscure corners to prolong his illusions. He decided to go out and seek food.

As he walked along the street, he saw the familiar tavern, the familiar steamed rolls. He passed them by, without even thinking about them or stopping before them, for somehow he knew that these were not for him, though he did not know what exactly he was looking for.

Wei was not a large village and Ah Q soon left it behind and found himself among the fresh green of the rice fields, relieved here and there by moving black dots, which were, of course, peasants at work. Ah Q did not stop to examine this picture of rural bliss, for he instinctively felt that it had no direct bearing upon his immediate need. Finally he found himself outside the walls of the nunnery.

It was also surrounded by rice fields, its white walls rising sheer above the fresh green fields. In the rear, a low mud wall protected a vegetable garden. Ah Q hesitated, looked around, and having made sure that no one was looking, climbed up on the wall, steadying himself by holding on to some vines. His legs shook and loosened some dirt from the wall. Then he caught hold of a mulberry branch and swung himself to the ground. Inside the walls, greenery again greeted him, but no wine or steamed rolls or any other form of eatables. Along the western wall in the bamboo grove there were new shoots but they had to be cooked before eating. The rape had gone to seed, the mustard was in bloom, and the cabbage, too, was getting tough.

Ah Q felt as misused and wronged as a student who fails his examinations. As he approached the garden gate he suddenly came upon a few furrows of large radishes. He squatted down and started to pull up some. A head, very smooth and round, stuck out through the gate, but it was immediately withdrawn. It belonged to the little nun. Ordinarily Ah Q had no fear of such as she, but in the present situation he decided it would pay to be careful. Hastily he pulled up four radishes and put them in the apron of his coat. In spite of his haste, the old nun was already on the scene.

"*Amitofo!* Ah Q, how could you have come to steal radishes from people like us? It is a great sin, a great sin, Amito Buddha!"

"When did I steal your radishes?" Ah Q said as he walked away.

"Are those not our radishes there?" the nun said pointing to his loot.

"Are they really yours? Then call to them and see if they'll answer you."

He darted off before he finished speaking, followed by a huge black dog, which had somehow turned up in the garden though its usual post was at the front gate. The dog growled and was almost near enough to snap at Ah Q's legs when a radish dropped and scared it. As the dog stopped to sniff at the radish Ah Q climbed up the mulberry tree, thence to the wall and rolled down, radishes and all, on the other side, leaving the dog barking up the empty tree and the old nun invoking the name of Buddha.

Still apprehensive of the dog, Ah Q hurried off with his radishes, picking up pieces of rocks and broken bricks as he went. But the dog did not follow him. Ah Q threw away his missiles and walked on, eating his radishes and thinking the while that he had better try his luck in the city as there was nothing for him in the village.

By the time he had finished the three radishes, his mind was made up.

AH Q'S RISE AND FALL

When Ah Q reappeared in Wei shortly after the festival of the Harvest Moon, the villagers were first surprised and then began to wonder where he had been; for Ah Q had not told any one of his impending visit to the city, as he used to do with great pride and gusto, and no one had noticed his disappearance. He might have told the old attendant of the temple; but the latter had not taken the trouble to broadcast the information and the village had no way of knowing. In Wei it was considered an event only when Their Honors Chao and Chien and the licentiate went to the city; even the fake foreigner's visit went unnoticed, to say nothing of the absence of Ah Q.

The manner in which Ah Q returned was different from former times and truly merited astonishment and wonder. He appeared in the tavern at dusk, with sleepy eyes; he approached the counter, reached his hand around his waist, took out some copper and silver coins, slapped them on the counter, and shouted, "No credit, this time! Give me wine!" He wore a new, lined coat and hanging from his waist cord was a big wallet sagging from the weight of its contents. In Wei it was the general policy to honor anyone who appeared as though he might be somebody. Though they knew that this was only Ah Q, yet they realized that this was not the old Ah Q of the tattered coat, and they were reminded of the ancient saying that a man should be looked upon with different eyes though he has been away only three days. Consequently, the waiter, the proprietor, the patrons and the passers-by all manifested a deferential wonder. The proprietor nodded to him and engaged him in conversation.

"Back, eh, Ah Q?"

"*Fatsai, fatsai.*[10] Where . . . ?"

"I have been to the city."

By the following day the news had spread through the entire village and had become a matter of absorbing interest. Every scrap of information that could be gathered in the tavern and teahouse and under the gate of the temple was sifted and pieced together, and as a result of this coöperative effort the history of the renascence of Ah Q with his heavy wallet and new coat came to be known in detail and gave Ah Q a new prestige.

According to his own story Ah Q had worked in the house of His Honor the provincial graduate. This announcement immediately raised his status in the villagers' eyes. His Honor's patronymic was Pai, but as he was the only graduate in the whole district, it was unnecessary to prefix his name to the title. This was not only true in Wei but true everywhere within a radius of a hundred *li* from the city, so much so that people almost began to think that His Honor the Graduate was the man's name. It was naturally a great honor to work in such a man's house. But Ah Q had quit his job because he said the graduate was entirely too much his mother's such and such. The announcement brought forth a general sigh of regret and satisfaction; satisfaction because after all Ah Q was hardly worthy of the honor and regret because it was a great pity to throw up such a fine job.

Another reason why Ah Q had returned to Wei was because he had become dissatisfied with city people's ways. The first complaint he had against them was an old one: they called a bench *t'iao teng* instead of *ch'ang teng* and used shredded onion instead of big sections of it in frying fish.

[10] May you grow rich.

The second complaint he had was the mincing gait of city women, which he had noticed on his last visit and which he found very offensive to his taste. There were, however, things to be said for city folks. For instance, in Wei they played only a game of dominoes of thirty-two pieces; the only exception was the fake foreigner, who could play mah-jong: but in the city even the little turtles working in the brothels could play mah-jong well. The fake foreigner might be very proud of himself, but when matched against a small turtle in his teens, he would fare no better than would a little demon in the hands of the King of Hell. The listeners were duly impressed by these pronouncements.

"And have any of you seen a decapitation?" Ah Q suddenly asked. "*Hai*, a grand sight it is to watch the beheading of the revolutionaries. *Hai*, a grand sight, really a grand sight!" He shook his head appreciatively and sputtered saliva in Chao the watchman's face. In the awed silence that followed, Ah Q looked around and suddenly raised his right hand and struck Wang the Beard on the back of his neck as the latter craned forward in his eagerness not to miss anything, and said, "Zip! like this."

The Beard jumped and withdrew his head like lightning, much to the amusement of the awed listeners. For several days after this he acted as though he had actually lost his head and kept a respectful distance from Ah Q as did everyone else.

Though it could not be said that the position which Ah Q now occupied in the village surpassed that of His Honor Chao, there is little danger of overstatement in saying that it was about the same.

Presently Ah Q's fame invaded the "inner apartments" of Wei. The term may sound somewhat pretentious as only the

Chaos and Chiens had homes of any size to speak of, while the rest of the villagers had only what might be called women's corners. But women do have a world of their own and it was strange that Ah Q's fame should have penetrated therein. Whenever women met, they all talked about the blue silk shirt which Sister Tsou had bought from Ah Q. It was secondhand, to be sure, but then she paid only nine dimes for it. Another fortunate woman was the mother of Chao the white-eyed—one report had it as the mother of Chao the watchman, a matter that needs further investigation—who bought from him a boy's red muslin gown, seventy percent new, for only three hundred *cash*, ninety-two to the hundred.[11] As a consequence, the women of Wei were all eager to see Ah Q. Instead of hiding from him as they had done for a while, they ran after him, and stopped him to ask:

"Ah Q, have you got any more silk shirts? No? How about a muslin gown? Surely you have a few more things to sell, haven't you?"

His fame was carried from the women's corners to the deeper inner apartments, largely through Sister Tsou, who had displayed her proud acquisition to Chao *tai-tai* and the latter had in turn remarked about it to His Honor. At supper that evening His Honor discussed the matter with his heir the licentiate, suggesting that there was something suspicious about Ah Q and that they had better look after their doors and windows. But the things that Ah Q had to sell were all right and he might have a few more good bar-

---

[11] It was customary to allow a certain percentage for the cost of the string with which the *cash* coins were strung together. The custom persisted even after the ten-*cash* copper supplanted the *cash*, though the new coin has no holes and is not strung together with strings.

gains. Moreover, Chao *tai-tai* was contemplating the purchase of a good but inexpensive fur vest. It was decided at this family conference to send Sister Tsou to look for Ah Q without delay and it was further decided that they would light the lamp for this special occasion.

The level of the oil burned down quite perceptibly, and still Ah Q did not appear. The entire Chao household was in a state of anxiety; some complained of Ah Q's uncertain whereabouts, some charged Sister Tsou with laxity, while all yawned because of the unaccustomed lateness of the hour. *Tai-tai* thought Ah Q might be afraid to come because of the conditions imposed upon him that spring, but His Honor reassured her, saying, "*I* have sent for him, you know." Indeed his honor was right, presently Ah Q came in with Sister Tsou.

"He insisted that he has no more, but I said to him you go and tell His Honor that yourself. He still insists that he has no more, but I told him . . . ," Sister Tsou said, panting.

"Your Honor!" Ah Q said with a half-smile, stopping under the eaves.

"Ah Q, I am told that you have prospered while you were away," His Honor said, surveying Ah Q from head to foot. "That's very good, very good. Now . . . I am told that you have some old articles. You may bring them and let me see everything—there is no other reason, I only want to take a look."

"I have told Sister Tsou. They are all gone."

"All gone?" His Honor could not suppress his disappointment. "How could they have gone so fast?"

"They were things belonging to a friend. There were not many in the first place."

"You must have something left."

"I have only a cloth door curtain left."

"Then let us have a look at that," *tai-tai* hastened to say, hopefully.

"In that case, bring it around tomorrow," His Honor stated, with less eagerness. "Now, Ah Q, if you should come by anything later on, show it to us first."

"We shan't pay you less than anyone else," the licentiate added.

Shao-nai-nai cast a glance at Ah Q to see if he had been favorably impressed by the reassurance.

"I want a fur vest," *tai-tai* said.

Ah Q muttered his consent and walked away with a careless air from which it was impossible to tell whether the interview had made any impression on him. This nonchalance disappointed, irritated and worried His Honor to such an extent that he stopped yawning. The licentiate was indignant, too, and said that the *wang-pa-tan* would bear watching and that they should perhaps have the constable banish him from the village. But His Honor vetoed this, saying that there was no sense in making enemies, that those engaged in such a line of business did not, as a rule, operate near their own nests, and that, therefore, they need not worry very much in Ah Q's own village, though it was never amiss to be a little careful. With this "family instruction" the licentiate was in complete accord; he withdrew his proposal and, moreover, cautioned Sister Tsou not to tell any one that such a proposal had been made.

But just the same Sister Tsou, on her way to the dyer's to have her blue skirt died black, broadcasted the family's suspicions about Ah Q, though she did take care not to mention the licentiate's proposal to have him banished. The consequence of these revelations was definitely prejudicial to

Ah Q. First the constable came to see him and took away the curtain; he ignored Ah Q's professions of innocence and said that he was going to speak to him later on about hush money. Then there was a noticeable change in the attitude of the villagers toward him. It was true that they were still wary of him and did not dare to take any liberties with him, but it was also clear that the reason back of this wariness was different from that which kept them at a distance after he "zipped" the Beard's head.

The interest of the idlers in his exploits persisted, however, and Ah Q was not reluctant to satisfy their curiosity. They learned then that Ah Q played only a minor role in these exploits; he climbed no walls, crawled through no breaches, but only stood on the outside and waited for things to be passed to him. One night as he was waiting expectantly after he had already received one bundle, he heard a commotion inside the house. Thereupon he ran away as fast as he could, climbed over the city wall and fled back to Wei, and had not dared to venture forth again. This confession hurt Ah Q's prestige even more than Sister Tsou's revelations. The villagers had been wary of him because they were afraid of antagonizing a dangerous character; they had not expected to find that he was not only a petty thief but a reformed one at that. Of such a person one needs to have no fear.

THE REVOLUTION

On the fourteenth day of the ninth month, the third year of the reign of Hsuan T'ung—that is, the day on which Ah Q sold his wallet to Chao the white-eyed—at the fourth beat of the third watch, a big, covered boat stopped at the Chaos' landing. In the darkness of the night while the villagers were sound asleep, its arrival had not been noticed; but as it was

almost dawn when the boat left, its departure was witnessed
by several early risers. It was soon established that the boat
belonged to no less a personage than His Honor the graduate.

The boat brought with it uneasiness to Wei, an uneasiness
which reached almost panic proportions by noon. The Chaos
had kept the mission of the boat a secret, but it was said in
the teahouse and the tavern that the revolutionaries were
about to occupy the city and that His Honor had come to
take refuge in the country. Sister Tsou, however, thought
otherwise, saying that the boat had only brought a few old
trunks, which the graduate wished to store with the Chaos,
but that his honor Chao had refused to take them. The truth
was that His Honor the graduate and the licentiate were not
on good terms, and the latter's family was not, therefore,
obliged to share their "vicissitudes and afflictions" in a time
like this. Sister Tsou must have been right, as she was a neighbor of the Chao family and was close to what happened in
that household.

But rumors were rife, the one having the widest currency
being that although the graduate did not call in person, he
sent a long letter to the Chao family and established, by
following the ramifications of their family trees, some sort
of remote kinship with them; that His Honor Chao had,
after considering the question from all angles, come to the
conclusion that he could not possibly come to any harm because of it; that His Honor had accordingly taken the trunks,
which were at that moment reposing under *tai-tai's* bed. As
to the revolutionaries, some said they had entered the city
that very night, all wearing white helmets and white armor
as a sign of mourning for the last emperor of the Ming
Dynasty.

Ah Q had long ago heard about the revolutionaries and

had seen the decapitation of one during his last venture into the city. Somehow he had come by a violent prejudice against them, regarding them as rebels and therefore his natural enemies. But now he could not help regarding them in a more favorable light since they were able to inspire terror in such a personage as His Honor the graduate; and he relished the plight that they had caused the accursed men and women of Wei.

"Revolution may be a good thing after all," Ah Q thought. We'll revolutionize them all, their mothers' ——, the detestable, loathsome things! I wouldn't mind joining the revolutionaries."

Ah Q had been very hard put to it recently and felt a grudge against the world. Furthermore, he had just drunk two cups of wine on an empty stomach and was feeling its effects. He walked on and thought about the revolutionaries, and was again sailing on airy feet. By some curious process of reasoning he came to feel that he was, indeed, one of the dreaded revolutionaries and that the villagers were his prisoners. In this state of mind he could not help shouting:

"Revolution! Revolution!"

The villagers looked at him with wonder and fear, and Ah Q, not used to the important role that he suddenly found himself in, relished it as one relishes an iced drink on a hot summer day. He shouted more lustily, mixing stray bits from popular theatrical pieces with his revolutionary slogans:

"Yes, Revolution! I'll take what I want and do whatever I like with any one . . .

"Da-da-dee-da, tong-tong . . .

" 'I regret having executed my good brother Cheng while I was drunk . . . I much regret, ah, ah, ah!'

"Da-da tong tong, da, tong-ling-tong!

" 'With the steel whip in my hand I shall smite thee . . . ' "

Standing at their gate, the two male members of the Chao household were also discussing the revolution with their two authentic kinsmen. Ah Q did not see them and passed by them singing.

"Q-lao,"[12] His Honor greeted him timidly.

"Da-da tong-tong, da, tong, tong-ling-tong, tong," Ah Q continued, never suspecting that any one would link his name with the honorific *lao*.

"Lao-Q!"

" 'I much regret . . . ' "

"Ah Q," the licentiate at last called him by his familiar name.

Only then did Ah Q stop and ask, half turning around, "What is it?"

"Lao-Q, now . . . ," His Honor did not know how to put it. "Now—you are doing well?"

"Doing well? Of course. I'll take what I want . . ."

"Ah—Brother Q, I suppose poor people like us are all right?" Chao the white-eyed asked timidly, seeking to discover the attitude of the revolution towards himself.

"Poor people? You got more money than I anyway," Ah Q said as he walked away.

They all felt uneasy. His Honor and his son went home and discussed the matter until after dark. Chao the white-eyed went home and gave his wallet to his woman to put at the bottom of the chest.

After fluttering about the village Ah Q returned to the temple where he found the old attendant unexpectedly affable. The latter treated him to tea and produced, upon Ah Q's demand, two rolls. After eating these Ah Q ex-

[12] *Lao* (old) is honorific as suffix, familiar as prefix.

tracted from him a partly used four-ounce candle and a candlestick. He lit the candle and the unaccustomed luxury gave him an indescribable feeling of well being. The candle flame danced with a festive air and his thoughts danced with it.

Revolution was a great thing, he decided. He saw the revolutionaries pass by the temple in white helmets and white armor, holding broadswords, steel whips, bombs, cannons, spears, and halberts, and he heard them call to him, "Come with us, Ah Q!" In his imagination he went with them.

What a pitiable lot were these cursed villagers! They all knelt before him, whimpering, "Ah Q, spare us!" He would not relent. First little Don and His Honor Chao must go, and the licentiate and the fake foreigner . . . Should he spare any? Wang the Beard might have been spared, but not now after his impudent behavior.

And the things he would help himself to! He would go straight in and open up the chests—silver ingots, dollar pieces, a muslin gown . . . He would first bring to the temple the Nanking bed that formed part of the dowry of the licentiate's wife, and then provide himself with tables and chairs from the Chiens—maybe he would take the Chaos' while he was at it. He would not bestir himself about these things. Little Don would be told to do it and he had better be quick about it if he did not want to get slapped . . .

The sister of Chao the white-eyed was too ugly. Sister Tsou's daughter? She was a mere child as yet. The fake foreigner's wife? Bah! She was no good since she had slept with a man without a queue. The licentiate's wife had a scar on her eyelid . . . Where had Wu-ma been keeping herself?—her feet were a bit too large anyway.

But before he was able to make up his mind, Ah Q had already begun to snore, while the flickering candle, which had burned down only about half an inch, lighted up his open mouth.

Suddenly he started up, looked around the room in fright, but the sight of the four-ounce candle reassured him and he fell back to sleep.

The next day he rose very late. On the street he found everything much the same as before. He felt hunger no less keenly. For a while he did not know what to do, then suddenly he made up his mind and started in the direction of the convent.

The convent, with its white walls and black gate, was as quiet as in the spring. After some hesitation, he knocked and was immediately answered by the menacing barks of the dog. Hastily arming himself with some broken bricks, he knocked again, a little more vigorously. But no one came to open it until he had made quite a number of pockmarks on the black door.

Hastily he got the bricks ready, assumed a fighting position, and prepared for the dog. The door opened only a crack, through which he saw the old nun. No dog rushed out.

"What have you come for?" she asked in astonishment.

"The revolution! Don't you know that?" Ah Q replied cryptically.

"Revolution, revolution! But we have had one already. How many times must you revolutionize us?" the old nun said pitifully.

"What did you say?" Ah Q was surprised in his turn.

"Don't you know that they have already been here and revolutionized us?"

"Who?" Ah Q was more surprised than ever.

"The licentiate and the foreigner."

Ah Q was paralyzed by the unexpectedness of this answer. Emboldened by his irresolution, the old nun shut the door in his face. It was bolted when Ah Q pushed against it, and when he knocked again there came no reply.

The robbing of the convent had occurred in the morning. The licentiate Chao was better informed than most people in the village, and as soon as he learned that the revolutionaries had actually entered the city during the night, he wound up his queue under his cap and went to call upon the fake foreigner, whom he had up to that time avoided. But a new epoch had just dawned and the two men found themselves completely in accord and became fast comrades in a common cause. For a while they did not know what their immediate mission should be. Finally, after a long conference and much exchange of views, they recalled the votive tablet in the convent bearing the legend, "Long live the Emperor, ten thousand years, ten thousand times ten thousand years!" This, they decided, must be revolutionized without any delay. Being true revolutionaries, they had set out immediately for their objective. Because the nun had dared to hinder the course of the revolution, they immediately declared her the personification of the Manchu Government itself and had fearlessly given her several whacks on her smooth-shaven head. After the departure of the revolutionary heroes, the nun carefully examined the place and found that besides the broken votive tablet, an incense burner, dating from the reign of one of the early Ming emperors, had disappeared from the altar before Kuanyin.

Ah Q regretted oversleeping that morning and felt offended that he had not been called upon to join the expedition. Then he comforted himself with the thought that they were perhaps not yet aware that he had entered the service of the revolution.

AH Q DENIED THE RIGHT OF REVOLUTION

Little by little normal conditions returned to Wei. It was learned that although the revolutionaries had occupied the city, there had been no untoward changes. The magistrate from the old regime kept his post under a new name; the graduate also became some sort of official, the correct name of which the villagers could not comprehend. The local garrison remained under the command of the same captain. The only outrages were perpetrated by the bad element among the revolutionaries, who started to forcibly cut off queues. It was reliably reported that the boatman Seven Pounds from a neighboring village fell victim to this outrage and was now without the mark that distinguished man from beast. This did not terrify the villagers, however; since they seldom went into the city, they were not exposed to the danger. Those who had intended to go changed their minds. Among them was Ah Q, who gave up the idea of visiting an old friend in the city.

It could not be said exactly that there was no change in Wei, for the number of those who knotted up their queues increased day by day. The first was, as we have already observed, the licentiate, followed by Chao the watchman and Chao the white-eyed, and finally Ah Q. If this had happened during the summer it would not have been conspicuous, but since it was late autumn, the queue-knotters could not be said to lack courage, nor could it be said that the village of Wei was insensitive to the spirit of change that characterized the times.

When Chao the watchman walked down the street with nothing dangling from his head people shouted: "There goes a revolutionary!"

Ah Q envied him. He had heard about the licentiate's knotted queue but had not thought that he could follow so illustrious an example. The watchman was, however, not beyond his emulation and he now made up his mind; with a chopstick he secured his queue on top of his head and after some hesitation went out boldly on the street.

His appearance attracted some attention but caused no comment. This neglect at first chagrined and then angered him. He had become dissatisfied and irritable of late— though his problem of living was no more difficult than before the revolution, though people were courteous to him, and though the tavernkeeper did not refuse him credit. He felt that the revolution should not be so prosaic and colorless. One day his ire was fanned to the exploding point when he encountered little Don.

For little Don's queue was also knotted on his head and secured with a bamboo chopstick. Ah Q never thought that little Don would be so brazen, and never would have permitted it if he had had his way. For what was little Don? He wished to seize the impudent pretender, break his chopstick in two, let down his queue for him, and to slap him as a punishment for forgetting his birth, for the crime of daring to become a revolutionary. But with magnanimity and restraint he let little Don off and only glared at him and spat in token of his contempt.

The fake foreigner was the only one who did dare to venture into the city. The licentiate had contemplated making a call upon His Honor the graduate for having stored the trunks, but thought better of it in view of the danger to his queue. Instead he sent a very ingratiating letter to His Honor through the fake foreigner, whom he also prevailed upon to propose his name for membership in the Freedom Party. Upon reimbursing the latter four dollars when he returned from the city, the licentiate received a peachlike ornament made of silver which he pinned to his breast. This inspired awe and admiration in the villagers, who divined that with the Shih Yu Tang[13] (Persimmon Oil Party) it was the equivalent of the mandarin's official button, almost the equivalent of a *hanlin*. His Honor Chao's prestige soared, soared infinitely higher than when his son passed his examination. He was so proud that he had no use for any one, including the very estimable Ah Q.

It then dawned upon Ah Q why he had been neglected: he realized that it was not enough to say that he had joined the revolutionaries, or to knot his queue on top of his head; it was necessary to make the acquaintance of the revolutionaries. He knew of only two: the one in the city had long ago been—zip!—beheaded; there remained only the fake foreigner. There was but one way out of Ah Q's neglected position; he must immediately discuss matters with the fake foreigner.

The gate of the Chien house was open. Ah Q edged in timidly. Inside, the fake foreigner was standing in the courtyard, dressed in a black outfit that must have been a foreign costume, a silver peach pinned to his breast, holding in his hand the stick with which Ah Q had already had some encounters; his growing queue was untied and hanging loose over his shoulder as in representations of the Taoist immortal

---

[13] Tzu-yu (freedom), being a new term, is corrupted by the illiterate peasantry into Shih-yu because of the similarity in sound.

Liu Hai. Around him were Chao the white-eyed and three idlers listening reverently and attentively to his discourse.

Ah Q tiptoed in and stood behind Chao the white-eyed. He wanted to greet the speaker, but did not know what form of address to use. "Fake foreigner" certainly would not do; "foreigner" was none too appropriate; "revolutionary" did not seem appropriate either; perhaps he should address him "Mr. Foreigner."

Mr. Foreigner did not notice the newcomer, being in the midst of an exciting chapter of the revolution.

"I have always been hot-tempered, you know. So when we met I always said to him, 'Brother Hung,'[14] let us strike now!' But he always said, '*No!*'—which of course you will not understand as it is in the foreign language. Otherwise we would have succeeded long ago. But from this you will see how cautious and careful he is. He has asked me to go to Hupeh several times, but I have not yet consented. Of course I would not think of accepting a post in a little district city like ours . . ."

"Hem, er," Ah Q tried to begin during this pause, forgetting to address him as Mr. Foreigner.

The four listeners turned around and looked at him in astonishment; Mr. Foreigner also noticed him.

"What do you want?"

"I . . ."

"Get out!"

"I want to join . . ."

"Get out!" Mr. Foreigner raised his funeral stick.

Chao the white-eyed and the other listeners shouted, "The gentleman tells you to get out. Can't you hear?"

Instinctively Ah Q raised his hands to protect his head as

[14] Li Yuan-hung, commander of the revolutionary forces.

he turned and fled. Mr. Foreigner did not give chase. Ah Q slackened his gait to a walk, his heart filled with a melancholy despair. The fake foreigner, his only entrée to the revolutionary party, had forbidden him to revolt; thenceforward he could no longer expect revolutionaries in white helmets and white armor to summon him to action—his talents, aspirations, hopes, and his career were all destroyed by the prohibition. In the face of these blasted hopes, the ridicule of such people as little Don and Wang the Beard, who would soon hear of it from the idle witnesses, seemed nothing.

Never before had he experienced such frustration, never before such a feeling of futility. His coiled queue seemed somewhat absurd even to himself. He began to despise it and he thought of letting it down to show how little he cared, but he did not do so. He wandered about until evening and then went to the tavern and gulped down two cups of wine, on credit. Gradually his spirits were restored and in his fertile imagination there again appeared fragments of shattered white helmets and white armor.

One day he had lingered in the tavern until closing time as usual and was on his way to the temple with slow heavy steps.

Bang! bang!

He suddenly heard a strange sound, like and yet unlike firecrackers. Always curious, Ah Q felt his way along in the darkness in the direction of the sound. He heard footsteps, and as he stopped to listen a man rushed by, as though fleeing from something. Ah Q turned around and fled after him. The man turned a corner; Ah Q turned also. The man stopped and Ah Q stopped, too. He looked back and found no danger threatening from behind; he looked at his man and found it was only little Don.

"What is up?" Ah Q said, somewhat annoyed.

"The Chaos . . . they have been robbed!" little Don said panting.

Ah Q's heart jumped. Little Don moved on, but Ah Q vacillated. After all he had been in "that line" and was on that account bolder than most people. He emerged from around the corner and listened attentively. He seemed to hear sounds. He looked and fancied he saw people in white helmets and white armor, carrying out chests, furniture—including the Nanking bed of the licentiate's wife—but he could not see very clearly in the darkness. He thought of going up nearer, but his legs would not move.

It was a moonless night. Wei village lay in peaceful quiet such as prevailed in the primeval days of Fu Hsi. Ah Q stood and watched until he began to feel weary of the endless procession of chests, tables, Nanking beds that he fancied he saw, and until he began to doubt the trustworthiness of his own eyes. He decided to return to the temple.

The temple was even darker than the streets. He closed the gate after him and stumbled into his own room. Lying in bed he turned the matter over in his mind; the men in white helmets and white armor had been here, no more doubt of that, and they had not asked him to join them. They had carried off a lot of things and he had not gotten his share of the loot. It was all the fault of the fake foreigner, who forbade him the revolution, otherwise, he thought, how could he have been denied his share? The more he thought about it the more indignant he became, until his heart was filled with hatred and bitterness, and he said, nodding his head with grim determination: "No revolution for me, eh? but only for yourself, eh? Fake foreigner, your mother's——! All right, revolt all you like: the punishment for revolt is death, sure. I shall inform the authorities, I shall see you arrested and dragged into the city, I shall see you beheaded—you and all your family—zip! zip! zip!"

THE GRAND HAPPY ENDING

The robbing of the Chaos caused in the villagers a mixed feeling of pleasure and uneasiness; and it produced the same sort of feeling in Ah Q. Four days later he was arrested during the night, without warning, and taken into the city. It was a dark night. A squad each of regulars, militiamen, and armed police, and five detectives, entered Wei, surrounded the temple under cover of darkness and trained a machine gun on the gate. But Ah Q did not rush the siege as anticipated. After a while the commander of the expedition became impatient and offered a reward of twenty thousand *cash*, whereupon two militiamen volunteered to dare and die. They climbed over the wall and opened the gate. The expeditionary force rushed in and dragged out the sleeping Ah Q, who did not fully wake up or realize what had happened until he had been placed beside the machine gun.

It was noon when the triumphant expedition entered the city. Ah Q was dragged into a dilapidated yamen, marched through several compounds and then thrust into a cell. The heavy grilled door closed after him as he stumbled in. He was surrounded by solid walls on the other three sides. Looking around carefully, he discovered two other men in the cell.

Although somewhat frightened, Ah Q was by no means distressed by his new surroundings, for his room in the temple was no more sumptuous than this one. The other prisoners looked like villagers, and as they got to talking one said he was being held for back rent that his grandfather had owed to His Honor the graduate, the other said that he did not know what he was held for. They asked Ah Q and Ah Q answered proudly and unhesitatingly:

"Because I want to revolt."

In the afternoon he was taken out of the cell and marched to the judgment hall. Behind a table in the center sat an oldish man with a clean-shaven head. Ah Q at first thought that he was a Buddhist monk, but when he observed the squad of soldiers standing below and the group of some ten personages in long gowns on either side—some with clean-shaven heads like the oldish man, some with hair about a foot long hanging down their shoulders like the fake foreigner, all with fierce features and staring at him menacingly—he decided that there must be something to that oldish man and his knee joints thereupon loosened and he knelt down.

"Stand up! Don't kneel!" shouted the personages in long gowns.

Ah Q, though he appeared to have understood the command, was unable to maintain a standing posture, his knees failed him, he sagged down and again lapsed into his kneeling position.

"Slave habit!" The personages in long gowns grunted with contempt, but did not insist on his standing up.

"You might as well confess the truth so as to avoid unnecessary pain. I know everything already. Confess and you will be set free." The oldish man with the clean-shaven head said very firmly and deliberately, his eyes fixed searchingly upon Ah Q.

"Confess!" the personages in long gowns echoed.

"I had intended to come and . . . ," Ah Q said after revolving the situation in his confused mind.

"Then, why did you not come?" the oldish man asked benignantly.

"The fake foreigner would not let me!"

"Nonsense! It is too late to say that you had intended to come. Now where are your accomplices?"

"What?"

"The men who robbed the Chao family that night, where are they?"

"They did not come for me. They carried off the things themselves," Ah Q said vehemently.

"Where did they go? You will be set free if you tell." The oldish man was more benign than ever.

"I do not know . . . they did not come for me."

At a glance from the oldish man Ah Q was again seized and thrust into the cell. When he was dragged out of the grilled door for the second time it was the forenoon of the second day.

Things were the same in the great hall. The oldish man again sat behind the table and again Ah Q knelt down.

The oldish man asked benignantly, "Have you anything else to say?"

Ah Q could not think of anything, so he answered, "Nothing."

Thereupon a personage in a long gown approached Ah Q with a sheet of paper and a writing brush which he was about to put into Ah Q's hand. At this Ah Q became confused, nay terrified out of his wits, for this was the first time that he had ever come into such proximity with a writing brush. He was pondering how it should be held, when the man pointed to a place on the sheet of paper and told him to sign.

"I—I—cannot read," Ah Q said with terror and shame as he grasped the brush in his hand.

"We'll let you off easily. You can just draw a circle."

Ah Q was willing but in spite of himself the brush shook in his hand. The man spread the paper on the ground. Ah Q stooped over and tried with all his might to make the circle as directed. But the mischievous brush was not only heavy but also unruly. Just as he was about to close the circle with his trembling hand, it jerked with a centrifugal motion with the result that the circle was shaped like a melon seed.

Ah Q felt humiliated that he had not made a good round circle, but the man assisting took the paper without finding fault with it. Ah Q was then taken behind the grilled door for a third time.

He did not feel particularly distressed. He probably thought that in a man's life there must be times when he would be seized and thrust behind grilled doors, and be required to make a circle on a sheet of paper. But he did feel keenly the blot on his "life and deeds" because he could not make a truly round circle. The last thought, however, troubled him only for a brief moment, for he soon decided that no decent man could draw a perfect circle anyway. He fell asleep.

Strangely enough His Honor the graduate could not sleep that night. He had had a disagreement with the captain; for he had held that the recovery of the loot was the most important thing while the captain, who had become very insolent of late, had insisted that the most important thing was to make an example of the prisoner. Pounding loudly on the conference table, the captain had shouted: "We must punish him as a warning to others. Look, more than ten robberies have occurred during the less than twenty days since I became a revolutionary. No arrests have been made until now. What is to become of my prestige? Now that I have made an arrest, you try to block me. It won't do. This is within my jurisdiction." The graduate had been greatly embarrassed but he stood his ground and threatened to resign his chairmanship of the citizens' revolutionary committee if the prisoner was not spared for the moment, so that he could lead to the recovery of the loot. At this the captain had only retorted, "Do as you like." As a result His Honor could not sleep that night. However, he did not resign the next day.

On the morning following His Honor's sleepless night Ah Q was again taken out through the grilled door. In the great hall the oldish man with the clean-shaven head sat as before and as before Ah Q knelt down.

"Have you anything more to say?" the oldish man asked benignantly.

Ah Q thought for a moment, found nothing to say, and so answered very candidly, "Nothing."

Thereupon personages in long gowns and others in short coats put a white vest on him, on which were written some characters. Ah Q was distressed by this, for white was the color of mourning and mourning was an unlucky thing. His hands were tied behind his back and he was taken out of the yamen.

Ah Q was then hoisted into an open cart, several short-coated personages sat down beside him, and the cart immediately started, preceded by a squad of soldiers and militiamen carrying foreign guns, flanked by numerous open-mouthed spectators, and brought up in the rear by—but Ah Q could not see that.

Suddenly the realization came upon him: was he not going to have his head cut off? His eyes went blank, his ears buzzed with a ringing sound, he felt faint. But he did not really faint away. He felt an acute distress at one moment but in another moment he was at peace with the world, probably feeling that it was in the nature of things that some people should be unlucky enough to have their heads cut off.

Why were they not heading him directly toward the execution ground? Ah Q had not lost his bearings, but he did not know that he was being paraded through the streets as a warning. If he had known, it would have only occurred to him that that, too, was in the nature of things.

Finally he realized that he was being taken to the execution ground in a roundabout way, that there was no question that he was going to have his head—zip!—cut off. Indifferently he looked to the right and left and was dimly conscious of crowds of people like ants. Then his eyes fell upon Wu-ma, whom he had not seen for a long time as she had in the meantime found work in the city. Suddenly he felt ashamed of himself because of his tameness, because he had not sung a few sentences from the plays to show how little he cared. Feverishly he considered his stock: "The Little Widow at Her Husband's Grave" was not dignified enough for the occasion; he had already done to death the song beginning with "I regret . . ." in the play *Struggle between Dragon and Tiger*; perhaps he had best sing "With the steel whip in my hand I shall smite thee." He thought of raising his right hand for effect, but suddenly realized that his hands were tied behind his back. He had to give up that, too, as he was something of a perfectionist.

"In twenty years I'll be here again . . . ,"[15] Ah Q sud-

[15] Common formula of defiance used by desperadoes on their way to the execution ground and signifying a sure return, in another incarnation, to carry on where they left off.

denly blurted out this immemorial defiance, which he had never heard said, in which he had never been coached, and which, therefore, he must have arrived at independently and instinctively in the crisis.

"Bravo!!!" a howl like that of wolves and jackals rose from the multitude.

As the cart rolled on amidst the applause, Ah Q cast another glance at Wu-ma. She did not appear to have seen him at all, but was lost in gazing at the guns carried by the soldiers.

Ah Q turned his glance upon the applauders.

Suddenly a scene from the past flashed through his mind. Four years ago he had met a famished wolf at the foot of the hills; it had followed him with dogged persistence, never too near and never too far, its mouth watering for his flesh. He was scared to death, but fortunately he had with him a woodcutter's axe and with it he was able to keep off the wolf and reach home. But he could never forget those eyes of the famished wolf, fierce and yet slinking, weird and hair-raising like jack-o-lanterns, as though piercing right through his skin and flesh. Now he beheld eyes even more horrible than those of the wolf. These were dull and lusterless eyes that yet seemed to glint with greediness, to relish his bravado and to be waiting for something that they would relish even more; and like the wolf they followed him, never too near, and never too far.

The myriad eyes seemed to merge into one, boring and gnawing relentlessly at his soul.

"Help!"

But before he had time to utter the word, all became black before his eyes, his ears rang, and his body seemed to break into tiny specks of dust.

The aftermath of the incident was felt more poignantly in the house of His Honor the graduate; the loot had not been recovered and his household was rent with lamentations. Next in order came the house of Chao, for not only was the licentiate's queue cut off by the more radical element of the revolutionaries, when he went into the city to report the case, but they had to pay the twenty-thousand *cash* reward. That household was, therefore, also rent with lamentations. From that time on they gradually began to manifest the symptoms of a man who has seen better days.

As to public opinion in Wei, there was no dissent from the natural conclusion that Ah Q must have been a bad character: the fact that he was shot was proof enough for anyone—otherwise, how could he have been shot? Public opinion in the city, however, was outraged and dissatisfied; most people contended that shooting was not as good a spectacle as beheading. And what a stupid and spiritless prisoner—not a single tune out of him all the time he was being paraded through the street! They had followed the procession for nothing.

A Hermit at Large

MY RELATIONS with Wei Lien-shu were, come
to think of it, rather odd, for they began with one funeral
and ended with another.

I used to hear his name mentioned when I was at the
city of S——. It was said that he was a very strange fellow: He
specialized in zoology and yet taught history in the middle
school; he was aloof and supercilious in manner and yet had
a tendency to mind other people's business; he insisted that
the family system must be destroyed and yet he always sent
part of his salary to his grandmother as soon as he received
it, with never a day's delay. There were many other stories
told about him. He was, in a word, a character in the city
of S——, an unfailing topic for idle conversation. In the fall
of one year I happened to be staying with some relatives at
Cold Stone Mountain. Their name was Wei and they were
Lien-shu's kin. But they knew even less than I about him and
seemed to look upon him as if he were a foreigner. "He is
different from us all," they said in summing him up.

This was not strange, for although modern education
already had a history of over twenty years in China, Cold
Stone Mountain did not even have a primary school. In this
mountain village Lien-shu was the only one who had gone
out to study. He was, therefore, really different. However,
they also envied him, for he was said to earn a lot of money.

Toward the end of fall, dysentery began to be prevalent.

I was rather alarmed by it myself and was thinking of returning to the city. I heard that Lien-shu's grandmother was among those afflicted and that she was in a very serious condition because of her age. There was no physician in the village. Lien-shu's immediate family consisted only of his grandmother, who lived a simple, quiet life with a maidservant. Lien-shu had lost his parents in his childhood and had been brought up by this grandmother. She suffered a great deal of privation in her day, but now she was without wants. Since Lien-shu was unmarried, his house was naturally a very quiet and lonely one. This was probably one of the things that caused people to look upon him as somewhat odd.

Cold Stone Mountain was one hundred *li* by land, seventy *li* by water, from the city, requiring at least four days for a special messenger to reach Lien-shu and back. In the monotony of village life, an event like this was news of the first magnitude, which everyone wanted to find out about. On the second day it was said that her condition had become critical and that a special messenger had been despatched. But she breathed her last during the fourth watch of the same night, her last words being, "Why can't I have a last meeting with Lien-shu?"

The head and nearer members of the clan, representatives from the grandmother's family, and idlers gathered in a crowded room to devise ways and means to cope with the situation. They figured that by the time Lien-shu arrived it ought to be encoffining time. The coffin and burial clothes had been prepared long in advance[1] and required no atten-

[1] Death being one of the three most important events in a person's life, the Chinese make preparations for it as well as for the other two— birth and marriage. It is not uncommon for elderly people to select their coffins and store them in a spare room in the house.

tion. The one problem was how to deal with the chief mourner, for they anticipated that he would want to introduce innovations in the funeral ceremonies. As a result of this council it was decided that the chief mourner must fulfill three conditions: he must wear white; he must kowtow; he must have Buddhist and Taoist priests to conduct funeral services.[2] In other words, everything must be done as it had always been done.

After they had decided upon these essentials they arranged to meet again in the front hall of the house of mourning on the day of Lien-shu's arrival and conduct a bold parley with him. They agreed to dispose themselves in strategic positions and to support one another in a concerted attack. All the villagers gulped with excitement and curiosity, as they waited for developments. They knew Lien-shu for a "revolutionary" who "eats religion,"[3] a man devoid of common sense and justice, and they anticipated a violent struggle between the parties, perhaps even something quite unexpected.

It was said that Lien-shu arrived in the afternoon. Entering the house, he only made a slight bow before the spirit tablet of his grandmother, whereupon the head of the clan proceeded with the prearranged program. He summoned Lien-shu to the front hall, and, after a rather long introduction, launched into the subject in hand. He was echoed from one end of the hall to the other, giving Lien-shu no chance to put in a word in rebuttal. Finally the relatives tired themselves out and silence fell on the room, with everyone watching tensely Lien-shu's mouth. But Lien-shu betrayed no

[2] The Chinese believe in the diversification of their other-worldly investments; hence a mixture of Buddhist, Taoist, and Confucian rituals is used at the more elaborate funerals.

[3] That is, living on the benefits derived from the missionaries by embracing Christianity: the "rice Christians" of American journalists.

emotion whatever. He simply said, "I'll do everything you say."

This was entirely unexpected. One burden fell from the hearts of those present, but at the same time a new and heavier burden seemed to take its place, for Lien-shu's acquiescence appeared too fantastic to be true and might really mean something else. The curious villagers were very much disappointed. "How strange it is," they said. "He says that he'll do everything they want. Let us go and see." He would do everything they wanted him to meant that everything would be done in the usual and customary way, which in turn meant there was nothing much to be seen. But the villagers wanted to be there just the same, and so after twilight they all foregathered in the funeral hall with eager anticipation.

I was among those who went to see the ceremony, sending beforehand incense and candles as an offering to the deceased. When I arrived at the house of mourning, I found Lien-shu already engaged in enshrouding the dead. He was a short man of lean, sharp features, with loose hair and a thick dark beard; his eyebrows occupied a good portion of his face, which was dominated by two bright and burning eyes. He did his job of enshrouding well; he did it in an orderly and methodical manner, as if he were an expert at it, and he impressed the spectators favorably in spite of themselves. According to the well-established tradition of Cold Stone Mountain, the representatives of the family of the deceased were bound to offer criticisms no matter how well things were proceeding. Lien-shu was never ruffled by these criticisms, but quietly and obligingly made whatever changes that were demanded. A white-haired old lady standing before me could not help emitting a sigh of appreciation.

The enshrouding was followed by kowtowing, then weeping, which the women did with improvised librettos. The body was then put in the coffin, followed by more kowtowing and weeping until the lid was nailed down. A momentary silence was almost immediately succeeded by a tenseness, a feeling of surprise and dissatisfaction in the atmosphere. It had suddenly occurred to everyone, as it occurred to me, that during all the time Lien-shu had not shed a single tear. He only sat distractedly upon the mourner's straw mat, his eyes glittering out of his swarthy countenance.

The encoffining was concluded in this atmosphere of surprise and dissatisfaction. The spectators were about to disperse, as Lien-shu continued to sit abstractedly on the straw mat. But suddenly his tears began to flow. They were followed by sobs which immediately turned into the long howls of a wounded wolf in the wilderness deep at night—cries of pain, fury, and sorrow. This was something uncalled for by old tradition; the assemblage, taken by surprise, did not know what to do. After a while, a few went up to him to persuade him to stop crying. Others joined the group until he was entirely surrounded, but he continued to utter his heartbreaking cries, oblivious of the people around him.

As their efforts to quiet him were of no avail, they desisted and walked away from him awkwardly. He wept for about half an hour, then suddenly stopped and went inside without a word of thanks to the mourners. Someone went in to peep and came back with the report that he had gone into his grandmother's room, that he was lying down and appeared to have gone off to sleep.

Two days later, the day before I was to start back for the city, I heard heated discussions among the villagers. They said that Lien-shu wanted to burn up most of the furniture as offerings to his grandmother and to distribute the rest to those who had served her in her lifetime and particularly to the maid who waited upon her at her deathbed. Moreover, he wanted to let the maid have the use of the house as long as she lived. His relatives and kin talked against it until their tongues were worn out and their lips were dry, but it was no use.

Probably it was chiefly out of curiosity that I stopped by his house on my way to the city to offer him my condolences. He came out wearing unhemmed white cotton, and looked very much the same as when I first saw him, very much aloof. I comforted him the best I could, but except for a few perfunctory grunts, he only said, "Thank you for your kindness."

Early in the same winter we met for a third time in a bookstore in the city of S——. We nodded to each other as acquaintances, but it was not until toward the end of the year, after I lost my position, that we came to know each other well. I went to see him often because I had nothing to do and wanted company and also because I was told that, though he was by nature aloof, he liked to associate with those in unhappy circumstances. However, fortunes rise and fall, and those in unhappy circumstances do not always remain so; consequently he did not have many friends of long standing. This reputation was indeed true for he received me as soon as I sent in my card. His guest room was simply furnished with some bookcases, tables, and chairs. Though he was known as one of those dreadful "innovators," there were few "new" books on the shelves. He had heard that I had lost my position. After the usual words of greeting, host and guest fell silent. He smoked furiously and did not throw away his cigarette until it burned almost to his fingers.

"Have a cigarette," he said, as he reached out for his second.

I took a cigarette and as we smoked we talked about teaching and books. But soon our conversation lagged again and I was about to leave when I heard footsteps and chatter; four children came rushing in. The oldest was about eight or nine, the youngest four or five, all very dirty and homely enough. However, Lien-shu's eyes lighted up with pleasure as he stood up and walked into the inner room, saying, "Big Liang, Little Liang, come here! I have got the mouth organs that you asked for yesterday."

The children followed him into the other room and soon emerged, each with a mouth organ. Almost as soon as they stepped out of the guest hall they began to quarrel. One of them was crying.

"There is a mouth organ apiece and they are all the same," he said to them, "so do not fight over them."

"Whose are they, all these children?" I asked.

"They are the landlord's. They have no mother, only a grandmother to take care of them."

"Is the landlord single?"

"Yes. His wife died three or four years ago and he has not married again. Otherwise he would not rent his spare room to a bachelor." He smiled a wry smile as he said this.

I wanted to ask him why he had remained single, but decided that we did not know each other well enough for that.

As I got better acquainted with Lien-shu I found him a good person to talk with. He had something to say on almost every subject and everything he said was marked with originality.

Some of his visitors were not very easy to put up with. They must have read *Lost*,[4] for they often referred to themselves as "unfortunate youths" or "forgotten men." They sprawled languidly on the chairs like so many crabs, sighing and smoking incessantly. Then there were the children, always quarreling, upsetting cups and saucers, demanding sweets, and generally making a nuisance of themselves. But as soon as Lien-shu saw them he lost his usual coldness; he seemed to cherish them more than his own life. I was told that when Third Liang had the measles he was so upset that his swarthy countenance looked darker than ever. It turned out to be a light case. The child's grandmother thought it a good joke and liked to tell about it.

"Children are always good. They have not yet been contaminated," he said to me one day as he noted my impatience with the children.

"That is not necessarily true," I said, indifferently.

"You are wrong. Children do not have the bad traits that grownups have. If they become bad later on—the kind of badness that you attack—it is because of their environment. They are not bad to start with. I think the only hope for China lies in that."

"I do not agree. If children do not have the seeds of badness in them, how can they bear bad flowers and fruits when they grow up? It is only because a seed carries within it the embryo of leaves, flowers, and fruits that it sends forth these things later on. How could it be otherwise?"

I was at the time reading Buddhist sutras, having nothing better to do—very much like the great who become vegetarians and talk about Zen the minute they are kicked out of

[4] A story by Yü Ta-fu published circa 1922.

office. However, I understood nothing about Buddhism, though I talked thus glibly of cause and effect.

Lien-shu became furious at me; he looked at me contemptuously and would not say another word. I was not quite sure whether he had nothing to say or whether he felt that I was beneath his dignity. But I noticed that he assumed the cold manner that I had not seen for some time. He smoked two cigarettes in silence. I fled as he reached for a third.

This difference between us was not cleared up until three months later, probably partly because he had forgotten about it and partly because he himself happened to have been abused by "innocent" children, and therefore felt that there was some justification in my blasphemy against them. This was, of course, only my guess. It came out at my lodgings, after we had been drinking some wine. Looking up reflectively he said with an air of sadness, "It is really very strange when you think of it. As I was coming towards your house I saw a very small child. He waved at me the reed leaf that he was holding and said 'Kill him!' He was hardly old enough to walk."

"It is because he has been corrupted by his surroundings."

I immediately regretted saying that, but he did not seem to mind, and went on drinking and smoking furiously.

"By the way," I said, trying to cover up my blunder by changing the subject, "what has brought you here? I know you are not in the habit of calling on people. We have known each other for more than a year but this is the first time that you have come to my place."

"I was just going to tell you: you must not come over to my lodgings to see me. There are two persons there, one old and one young, that will nauseate you."

"One old and one young? Who are they?" I asked with surprise.

"My elder cousin and his younger son. *Huh*, the son is exactly like his father."

"I suppose they have come to see you and at the same time take in the sights of the city?"

"No. He says that he wants to talk to me about my adopting that boy."

"Oh," I said with astonishment. "But you aren't married, are you?"

"They know that I am not going to marry. But that does not matter. What they really want is to adopt that old house of ours in Cold Stone Mountain. I have nothing besides this old house as you know; I spend everything as soon as I get it. This dilapidated house is the one thing I own. The only interest that my cousin and his sons have in life seems to be to drive out the old maidservant who is living in it."

The bitterness with which he said this chilled me. I tried to comfort him: "I do not think that your kinsmen could be that bad. Their only fault is that they are somewhat old-fashioned and reactionary in their thinking. I remember that they were very solicitous and eager to comfort you when you cried so sorrowfully at the funeral."

"They were just as solicitous and eager to comfort me when my father died, though that did not prevent them from trying to make me sign away my house." He looked up and stared into empty space as if trying to form a picture of just what had happened then.

"In a word, the crux of the matter is that you have no children. Why is it that you would not marry?" Finally I hit upon the subject which I had had in mind for so long a time;

this seemed a more appropriate moment to discuss it than any other since I had known Lien-shu.

He looked at me with surprise and then cast his eyes down and stared at his knees. He lit a cigarette and continued to smoke, without answering my question.

Dreary and cheerless as Lien-shu's circumstances were, he was not allowed to live his life in peace. Gradually there appeared in the tabloid papers anonymous attacks upon him, and gossip about him became more frequent among the teaching fraternity. Now, the gossip was not that of curiosity and amusement, as formerly, but that of malice and was intended to do him harm. I knew the reason: it was because he had recently published some articles. I paid no attention to the attacks and gossip. The people of the city of S—— hated most outspoken and indiscreet utterances and never failed to punish those who were guilty of such indiscretions. It had always been so; Lien-shu himself knew this. In the spring I heard that he had been relieved of his post by the principal of the school. It seemed rather sudden but in reality it was the logical sequel; it seemed sudden and unexpected only because I had been hoping that those I knew might avoid this fate. The people of S—— did not, on this occasion, go out of their way to do Lien-shu ill; it was merely their customary way of dealing with nonconformers.

I was occupied with my own problems at the time and was making preparations for going to Shan-yang to teach in the following fall. So I did not have time to go to see him. When I finally found time, it was more than three months after Lien-shu had been relieved of his post. Even then it did not occur to me to call on him. Walking by the main street one day, I stopped at one of the secondhand book stands and something I saw gave me a shock. It was an early printing of the Chi-ku-ko edition of the *Shih-chi so-yin,* which I recognized as having belonged to Lien-shu. He liked books but was not a collector. To him this must have been a rare edition that he would not have parted with except under absolute necessity. However free with his money he might have been, could it be possible that he had come to this only three months after he lost his position? Thereupon I decided to call on Lien-shu. I bought a bottle of kaoliang spirits, two packages of shelled peanuts, and two smoked fish heads.

The door to his room was closed. I called to him but there was no answer. I thought he might be sleeping, so raised my voice a bit, at the same time knocking on the door.

"He must have gone out," Big Liang's grandmother—that fat woman with triangular eyes—stuck out her gray head from the window across the yard and said in a loud and impatient voice.

"Where has he gone to?" I asked.

"Where has he gone to? How is one to know? But he cannot have gone far, so you might as well wait. He will be back by and by."

I pushed the door open and walked into the guest room. Truly, "an absence of one day is like three autumns." The room was dismal and empty. Not only was there little furniture left, but of his books there remained only those bound in foreign style which no one in the city of S—— could possibly want. The round table was still there, the table which used to be surrounded by languid and sad-looking young men, neglected geniuses, and dirty, noisy children, but which was now so quiet and covered only with a thin layer of dust. I put the bottle and packages on the table, pulled up a chair and sat down facing the door.

The landlady was correct. "By and by" the door opened and a man came in as quiet as a shadow. It was Lien-shu. It might have been due to the lateness of the afternoon, but he did seem to me darker than ever, though he was otherwise the same.

"Ah, so you are here! How long have you been here?" He seemed glad to see me.

"Not very long," I said. "Where have you been?"

"Nowhere in particular. I just went out for a walk."

He also pulled up a chair and sat by the table and we began to drink and to talk about his losing his position. However, he did not want to talk much about that. He regarded it as something to be expected, something which he was now used to and which should cause no surprise, something hardly worthy talking about. He kept on drinking as he always did and talked about society and history in general. I noticed his empty bookcases and, recalling the early printing of the Chi-ku-ko edition of the *Shih-chi so-yin*, I felt a sense of melancholy and sadness.

"Your guest room seems so desolate. Don't you have many visitors nowadays?"

"No. They don't want to come because I am depressed. A man in low spirits makes others uncomfortable. No one likes to visit the park in the winter." He took two draughts in succession without saying anything. Suddenly he looked up at me and asked, "I don't suppose you have any assurance of getting a position either?"

I was about to give vent to my feelings on the subject when he cocked his ears to listen and went out with a handful of peanuts. Outside was the sound of talk and laughter of Big

Liang and his brothers. The children fell silent the moment he went out and seemed to have gone away. He followed and talked to them, but they did not answer him. He came back into the room as quietly as a shadow and put the peanuts back in the package.

"They don't even want to eat my things," he said in a low, mocking, defiant tone.

I felt saddened, but I said with a forced smile, "Lien-shu, I think you take things too hard. You are too misanthropic . . ."

He smiled a wry smile.

"I have not yet finished what I was going to say. I suppose you think that we, we who occasionally drop in to see you, come here because we have nothing else to do and are only trying to use you as an object of amusement?"

"No, not always, though I think that way sometimes. People like to shop for material for conversation."

"You are wrong there. People are not in reality like that. The truth is that you have woven yourself a cocoon of loneliness and wrapped yourself up in it. You ought to try to concede more light in the world."

"Perhaps it is so. But tell me, where comes the silk filaments with which the cocoon is made? Of course there are many people like that in this world. My grandmother was one of them. Though I have not shared her blood I might yet inherit her fate. It does not matter very much, for I have mourned both for her and for myself."

I recalled vividly his grandmother's encoffining, every detail reappearing before my eyes.

"I never understood your heartrending cries at the time," I bluntly stated.

"You mean at my grandmother's encoffining? Yes, it

would be hard for you to understand it," he said as he lit his lamp. "Yes, it happens that our acquaintance began at that time. You wouldn't know, of course, that that grandmother of mine was my father's stepmother; his own mother died when he was three years old." He reflected, drank some spirits, and finished his fish in silence.

"I did not know these things at first, of course, though there was one incident which troubled me even as a child. My father was still living and our family circumstances were fair. In the first month it was the custom in the family to hang up our ancestral portraits and to make offerings before them. I loved to look at those portraits of gorgeously costumed men and women; it was an occasion which came but rarely. The maidservant who held me in her arms always pointed to one portrait and said: 'This is your real grandmother. Kowtow to her and ask her to protect you and make you grow up fast and as strong as dragons and tigers.' I could not understand why I should have another 'real grandmother' when there was one in the house already. But I loved this 'real grandmother,' who was not so old as the grandmother in the house. She was young and beautiful, and wore a red dress embroidered with gold, and a pearl hat. In the portrait she looked almost as young as my mother in hers. Whenever I looked at her, her eyes were always fixed on me and her smile seemed to become brighter. I knew that she must love me very much.

"However, I also loved the grandmother in the house, the grandmother who was always sitting and sewing slowly, under the window. No matter how gaily I played in front of her and called to her, I could not make her happy and laugh. She always seemed so sad, so different from other people's grandmothers. But I loved her just the same, though

later on I began to drift away from her. This was not because
I realized as I grew older that she was not the true mother
of my father but because she was always, day in and day out,
year in and year out, sewing and sewing, sewing away like
a machine. I could not understand why she was like that and
I was impatient with her machinelike ways. But she kept on
sewing as she always did; she took care of me and looked
after me. She never scolded or punished me, though she
never smiled or laughed. She was like this after my father
died. Later on we depended almost entirely upon her sewing
for our support. Naturally she became even more of a
stranger to gaiety and laughter. She managed to send me
to school ——"

The lamp burned low, the kerosene was about dry. He
got up, took a small tin from the bookcase and replenished it.

"Kerosene has gone up twice this month," he said as he
adjusted the wick. "Living is going to be more and more difficult—Her life went on like this even after I graduated and
got a job and our life became more secure. She probably
never stopped sewing until she grew ill and had to lie down.

"Her last years were, I suppose, not so very hard and she
lived to a ripe old age. I need have shed no tears, especially
when there were so many to mourn at her funeral. Even
those who had persecuted her in her lifetime appeared saddened. But I—somehow I saw then before my eyes the whole
of her life, the lonely and solitary life that she had woven for
herself and which she spent her days in ruminating upon.
Moreover, I felt that there were many people in the world
like her. It was for those people that I cried. I was still the
plaything of my emotions.

"The way you feel about me is the same as the way I used
to feel about her. But I was mistaken. Her loneliness was not

of her own making entirely; I know that I myself had gradually drawn away from her and had neglected her as far back as I can remember."

He lapsed into another silence, his head lowered in thought, while his cigarette burned on. The lamp flickered.

"Ah, how bitter it is to think that no one would mourn for you after you are dead," he said as if to himself. After a while he raised his head and said to me, "I suppose there isn't anything that you can do. I must find something to do as soon as possible."

"Don't you have any other friends to call upon?" For I was then at the end of my own resources.

"There are still a few, but most of them are situated much as I am."

When I left Lien-shu the round moon was in the middle of the sky. It was a very still night.

Conditions in the educational world at Shan-yang were very bad. Two months after I got there I had not received a penny of my salary. I had to cut out even cigarettes. But the officers of the school, although they earned only fifteen or sixteen dollars a month, were every one of them contented men who knew their places and who worked from morning till night, in spite of their sallow faces and skinny bodies, thanks to the "copper sinews and iron bones" they had gradually cultivated. Moreover, they had to stand up every time they met their superiors. They were not people who "must have enough of food and clothing before they can be expected to know the rites and proper conduct." These things always reminded me of the words of Lien-shu when I took leave of him. His circumstances had gone from bad to worse. There was an air of diffidence about him, whereas before he had been merely silent and aloof. Hearing that I was about to leave the city, he came to see me at night and said haltingly, "I wonder if there is anything you can do for me there?— Even if it is just a clerical job at twenty or thirty dollars a month, it would be all right. I . . ."

I was very much surprised. I never thought that he would demean himself to this. I did not know what to say.

"I . . . I want to live a few more years . . ."

"I'll see what I can do there. You can be sure that I'll do the best I can."

This was my promise and it recurred to me often and with it Lien-shu's face and his halting, diffident words—"I want to live a few more years." Then I would try to recommend him for jobs. But what was the use? There were more people than jobs and the net result of my efforts was that I received a few words of regret from those I approached and Lien-shu received a few words of apologies from me. As the end of the semester approached, things grew worse. The *Weekly Student*, published by the local gentry, began to attack me. My name was, of course, never mentioned, but the attacks were so cunningly phrased as to give the unmistakable impression that I was trying to stir up trouble in the educational world, my attempts to find work for Lienshu being alluded to as an effort to place my own kind.

I was forced to lie low and to shut myself up in my room after classes; I was even afraid that my cigarette smoke might arouse suspicion that I was trying to stir up trouble. Naturally I had to abandon my efforts to help Lien-shu. Thus time dragged on until the middle of winter.

It had been snowing all day and it continued to snow into the night. It was so quiet outside that you could almost hear the stillness. I sat alone with eyes closed in the dim lamplight and seemed to see the falling snow flakes add to the vast expanse of snow. In my native home everyone was busy making preparations for the New Year celebrations. I was again a young boy and was making a snow Lohan, with my playmates in the backyard. The Lohan's eyes were made by sticking in two pieces of coal, and they appeared very black against the snow. The eyes blinked and became Lien-shu's eyes.

"I want to live a few more years," I heard a familiar voice say.

"Why?" I asked without any apparent reason; the question sounded idiotic the moment I uttered it.

This idiotic question woke me from my reveries. I sat up and lit a cigarette. I opened the window and looked out: the snow was falling thicker than ever. Someone knocked on the gate; there was a sound of footsteps which I recognized as those of the porter. He pushed open my door and handed me a letter in a long envelope. The handwriting was very cursive but I made out in a glance the words "Sealed by Wei." It came from Lien-shu.

This was the first letter which I had had from since I left S——. I knew of his lazy habits and did not miss his letters, though sometimes I could not help resenting his silence. Now his letter aroused my curiosity and I opened it hastily. The handwriting inside was also very cursive. The letter read as follows:

SHEN-FEI ——:

How should I address you?[5] I'll leave the space blank and let you fill in whatever you like. It does not make any difference to me.

[5] Chinese usage requires some such word as "elder brother" or "friend" after the name.

Since we parted I have received three letters from you and have answered none of them.

You may like to know something about me and so here is the story in brief: I have now become a failure. I used to consider myself a failure, but I know now that I was not then a failure. It is now that I am definitely a failure. Formerly, when there was someone who wanted me to live a few years longer, when I wanted myself to live a few more years, it was impossible for me to live. Yet now, when there is little reason for me to live, I keep on living . . .

But should I go on living as I am?

The man[6] who wanted me to live longer is no longer living. He was murdered by his foes. Who were his murderers? No one knows.

How fast life changes! During the past year I almost came down to begging, I might say that to all intents and purposes I did come to that. But there was something that meant something to me, something for which I was willing to beg, to starve, to suffer loneliness, and to toil. I was not willing to suffer the annihilation of death. See how much the mere fact that someone wants me to live can mean to me. But now this is no more, this someone no longer lives. At the same time I feel that I have no justification for living. How do others think? They do not think I have any right to live either. At the same time I feel that I must go on living to spite those people that do not want me to live. Fortunately there is no longer anyone who wants me to live; fortunately, I shall cause no one any unhappiness. I do not want to cause anyone who wants me to live any unhappiness. Now there is no such person left—not a single one. I am glad, I am really happy: I have begun to do myself the things that I used to hate; and to oppose and to reject everything that I used to admire and to believe in. I have truly failed—and at the same time I have become a success.

Do you think that I have gone mad? Do you think that I have become a hero or a great man? No, no. It is all very simple; I have

[6] It is often impossible to tell whether the person referred to is "he" or "she," as here.

recently become an advisor to General Tu at eighty dollars cash[7] a month.

Shen-fei ——: What do you think of me now? Think whatever you like; it makes no difference to me.

Perhaps you still remember my guest room, the room where we met for the first time in the city and where we met before we parted. I am still using the same guest room. But here there are now new guests, new gifts and presents, new flatteries, new wire-pullings, new kowtowing and bowing, new mah-jong games and drinking matches, new hatreds and new nausea, new sleeplessness and pulmonary hemorrhages . . .

In one of your letters you said that you were not very happy in your new teaching post. Do you want to become an advisor too? Tell me if you do and I'll get you an appointment. It really doesn't matter if one becomes a mere gatekeeper, for there will also be new guests and new gifts and presents, new flatteries . . .

We have had a heavy snow here. How is it where you are? It is now late at night. I have just spit some blood and I feel wide awake. I suddenly realize that you have written me three letters since fall. What pleasant surprises they were. I must send you some news of myself. I hope you are not too disappointed.

I don't suppose I shall write again; you know how I am about letters. When are you coming back? If early enough we might yet see each other. But I am afraid that we have to go our separate ways. So you had better forget about me. I thank you from the bottom of my heart for your efforts to help me. But you had better forget me, for I am now "all right."

LIEN-SHU.

DECEMBER 14

Although I was not "too disappointed," I had a depressed feeling after rereading his letter carefully, a feeling which was not, however, unmixed with gladness. In any case, I thought, his livelihood was no longer a problem with him, which meant that I need not worry about him, though on

[7] Around the 'twenties there was a general depreciation of paper currencies.

my part I had done nothing concrete to help him. I had an impulse to write an answer, but the impulse vanished immediately as I did not have anything adequate to say.

I really began to forget him; his face no longer appeared so frequently in my memory. But in less than ten days after I got his letter I suddenly began to receive the *Academic Weekly* published in the city of S——. I rarely read these things, but since they were mailed to me, I naturally glanced through them. These reminded me of Lien-shu, for there were often poems and other items about him in the *Weekly*, such as "A visit to Mr. Lien-shu on a Snowy Night," "A gathering in the Study of Advisor Lien-shu," and the like. In the column headed "Chats of an Academician" there were frequent accounts of Lien-shu's oddities, now described as anecdotes and there was always a suggestion that "an unusual man always has his unusual ways."

I did not know why it was but while I was receiving these reminders of Lien-shu his face grew more and more vague in my memory. Yet at the same time I felt more strongly bound to him and often experienced for him an anxiety that I could not understand. In the spring the *Weekly* ceased to come. Meanwhile the Shan-yang *Weekly Student* began to publish serially a long article entitled "Truth behind Humors." In it the writer alluded to the unsavory activities of certain persons which well-informed people had known about and deplored for a long time. I was among these certain persons and again I found it necessary to be extremely careful, to take care not even to let cigarette smoke fly out of my window. Such caution kept one busy and enforced inactivity. I ceased to think about Lien-shu. I might say that I had really forgotten him.

In spite of all my efforts to be discreet, I did not last

through the semester. I left Shan-yang toward the end of May.

From Shan-yang I went to Li-cheng and from there to Tai-ku. After more than half a year of wandering I was still without a job, and I decided to return to the city of S——. It was in the afternoon of an early spring day when I arrived; the sky was overcast and everything was enveloped in gray. There was a vacant room in my former lodginghouse and again I put up there. I had thought of Lien-shu on the homeward journey, and decided to go over to see him after supper. Carrying with me two packages of the steamed cakes for which Wen-hsi was famous, I walked through miles of wet road, avoiding the numerous dogs that lay indolently in the street, and finally arrived at the house where Lien-shu lived. It was bright inside. I smiled as I thought that this must be because he was now an advisor to General Tu. But when I looked up I discerned clearly a strip of paper pasted at an angle on either side of the door. Big Liang's grandmother must have died, I thought as I stepped into the gate and went toward the inner court.

There was a coffin in the dimly lit court. Beside it stood a soldier or bodyguard in military uniform talking to someone who turned out to be Big Liang's grandmother. There were also a few laborers in short coats. My heart began to beat violently. The old woman turned around and saw me, whereupon she cried, "Ah, you have returned? Why couldn't you have come back earlier?"

"Who—who has died?" I asked though there was little doubt now in my mind as to who it was.

"His Excellency Wei. He passed away day before yesterday."

Looking around I found the guest room rather dark, prob-

ably lit with only one lamp. But the center room was hung
with mourning curtains and outside stood Big Liang and his
brothers.

"He is laid out in there," Big Liang's grandmother said,
pointing to the room. "After His Excellency received his appointment I gave up the center room to him. He is laid in
there now."

Before the mourning curtains stood a long narrow table
and in front of that, a square table. On the latter were laid
out ten dishes of food. I was stopped by two men in long
white robes as I stepped into the room; they stared at me
with fishy eyes betraying surprise and suspicion. I told them
who I was and of my friendship with Lien-shu, attested to
by Big Liang's grandmother, whereupon their eyes and
hands relaxed and they allowed me to go in.

No sooner did I bow than there came the sound of weeping from below. I looked in that direction and saw a boy of
over ten years of age prostrated on a straw mat. He was in
white, a large string of hemp tied around his closely cropped
head.

After I had exchanged greetings with the men in white
and had learned that they were the closest relations of Lien-
shu, I begged to be allowed to take a last look at an old
friend. They tried to dissuade me, saying that they would not
think of putting me to the trouble, but my persistence prevailed and they lifted up the mourning curtains.

Now I beheld Lien-shu in death. How strange it was!
Though his short coat and his trousers were wrinkled and
bore traces of blood and though his face was painfully thin,
he looked very much the same as I used to know him. His
mouth and eyes were closed and he seemed to be sleeping

peacefully. I almost wanted to hold my hand over his nose to see if he was not actually still breathing.

All was still as death, the living as well as the dead. I came out from the room, followed by his cousin who spoke a few appropriate words, saying that his "brother" had "joined the ancients" when he was just in his prime and on the threshold of great things, and that this was not only a great misfortune to his "decaying clan" but was also a severe shock to his friends. He seemed to be making apologies for Lien-shu; such eloquence as this was rarely encountered in one from a mountain village. After this speech everything was again still as death, the living as well as the dead.

I felt weary but I was not particularly sorrowful. I joined Big Liang's grandmother in the yard and talked with her. I learned from her that the encoffining time was near, that they were only waiting for the burial clothes, and that when the coffin lid was nailed down those born in the years of the Rat, Hare, Ox, and Cock must not be present. She became very much interested in her subject and poured out a stream of words. She spoke of his illness, of the last months of his life, and of her candid opinion of him.

"Do you know that His Excellency became quite a different person after he came under his lucky star? His head was raised high and he looked self-assured. He no longer acted so stiff and formal before people. You know, of course, that he used to act like a dumb person, he used to address me as *lao-tai-tai* [venerable madam]. But later he called me an old wench. Yes, it was great fun. Once he received a present of *pai-shu*[8] from Hsien-chü. He didn't take such things himself, so he threw it out into the yard—right here—and said,

[8] *Atractylis lancea,* variety of *ovata formalyrata,* used for medicine and in soups.

'Old wench, you take it and stuff yourself with it.' People
came and went all the time after he came under his lucky
star. I gave up the center room to him and moved into one
of the side chambers myself. He was so different from ordinary people after he came into the 'red period in his horoscope'—we used to talk and joke a lot. If you had come a
month earlier, you would have been in for some good fun, for
there were banquets two days out of three: with jolly conversation, laughter, singing, versifying, games . . .

"He used to fear the children more than children feared
their father. He was always so gentle and patient with them.
But he was quite different of late. He teased and joked with
them and Big Liang and his brothers all liked to play with
him and went to him whenever they had the opportunity.
He had so many ways of teasing them; he would make them
bark like dogs or kowtow to the ground before he would buy
them what they wanted. Oh, it was such fun. Two months
ago Second Liang asked him to buy a pair of shoes for him.
He had to kowtow three times. He is wearing those shoes
now, still in good condition."

She stopped when one of the men in long white robes
came out. I asked her about Lien-shu's illness. She did not
know much about that. She said that he had been growing
thinner and thinner but no one paid any attention to it, as
he always seemed to be in such good spirits. A month or so
ago he had several hemorrhages, but did not seem to have
consulted any physician. Then he had to stay in bed. He lost
his speech three days before he died and could not say a
word. His Honor Thirteen came from Cold Stone Mountain
and asked whether he had any money saved up, but he did
not say a word. His Honor Thirteen was suspicious and
thought he was only pretending to be unable to speak, but

Big Liang's grandmother was not sure about that. Some people say that consumptives lose their power of speech before their death.

"But His Excellency was a very strange man," she said suddenly, lowering her voice. "He would not try to save anything, but spent his money like water. His Honor Thirteen is inclined to think that we have gotten something out of him. But the truth is that we never got even a whiff of his money. He spent everything no one knows how or on what. He would buy something one day and sell it the next. Or he would destroy what he bought—no one knows how or why. When he died he left nothing. He had squandered everything. Otherwise it would not be so quiet around here now . . .

"Yes, he was a reckless one. He would not think about the most important things in life. I have tried to advise him that he should get married, at his age. It would have been easy for him to find a good match in his recent circumstances. He might at least have bought a couple of concubines, if he could not find a suitable match. One must try to be respectable. But he only laughed at me saying, 'Old wench, are you still trying to be a matchmaker?' He took nothing seriously and would not heed any advice no matter how sincerely it was offered. If he had listened to my words, he would not have to feel his way around in the other world all by himself. At the very least he would have some dear one to mourn for him."

A store clerk arrived with a package of clothes. The relatives of the deceased took out the clothes and went behind the mourning curtains. Presently the curtains were pulled back. The underclothes had been changed; now they proceeded to put on the outer garments. These occasioned some surprise to me, for he wore khaki military trousers with wide red stripes and they were putting on a military coat with bright gold shoulder stripes. I did not know what rank the stripes represented nor how he won that rank. He was put in the coffin in a rather awkward position; at his feet were placed a pair of brown leather shoes, a paper sword by his side and, to one side of his pale dark face, a military cap with a gold band.

The three relatives wept for a while over the coffin, then stopped and wiped off their tears. The boy with a string of hemp tied on his head withdrew; Third Liang also went out of sight. They must have been born under the signs of the tabooed animals.

I went up to take a last look at Lien-shu as the laborers lifted up the coffin lid.

He lay peacefully in his ill-fitting and incongruous clothes, with his mouth and eyes closed and the corners of his mouth curled in a cold smile, as if he were amused by his amusing corpse.

Mourning wails began simultaneously with the hammering of the laborers. The mourning distressed me. I retreated into the yard and continued to retreat until I was out on the street. The damp roadway was clearly visible. Looking up I found that the thick clouds had disappeared and the full moon was exuding a cold, still brilliance.

I walked very rapidly as if trying to break through something heavy and oppressive, but I could not. Something seemed to be trying to struggle its way out of my ears. After a long while it succeeded in freeing itself. It was as a long howl, the howl of a wounded wolf in the wilderness deep at night, a howl that conveyed pain, fury, and sorrow.

My heart felt lighter, and I walked on serenely on the damp, stone-paved road under the moonlight.

Remorse

I WANT to write down, as far as possible, my remorse and my sorrow, for the sake of Tzu-chun and for myself.

How quiet and empty it is in this dingy room, secluded in a forgotten corner of the Provincial Guild! And how quickly time flies! It is now more than a year since I fell in love with Tzu-chun and through that love escaped this quiet and emptiness. How ironic that this same room should be the only one available when I came back here. Everything is as it used to be—the same broken window looking out on the same hollow locust tree and ancient wisteria, the same square table in front of the window, the same cracked wall, and by it the same bed. It is the same as before Tzu-chun and I lived together, it is as if the past year had been entirely eradicated, as if it had never existed, as if I had never moved out of this dingy room and established a tiny home full of hope in Chi-chao Hutung.

Not only this, but the quiet and emptiness a year ago were not quite the same as they are now, for they were then tempered with expectation, the expectation that Tzu-chun would soon arrive. After a long, impatient wait, how I used to come suddenly to life as soon as I heard the crisp sound of her high-heeled shoes upon the brick walk! Then I would see her dimpled, pale, round face, her thin arms, her striped cotton blouse and her black skirt.[1] She would bring in some

[1] The regulation dress of girl students during the first ten or fifteen years of the republic.

new leaves from the locust tree and draw my attention to
the clusters of purplish white flowers on the iron-colored
vines of the ancient wisteria.

The quiet and emptiness are the same as before, but
Tzu-chun will not come again—she will never, never come
again.

When Tzu-chun was not with me in my dingy room, I
could do nothing. In my boredom I would take a book,
whether science or literature, it did not matter, and read
and read. Before I could realize it, I had already turned over
ten pages, but I could not remember a thing I had read. My
ears, however, were unusually keen, and I fancied that I
could detect among the footsteps outside the gate those of
Tzu-chun and that they were drawing nearer. More often
than not the footsteps would die away and lose themselves
in the sound of others. I detested the son of the servant whose
cotton-cloth soled shoes did not sound like Tzu-chun's at
all; I detested that foppish ape in the next compound who
used vanishing cream and whose new leather shoes sounded
too much like hers.

Had her ricksha overturned? Had she been run over by
the street car?

I wanted to take my hat and go look for her at her uncle's
home, but her uncle had once berated me to my face.

Suddenly the sound of her shoes approached, louder and
louder. When I went out to meet her, she had already passed
the wisteria vines, her face dimpled with smiles. She probably had not had any trouble with her uncle, I thought, and
I felt relieved. After we had gazed at each other in silence
for a moment, the room would be gradually filled with our
chatter. We talked about the oppression of the family system, about the necessity of destroying old traditions, about
equality for men and women, about Ibsen, about Tagore,

about Shelley . . . She always smiled and nodded, her eyes filled with the light of childish curiosity. On the wall was tacked a half-length portrait of Shelley in half-tone, cut from a magazine, the best portrait of the poet. When I pointed it out to her, she cast only a brief glance at it and then lowered her head as if embarrassed. In these things Tzu-chun did not quite free herself from the fetters of traditional thinking. Afterwards I thought of taking the portrait down and hanging in its place the picture showing Shelley after his drowning in the sea, or a picture of Ibsen, but I never got around to it, and now even the magazine print of Shelley has disappeared.

"I belong to myself and none of them has any right to interfere!"

This was what she said, clearly and with quiet determination, following a moment of silence when, after we had known each other for about half a year, we happened to bring up again the subject of her uncle, with whom she was staying, and her father, who was living in her native village. By that time I had told her all about myself and my opinions and faults; I held back nothing and she seemed to have understood everything. These brave, determined words of hers stirred my soul and echoed in my ears for many days thereafter. I was filled with an indescribable happiness, for I felt certain then that the outlook for Chinese womanhood was not as hopeless as the pessimists made it out to be and that in the near future we should see the bright dawn.

When I escorted Tzu-chun to the gate, we invariably kept about ten steps apart, for the face of the disgusting old man with the catfish moustache was always glued close to his dirty window, his nose flattened against the pane, while in the outer compound the face of that foppish ape, thickly covered with vanishing cream, peered out from behind a bright pane of glass. But Tzu-chun walked on proudly without deigning to notice them and I would return as proudly to my room.

"I belong to myself and none of them has any right to interfere!" Her spirit of revolt appeared to be of the thoroughgoing kind, even more thoroughgoing, even more resolute than my own. What are Vanishing Cream and Flat Nose to her?

I can no longer remember distinctly how I professed to her my pure, true and passionate love. Not only have I forgotten now the details of that episode, but I had difficulty in recalling them even then. When I thought about it later in the same night, only fragments remained. A month or two after we began to live together, even these fragments became dream bubbles that eluded my grasp. I only recall that for more than ten days before it happened I carefully studied the various manners of approach, the sequence of my speech, not forgetting the possibility of her refusal. But when the time came, all that I had carefully rehearsed turned out to be unnecessary. In my nervousness I unconsciously adopted the method that I had seen in the motion pictures. Whenever I recalled it afterwards, I always had a feeling of embarrassment, yet in my memory this alone has found a permanent place. Even now it is like a lone lamp in a dark room, revealing the indelible scene: I kneel on one knee beside her; with tears in my eyes, I hold her hands in mine.

Not only have I forgotten what I said and did, but I was not even clearly aware of Tzu-chun's words and behavior: I only realized that she had given me her consent. I seem to remember vaguely that her face first became pale and then turned pink, a pink that I had never seen before and have never seen since, that her eyes, though they avoided mine, shone with sorrow and happiness, mixed with surprise and incredulity, and that she looked as if terror stricken, as if she was about to break through the window and fly away. I knew that she had given me her consent, but I did not know what she did or did not say.

She remembered. everything though: she could recite as out of a familiar book every word I said, and my behavior to her was like a picture invisible to myself, which she could describe with vividness and detail, including, naturally, the gaudy motion-picture flash that I so much wanted to forget. The stillness of the night was our reviewing time. I was frequently questioned, tested, required to repeat the words of that occasion. But I had to be prompted and corrected again and again, like a "D" student.

These reviews became less frequent, but whenever I saw that faraway look in her eyes, her abstraction, the gentle expression assumed by her face, her deepening dimples, I knew that she was again reviewing the ancient lesson herself. I dreaded the moment when she would come to the movie scene, but I knew that she would inexorably come to it, and would insist on dwelling upon it.

She did not think it funny; she did not even laugh at what I considered funny or shameful. The reason for this was clear to me: it was because she loved me, because she loved me so much and so truly.

The late spring of the past year was my happiest and busiest time. My heart was at peace, though at the same time I became very much occupied with a thousand things. We began to walk on the street together. We went to the park a few times, but most of the time we were hunting for a place to live in. I sensed the curious gazes that we encountered on the street, the disparaging remarks, the indecent and the insulting glances, which caused me, if I was not on my guard, to shrink from embarrassment. But I managed to summon up enough courage to face them proudly. She, however, was without embarrassment. She walked on calmly in the face of these hostile manifestations as if there was no one in the world besides herself and me.

It was no easy matter to find a place to live in. Most of the time we were refused upon one pretext or another, and the rest of the time we rejected the place as unsuitable. At first we were rather particular—we were not really particular, but the places we saw did seem unsuitable—later on we only wanted to find someone who would take us. After looking at more than twenty places, we finally discovered one that more or less answered our purposes. It consisted of a two-*chien* southern room in a house in Chi-chao Hutung. The landlord was a petty official, but was quite broadminded. He occupied the central (northern) unit of the house and the side chambers with his family, which consisted of his wife and a girl less than a year old and a peasant woman servant. It was a quiet place as long as the child did not cry.

Our household furnishings were simple enough, but it already required more than half of the money that I had managed to get together. Tzu-chun sold her gold ring and earrings, the only jewelry she had. I would not let her at first, but she insisted and I gave in. I knew that if I did not let her contribute her share she would not be happy.

She had broken openly with her uncle long before this. He now disowned her as his niece. I also broke off one by one with those of my friends who professed to offer advice for my own good but who really feared for me or were jealous of

me. But we did not mind this. Although it was always near
dusk when I was through at the office and the ricksha man
was always so slow, the hour always arrived when we would
be at last together. We would first gaze upon each other in
silence and then talk freely and intimately. We would be
silent again as we bowed our heads in thought, thinking
about nothing. Little by little I read all of her body and all
her soul, and in three weeks I understood her even better
than I had done before; I discovered many things about her
which I thought I had understood but which I really did not.
These had been the real barriers between us.

Tzu-chun became more lively every day. I bought two
potted plants for her at the temple fair, but she did not care
for flowers, and neglected to water them. At the end of four
days they dried up in the corner—I did not have time to attend to everything. She had, however, a weakness for animals, in which she was probably influenced by the wife of the
petty official. Inside of a month the family grew; four chicks
strutted about the yard with more than ten belonging to the
landlady. Each of the women recognized the markings of
the chickens, however, and knew which were her own.
There was, in addition, a black and white Pekingese, also
bought at the temple fair. I think it had a name when we
bought it, but Tzu-chun renamed it Ah Sui. That's the name
I called it by, though I did not like it.

This is true: Love must be renewed, must be made to
grow, must be creative. When I told Tzu-chun this, she
nodded understandingly.

Ah, what quiet, happy nights those were!

But peace and happiness have a way of stagnating and be-
coming monotonous. When we were at the Provincial
Guild we used to have occasional differences and misunder-

standings, but since we had come to Chi-chao Hutung there was not even this. We merely sat facing each other by the lamp and ruminated over the joy of reconciliation after those clashes.

Tzu-chun began to take on weight, and color and life appeared on her face. Only she was always so busy. With all her household duties, she did not even have time to talk, much less to study or take walks. We often said that we must engage a maidservant.

One of the things that irritated me was to find her in ill humor when I came home toward evening, especially when she tried to hide it by forced smiles. When I inquired into the cause of her irritation it was usually because of a silent duel with our landlady, with the chickens as the fuse. But why wouldn't she tell me about it? One must have the privacy of an independent home, I told myself. We could not go on living at a place like this.

My routine was fixed. Six days a week I went from the house to the office and again from the office to the house. At the office I sat at a desk and copied, copied, copied documents and letters: at the house I sat with her and helped her make the fire in the stove, cook the rice or steam the bread. It was during this period that I learned to cook.

My food was much better than it had been at the Guild. Although cooking was not Tzu-chun's forte, she did devote her entire energies in this direction. Since she herself worried about these things day and night, I could not help but worry about them too and thus it could be said that I shared her pleasures and her tasks. Her face was covered with sweat all day, the short hairs stuck to her forehead, and her hands became coarser.

In addition there was Ah Sui to care for and the chickens to be fed—all chores that she must do herself.

Once I did suggest that it did not matter if I did not have tempting things to eat and she must not work so hard. She did not say anything, but from the glance that she gave me I knew that she was hurt. And so I refrained from mentioning the subject again and she continued to direct all her energies to household duties.

The blow that I had been dreading finally fell. On the eve of the Double Ten Festival I was sitting in our room while she was washing dishes. There was a knocking at the gate. When I opened it, I discovered the office messenger. He handed me a stenciled form. I looked at it under the lamp and found it was what I had feared. It read:

> By order of the Director, Shih Chuan-sheng is hereby informed that his services are no longer required at the Bureau.
>
> The Secretary's Office. Oct. 9.

I had foreseen this when I was still at the Guild. Vanishing Cream was a gambling companion of the son of the Director and must have told him about Tzu-chun and myself, with inventions and embellishments of his own. What surprised me was that it should have been so slow in taking effect. It was not, to tell the truth, such a blow after all, for I had decided beforehand that I could get a clerical job elsewhere or find a position as tutor or do some translating work, though the last would have required greater exertion. I thought of the possibility of selling more translations to *The Friend of Liberty*; the editor was an acquaintance of mine and I had exchanged letters with him about two months earlier. But my heart beat violently just the same, and it pained me even more to see Tzu-chun's face turn pale, she who had always been so brave and fearless, but who seemed to have grown weak and timid of late.

"What does it matter? *Heng,* we'll find something new to do. We . . ."

She did not finish her sentence. I did not know why, but her voice sounded vague and unconvincing. The lamplight seemed dimmer than usual. What timid and laughable things human beings are! How profoundly affected they can be by little things like that! We first stared at each other in silence, then we began to talk about the situation, and we decided that we must do our best to stretch out as far as possible the little money we had, that we should put a classified advertisement in the papers for a copying or tutoring job and at the same time write to the editor of *The Friend of Liberty,* telling him of our present difficulties and asking him to help us by using some of my translations.

"Let us begin at once! Let us open up a new road!"

I turned resolutely to the table, pushing aside a bottle of sesame oil and a dish of vinegar while Tzu-chun brought to me the dim lamp. I first drafted an advertisement and then selected some books that I might translate. I had not opened any of them since we moved and they had been gathering dust. I left the letter to the last.

It was difficult. I did not know how to word it. When I stopped and tried to think, I would catch a glimpse of her face, so sad and crushed, in the dim lamplight. I never thought that such a little thing would cause such a noticeable change in Tzu-chun, who had been so resolute and fearless. The truth was that she had become very weak and timid of late—not only this evening. I felt more distressed than ever and in my distress I had suddenly a flash of the peaceful and serene life that had been mine in the dingy room at the Guild; in another moment I saw nothing but the dim lamplight.

After a long while the letter was finished. It was a lengthy letter and I felt tired, for I, too, seemed to have become weak and timid as compared with my former self. We decided that both the advertisement and the letter should be dispatched the next day. Unconsciously we both straightened our backs and seemed to feel, though neither of us said a word, a new courage and unconquerable spirit, and to see a new budding hope.

So this blow actually had an effect of awakening a new spirit in us. My life at the bureau was very much like that of a bird in the hands of a bird-peddler, who gives it just enough millet to keep it from starving but not enough to grow fat on. After a while its wings become feeble from disuse and it can no longer fly even if it should be let out of the cage. Now I have in any case escaped from the prison cage; I want to test my wings in unexplored and spacious skies before I have forgotten how to flap them.

A classified advertisement cannot be expected to produce results right away, naturally. Even translating is no easy matter. Things which I had read before and which I thought I had understood presented a thousand difficulties, when it came to actual translation. Thus my work was slowed down. But I was determined to overcome my difficulties, and the soiled edges of my dictionary (which had been almost new half a month ago) testified to my conscientiousness. The editor of *The Friend of Liberty* had told me that his publication would never turn down a good manuscript.

Unfortunately I did not have a quiet room to work in.

Tzu-chun was not as quiet and considerate as she used to be. The room was always cluttered with bowls and dishes and filled with smoke from the stove, making work difficult. I had only myself to blame for not being able to afford a study, but there was Ah Sui, and there were the chickens— growing larger and larger, and more and more frequently the cause of quarrels between the two families.

On top of everything else, there were the meals, as "unceasing as the flowing rivers." It seemed that Tzu-chun's only interest and achievement in life was expressed in this matter of meals. After eating there was the problem of money; after the money had been raised, again there was the matter of eating; then Ah Sui had to be fed, and the chickens. Tzu-chun seemed to have forgotten everything that she had ever known; she did not realize that my train of thoughts was frequently interrupted by her repeated announcements that dinner was ready. Even if I should take no trouble to hide my annoyance at table, she did not seem to sense it, but ate heartily as if nothing had happened.

It took five weeks to make her see that my work could not be regulated to fit in with the schedule of meals, and when she finally saw the situation, she probably did not like it, though she said nothing. As a consequence, my work began to proceed more rapidly. I turned out about fifty thousand words in a short time, which after some revision I would be able to send out, together with two other short pieces, to *The Friend of Liberty*. Food, however, remained a cause of annoyance. I did not mind its being cold but I did mind when there was not enough of it. Sometimes there was not even enough rice, though my appetite was considerably smaller than it used to be, as I stayed home at the desk all day. There was not enough to eat because she fed Ah Sui first, including the mutton that we so rarely treated ourselves to nowadays. Ah Sui had grown so pitiably thin, she said. The landlady sneered at us and she could not stand other people's sneers. Since Ah Sui ate before we did, there were only the chickens to eat our leftovers. It took me some time to discover all this and to realize that my place in the household was somewhere between the lapdog and the chickens, just as certain observations made it possible for Huxley to fix "Man's Place in Nature."

Later on, after many quarrels and at my insistence, the chickens gradually became part of our meals, and for some ten days both we and Ah Sui enjoyed this long-forgotten treat—though the fowls were lean because their regular diet had been reduced to a few grains of kaoliang each. The gradual disappearance of the chickens resulted in a greater quiet, but Tzu-chun missed them and seemed distracted and lost, to the extent of feeling disinclined to talk. How easy it is for people to change, I thought.

Soon we found it necessary to part with Ah Sui. We had given up hope of receiving any replies to our letters and for a long time Tzu-chun had nothing with which to tempt the little dog to sit up and paw the air. Winter came on with distressing speed and with it the problem of keeping a stove. Ah Sui's food was a burden that we had felt for a long time; now there was nothing to do but to part with the dog.

If we had taken it to the temple fair, we might have gotten a little something for it, but neither of us could or would do such a thing. In the end I blindfolded Ah Sui, took him outside the city wall and left him there. He tried to follow me back and I had to push him down a ditch, which, however, was not too deep.

I returned home feeling that I was rid of another load, but

Tzu-chun's face alarmed me—in it I saw something I had never seen there before. It was, of course, because of Ah Sui, but I did not think that it could affect her to this extent. I did not tell her I had to push him down the ditch.

In the evening there appeared a chilliness in her countenance, where before it had been only sad and mournful.

"Why are you like this today, Tzu-chun?" I could not help asking.

"What?" she said without looking at me.

"Your face looks . . ."

"Nothing. Nothing at all."

But I could tell by her face and from the way she spoke that she had come to look upon me as a cruel man. The truth was that it would have been much easier for me if I had been alone. Although I was too proud to associate, in my present circumstances, with friends of the family, and had even kept away from my former friends since we moved, there were many roads open to me if I were free and could go where I pleased. The reason I accepted the oppressive burden of our present life was because of her, and that, too, was the reason why I got rid of Ah Sui. How could she be so childish as not to see this?

I took the first opportunity to explain to her this line of thought. She nodded as if she understood, but from the way she acted I could tell that she either did not understand or refused to believe what I said.

The chilliness of the weather and the chilliness of Tzu-chun made it difficult for me to stay at home. But where was I to go? Though there is no human chilliness on the streets and in the parks, the wind was too cold and biting for comfort. Finally I found my paradise in the public library.

No admission ticket was required and there were two iron

stoves in the reading room. Even though there was barely enough coal to keep the fires going, yet the very sight of them had an effect of making one feel warm. As to the books, there were none worth reading: they were all ancient works —almost no new publications to speak of.

I did not mind this as I did not go there to read. There were usually a few men besides myself, sometimes as many as ten or fifteen, all thinly clad like myself, and all trying to keep warm under the pretext of reading. This suited me well. On the street I was always in danger of meeting people I knew and receiving from them contemptuous glances. There was no such danger in the library, for my more fortunate acquaintances preferred to sit by other iron stoves that they had access to, or by their own earthen stoves.

Though there were no books that I cared to read, I did find the atmosphere quiet and conducive to meditation. As I sat in the reading room and reviewed the past, I realized that during the past seven or eight months I had neglected— because of love, this blind love—other things in life just as important. The first of these is life itself, which is necessary for the embodiment of love and without which love cannot exist. There are still in this world roads to life for those who are willing to make the struggle, and I had not yet forgotten how to flap my wings, though I had become so much more ineffectual than I used to be.

The room and readers gradually disappear and I see fishermen in angry storms, soldiers in trenches, rich men in motor cars, opportunists in foreign concessions, unknown heroes in the fields and hills, professors on the platforms, politicians and thieves who carry on their work in the depth of the night.

As for Tzu-chun, she was not with me in these visions. She

had lost her courage, she was distressed because of Ah Sui and was worried only about cooking. The strange thing was that she had not grown thin.

The room began to get cold and the half-dead coal finally burned itself out. It was closing time, time for me to go back to Chi-chao Hutung and face Tzu-chun's chilliness. There had been occasional spells of warmth, which only added to my distress. I remember that one evening her eyes suddenly sparkled with childlike innocence as she talked about the days at the Guild. I detected, however, a note of fear and anxiety in her cheerfulness and I realized that I had become indifferent to her indifference and this, in turn, had aroused in her fear and uncertainty. I tried to smile and to give her some measure of comfort. But no sooner did the smile appear on my face and the comforting words come out of my mouth than they began to seem hollow and meaningless, a meaninglessness which reëchoed in my ears with insufferable mockery.

Tzu-chun appeared to sense it. She lost her phlegmatic calm and tried to conceal, not always with success, her fear and uncertainty. She became more considerate of me.

I wanted to tell her the truth but did not have the courage. I was several times on the point of speaking to her, but a glance at her childlike eyes would shake my determination and force me to assume a forced smile, which immediately mocked at me and caused me to lose my calm.

Now she again commenced to review the past, devising new tests and forcing me to give her reassuring but false answers. These false answers might have given her some comfort and reassurance, but they choked my heart and oppressed me with their falsity. It is true that it takes a great deal of courage to speak the truth; one who does not have this courage but is always ready to compromise with falsehood is never a man to blaze new trails in life. Not only is he not such a man, but he might as well have not existed at all!

One morning, one very early and cold morning, I found Tzu-chun in an ill-humored mood. This was unusual for early morning. Her mood might have been the result of my own, for I was filled with resentment against her and was secretly sneering at her. I suddenly realized more clearly than ever before that her intellectual interests and her vaunted courage were only a pretense and that she did not seem to realize this pretense. She no longer touched any books, no longer seemed aware that the first step in life is to seek a way to make life possible; that in this quest we must either struggle hand in hand or part company and seek our own salvation; and that one who can only hang on to another's coattail will interfere with the bravest of warriors and bring destruction upon all.

I felt that our hope lay in separation. I felt that she ought to have the courage to leave me. The thought of her death occurred to me, but I immediately repented and cursed myself for the thought. Fortunately it was early in the morning. There was plenty of time in which to prime myself for speaking the truth. This was my chance to hew out a new road.

I chatted with her, taking care to direct our conversation to the past; I spoke of literature, of certain foreign writers and their works, of Nora in *A Doll's House* and of *The Lady of the Sea*, and I praised Nora's courage and determination. These were the things we used to talk about the year before in the dingy room in the Guild; now they sounded hollow and meaningless in my own ears; they sounded more like the mockery of a naughty boy behind one's back.

She listened attentively, nodding in assent, and I managed to finish my speech, which was followed by a silence.

"It is true," she said after a while, "but Chuan-sheng, I feel that you have changed. Is it true? Tell me the truth."

The directness of this question stunned me, but I immediately recovered and explained my ideas and my proposal: the hewing of a new road, the creation of a new life, the necessity of this decisive step if we were both to avoid the fate of perishing. Summoning up all the resolution I was capable of, I concluded with the following words: "Moreover, nothing needs to hold you back from resolutely embarking upon a new life because . . . You want me to tell you the truth. That is a fine thing, for people must not be false. Now I'll tell you the truth: nothing needs to hold you back because I no longer love you. This is a fortunate thing for you, because now you can live your own life without worrying about me . . ."

I had expected violent reaction to this, but there was only silence. Her face turned deathly pale and yellowed, but she recovered almost immediately. Her eyes sparkled with their childlike innocence, and while trying to avoid my eyes, flitted about the room like those of a hungry child looking for its mother.

I could bear it no longer. Fortunately it was in the morning. I went out into the cold wind and hastened toward the public library.

There I saw *The Friend of Liberty* and found that it had published all the short pieces that I had sent. This was a surprise and gave me some new hope. There are yet many ways to live, I said to myself, but the present mode will not do.

So I started to visit friends with whom I had long lost contact. This I did only two or three times. Their rooms were warm, it was true, but the way they received me chilled me to the marrow. At night I returned to a room colder than ice.

Icy needles kept pricking at my soul, causing me to suffer constantly from a numb pain. There are still many roads to life and I have not yet forgotten how to flap my wings, I thought determinedly to myself. Again the thought of her death—again I cursed myself immediately and repented.

In the public library I often got glimpses of light, of a new road to life ahead of me. Tzu-chun, suddenly awakened to the situation, had resolutely walked out of our icy home; she was, moreover, without the least trace of bitterness. I felt as light as clouds floating in space, with deep blue skies above and mountains and seas below, expansive mansions, battlefields, motor cars, foreign concessions, grand houses, bustling market places, dark night . . . What was more, I actually had a feeling that this new life was about to open up before me.

We managed to live through the winter, a harsh Peking winter. We were like a dragon fly that had fallen into the hands of a naughty boy, and was tied to a fine thread, teased and cruelly abused. Though it might come through alive, it would be only half alive and would soon die.

Finally, after I had written him three letters, I heard from the editor of *The Friend of Liberty*. He enclosed only two book coupons of twenty- and thirty-cent denominations, while it cost me nine cents in cash for postage. Thus we went hungry one whole day for nothing.

However, what I had expected to happen finally did happen around the end of winter and the beginning of spring. The wind was no longer so cold and I had been in the habit of staying out for longer and longer periods. It was after dark when I came home. Yes, I had returned home at this hour many a time, weary and dispirited, and feeling all the more so as I saw our gate and slackened my pace still further. Eventually I entered our own room. There was no light. When I found the matches and lit the lamp, the room seemed more than usually solitary and empty.

As I was trying to take in the situation, the landlady came to our window and asked me to come out.

"Tzu-chun's father came today and took her home," she said simply.

This was not what I had expected and I was taken aback and stood there speechless.

"Has she gone?" this was the only question that I was able to frame.

"She has gone."

"She—did she say anything?"

"No, she did not say anything. She only asked me to tell you when you came back that she had gone."

I could not believe it, although the room had impressed me as so strangely solitary and empty. I looked around, half expecting to find Tzu-chun, but I saw only a few pieces of old, decrepit furniture, all testifying to her inability to hide anything from anyone. Perhaps she had left a letter or note; but there was none. I found, however, that she had gathered up in one heap the salt and dried peppers, flour, and half a head of cabbage and had placed by it twenty or thirty coppers. These were our entire resources and she had left them all to me so that I might manage to live on them until something else turned up.

I felt oppressed and rushed out into the darkness of the courtyard. The landlady's room was bright and resounded with children's laughter. My heart calmed down and there gradually emerged out of the oppressiveness of my situation a path into life: hills and lakes, foreign concessions, elaborate banquets under bright electric lights, ditches and moats, a dark, dark night, a blow of a sharp sword, noiseless footsteps . . .

I felt somewhat relieved and lighter; I even uttered a contemptuous "pooh" when I thought of the practical matter of traveling expenses.

Lying in bed, the future, as far as I was able to imagine it, soon exhausted itself before my eyes. In the darkness I seemed to see a pile of food, then the sallow, pale face of Tzu-chun, looking at me imploringly with her childlike eyes. When my gaze steadied, I could see nothing.

My heart again grew heavy. Why could I not have endured it a few days longer? Why must I have so impulsively told her the truth? Now that I had told her, there was nothing for her to look forward to but the harshness, as harsh as the burning sun, of her father—her creditor—and the chilly glances, chillier than frost and ice, of her friends and relatives. Outside of these there was only emptiness. How fearful was the prospect of walking along the so-called road of life with this heavy burden of emptiness on one's back and with nothing to encourage one except harshness and chilly glances! Especially when at the end of the road there was only—a tomb without even a tombstone!

I should not have told Tzu-chun the truth. Since we had loved each other once, I should have lied to her and told her that I loved her still. Truth cannot be such a precious thing if it has nothing better to offer Tzu-chun than this heavy burden of emptiness. Falsehood would, it is true, also lead to nothing in the end, but at the worst its burden could hardly be any heavier.

I thought that after I had told Tzu-chun the truth she would be able to walk resolutely ahead with absolute freedom, as resolutely and courageously as when we had decided to live together. But I am afraid that I was wrong. Her courage and her fearlessness of that time were born of love.

Because I did not have the courage to bear the burden of falsehood, I had loaded upon her the burden of truth. Ever since she fell in love with me, she had assumed this heavy burden and walked with it along the so-called road of life, with nothing but harshness and chilly glances to encourage her.

I thought of her death . . . Now I saw myself as a coward, a coward who should be ostracized by the strong, whether they be liars or truthful men. Yet in spite of my cowardice she had been anxious to help me maintain my livelihood as long as possible.

I wanted to leave Chi-chao Hutung, where it was so strangely solitary and empty. If I could only leave this place, I thought, it would be as though Tzu-chun were still here in the city. She might one day unexpectedly come to see me as she used to when I was at the Guild.

The new road to life continued to elude me; all my inquiries and letters failed to get any favorable response. As a last resort I went to see a friend of my family, a boyhood schoolmate of my uncle's, a specially presented licentiate known for his selfrighteousness. He was an old resident of the capital and had a wide circle of friends.

It was probably because of my worn old clothes that I was received with contemptuous and suspicious glances by the gatekeeper. When at last I was admitted, the man I had come to see recognized me, though he was very cold. He knew everything that had happened.

"Of course, you cannot live here any longer," he said after I had told him of my desire to go elsewhere to find a position. "But where to go? It is very difficult. Your— what should we call her? Suppose we call her your friend. Do you know that she has died?"

I was speechless.

"Is it true?" I asked finally.

"Of course it is true. Our servant Wang Sheng comes from the same village as she did."

"But—how did she die?"

"Who knows? She just died, that's all."

I have forgotten how I left him and how I managed to get back to my lodgings. I knew that he was not one to tell stories. Tzu-chun would never come again to see me as she used to last year. Even if she had wished to walk along the so-called road of life with a heavy burden of emptiness on her back and with nothing to encourage her except harshness and cold glances, it was now no longer possible. Her fate was sealed when I presented her with the truth and she had died in a loveless world!

Of course I could no longer live here, but truly "where to go?"[2]

All around me was limitless emptiness and a deathly stillness. I seemed to see the blackness faced by those who die loveless and to hear the sound of their tragic and hopeless struggle.

I still waited for something to happen, something I could

[2] The repetition with quotation marks of the question that the narrator's friend put to him has the effect of emphasizing the helplessness of the situation and perhaps of the speaker's perfunctory solicitude. It is a device which Lusin uses frequently, though its full effect is not felt in translation.

not define, something I could not foresee. But day after day, day after day, there was only deathly stillness.

I went out even less than I used to do. I only sat and lay in a limitless expanse of emptiness and allowed the deathly stillness to eat away my soul. Sometimes this deathly stillness seemed to tremble for fear of itself, seemed to retire of its own will. It was at such times, when the deathly stillness was in temporary retirement, that the undefinable, unexpected new hope flashed before me.

One dark forenoon, before the sun had been able to struggle out from behind the clouds, when even the air seemed weary, I heard the patter of light footsteps and a sound of sniffing. I opened my eyes, and I glanced around the room; it was empty, as usual. But I chanced to look down, and there, curled up on the floor I saw a tiny creature, lean, weak, half dead and covered with dirt.

I steadied my glance and my heart stopped. I jumped up. It was Ah Sui. He had come back.

It was not only because of the chilly glances of the landlady and her maidservant that I left Chi-chao Hutung; it was mostly because of Ah Sui. But "where to go?" There were, indeed, many new roads to life of which I had some vague knowledge. Sometimes I seemed to catch actual glimpses of them right in front of my eyes; but I did not know the necessary first step which would enable me to break into those new regions.

After many deliberations and comparisons, the Guild appeared to be the most suitable place as far as lodgings were concerned. So I came here. It is the same dingy room, the same bed of boards, the same half-dead locust tree and wisteria, but that which used to fill me with hope, joy, love, and life is now entirely gone, leaving only an emptiness, an emptiness which I have exchanged for truth.

There are still many new roads to life and I must continue my quest as long as I live. But still I do not know how to take the first step toward those new roads. Sometimes the road to life appeared like a long white snake, wriggling and rushing toward me. I waited and waited but it disappeared into the darkness when it came close.

The spring nights grew longer; night after night, I sat and sat as if lost. One evening I recalled a funeral procession that I had seen on the street that morning. In front of the procession there were paper effigies of men and horses; in the rear walked the mourners uttering sing-song cries. How wise they were, what a simple and sensible way of treating death!

Then I had a vision of Tzu-chun's funeral: she bore, alone, the burden of emptiness as she went to her grave along the long gray road. But bitter as it was, this vision gave way to something even worse—the harsh judgment and chilly glances that followed her.

I wish there were such a thing as ghosts and spirits; I wish there were really such a thing as hell. Then, no matter how furiously the winds of hell roar, I shall go and look for Tzu-chun, and tell her of my sorrow and repentance and ask for her forgiveness. If this is impossible then let the vicious fires of hell enfold me and fiercely consume me and cleanse me of remorse and sorrow.

In the midst of the furious winds and vicious fires of hell, I would embrace Tzu-chun and beg for forgiveness; perhaps I would make her happy . . .

But speculations like these were even idler than thoughts of the new roads to life. The only thing I am sure of is that

spring nights are long. As long as I live, I must step onto
the new road to life, but the first step that I have been able
to take was only to write down my remorse and my sorrow,
for Tzu-chun and myself.

Like the mourners I saw this morning, I have nothing but
sing-song cries for Tzu-chun's burial, her burial in oblivion.
And I, too, want only oblivion; for my own sake I do not
even want to remember that I have had nothing better to
offer for Tzu-chun's burial than oblivion.

I want to take my first step onto the new road of life. I
want to hide truth deeply in the wounds of my heart and to
walk on silently and resolutely, with oblivion and falsehood
as my guide . . .

The Widow

THE YEAR-END according to the old calendar is, after all, more like what a year-end should be, for the holiday spirit is not only reflected in the life of the people, but seems to pervade the atmosphere itself. Frequent flashes light up the heavy, gray evening clouds, followed by the crisp report of firecrackers set off in honor of the Kitchen God. Those fired in the immediate neighborhood, explode of course, with a louder noise, and before the deafening sound has ceased ringing in one's ears, the air is filled with the acrid aroma of sulphuric smoke. On such an evening I returned for a visit to my native village, Luchen. As we no longer had a house there, I stayed with His Honor Lu the Fourth. He was my kin—my Uncle Four, as he was one generation above me—and a very moral and righteous old graduate. He had not changed much since my previous visit; he had grown a little older, but he did not yet have a beard. After we had exchanged greetings, he remarked that I was stouter, and immediately thereafter launched into a tirade against the reform movement. I knew, however, that his tirade was not directed against me but against the ancient reformers of the nineties, such as K'ang Yu-wei. In any case we could not be said to understand each other, and I was left alone in the study shortly afterwards.

I got up very late the next day. After the midday meal I went out to call on friends and relatives. On the third day

I did the same thing. None of them had changed much, they were merely a little older. All were busy with preparations for the Invocation of Blessings, the most solemn and elaborate ceremony of the year, at which they offered the most generous sacrifices to the God of Blessings and prayed for good luck for the coming year. Chickens and ducks were killed and pork was bought at the butcher's. Carefully washed by women (whose hands and arms—some adorned with silver bracelets—became red from long immersions in the water), and then boiled and studded with chopsticks, they were offered with candles and incense in the early hour of the fifth watch. Only the male members of the family participated in the ceremony, which was always concluded with firecrackers. Every year it was like this in families that could afford it, and so it was this year.

The overcast sky grew darker and darker, and in the afternoon it began to snow. The dancing snowflakes, as large as plum flowers, the smoke from burning incense and from the chimneys, and the bustle of the people all gave Luchen a festive air. When I returned to Uncle Four's study, the roof tops were white, making the room lighter than usual at that hour. I could make out very clearly the large *shou* [longevity] character on a scroll hung on the wall, a rubbing based on what was supposed to be the actual handwriting of the Taoist immortal Ch'en T'uan. One of the side scrolls had come off and lay loosely rolled up on the long table against the wall; the one still hanging on the wall expressed the sentiment "Peace comes with understanding." I strolled over to the desk by the window and looked over the books. There were only a few odd volumes of the K'ang Hsi Dictionary and an annotated edition of the *Analects*.

I decided that I must leave the next day, whatever happened. What had depressed me most was a meeting with Sister Hsiang-lin the day before. I encountered her in the afternoon as I was returning home along the river bank after visiting some friends in the eastern part of the village, and by the direction of her vacant stare I knew that she was heading for me. Of the people that I had seen at Luchen on this visit no one had changed as much as she. Her gray hair of five years ago had turned entirely white; she was not at all like a woman of only forty. Her face was intolerably drawn and thin; it had lost its sad and sorrowful aspect and was now as expressionless as if carved of wood. Only an occasional movement of her eyes indicated that she was still a living creature. She held in one hand a bamboo basket containing a chipped and empty bowl; with the other hand, she supported herself with a bamboo stick, a little split at the lower end. She had evidently become a beggar.

I stopped, expecting her to ask for money.

"Have you come back?" she asked.

"Yes."

"I am very glad. You are a scholar, and you have been to the outside world and learned of many things. I want to ask you about something." Her lusterless eyes suddenly lighted up, as she advanced a few steps towards me, lowered her voice, and said in a very earnest and confidential manner, "It is this: is there another life after this one?"

I was taken aback by the unexpectedness of the question; the wild look in her eyes, which were fixed on mine, gave me a creepy sensation on my back and made me feel more uncomfortable than I used to at school when an examination was sprung upon us, with the teacher watching vigilantly by our side. I had never concerned myself with the after life. How was I to answer her now? Most people here believe in the survival of the soul, I thought rapidly as I considered an answer, but this woman seemed to have her doubts. Perhaps it was a matter of hope with her, the hope that there was an after life and that the after life would be a better one than this. Why should I add to the unhappiness of this miserable woman? For her sake I had better say that there was another life after this one.

"Maybe there is . . . I think," I said haltingly and without conviction.

"Then there would also be a hell?"

"Oh! Hell?" I was again taken unawares and so I temporized, "Hell?—It would seem logical . . . though it may not necessarily exist . . . but who cares about such things?"

"Then we will meet members of our family after death?"

"Er, er, do we meet them?" I then realized that I was still a very ignorant man and that no amount of temporizing and cogitation would enable me to stand the test of three questions. I became less and less sure of myself and wished to recant all that I had said. "That . . . but really, I cannot say. I cannot really say whether souls survive or not."

Before she could ask any more questions, I fled back to Uncle Four's house, very much agitated in spirit. I told myself that my answer to her questions might lead to something unfortunate and that I should be held responsible for what might happen. She probably felt lonely and unhappy at a time when others were celebrating; but was that all, or had she formed a definite plan of action? Then I laughed at myself for taking such a trivial incident so seriously, for pondering upon it and analyzing it. The psychologists would undoubtedly call such a morbid interest or fear pathological. Besides, had I not explicitly said "I cannot really say," thus annulling all my answers and relieving myself of all responsibility?

"I cannot really say" is a very useful sentence. Inexperienced youths are often rash enough to give answers to the difficult problems of life and prescribe remedies for others, and thus lay themselves open to blame when things go wrong. If, however, they qualify their statements by concluding them with "I cannot really say," they will assure themselves of a safe and happy life. I then realized the indispensability of this sentence, indispensable even when one is talking with a beggarwoman.

But my uneasiness persisted; I kept recalling the meeting with a presentiment of evil. On this dark, heavy, snowy afternoon in that dreary study my uneasiness became stronger. I felt I had better go away and spend a day at the county seat. I recalled Fu-hsing-lou's excellent shark's fin cooked in clear broth at only a dollar a plate, and wondered if the price had gone up. Although my friends of former days had scattered hither and yon, I must not fail to feast upon this delicacy, even if I had to eat by myself. Whatever happens, I must leave this place tomorrow, I repeated to myself.

Because I have often seen things happen which I had hoped would not happen, which I had told myself might not necessarily happen, but which had a way of happening just the same, I was very much afraid that it would be so on this occasion. And surely something did happen, for towards evening I overheard a discussion going on in the inner courtyard. Presently it stopped, and after a silence I distinguished the voice of Uncle Four.

"Of course a *thing like that* would choose of all times a time like this."

I was first puzzled and then felt uncomfortable, for the

remark sounded as if it might have something to do with me. I looked out the door but did not see anyone that I could ask. Not until the hired man came in to replenish my tea toward suppertime did I have an opportunity to make inquiries.

"With whom was His Honor Four angry a little while ago?" I asked.

"Who else but Sister Hsiang-lin?" he answered very simply.

"Sister Hsiang-lin? What did she do?" I hurriedly pursued.

"She died."

"Died?" my heart sank and I almost jumped. My face must have changed color. But the man did not raise his head and so did not notice it. I calmed myself and continued:

"When did she die?"

"When? Last night or early this morning. I can't really say."

"What did she die of?"

"What did she die of? Why, what else would it be if not poverty?" the man answered in a matter of course way and went out without ever raising his head to look at me.

My terror was transient, for I realized that, since that which was to come to pass had come to pass, there was no longer need for me to worry about my responsibility. Gradually I regained my composure; a sense of regret and disquiet only occasionally intruded. Supper was served, with Uncle Four keeping me company. I wanted to find out more about Sister Hsiang-lin, but I knew that though he had read that "Ghosts and spirits are only the manifestations of the two cardinal principles of nature," he was still subject to many taboos; that such topics as sickness and death should be carefully avoided at a time when New Year blessings were about to be asked; and that if I must satisfy my curiosity, I should resort to some well-considered euphemism. As I unfortunately knew no such euphemisms, I withheld the question I was several times on the point of asking. From the look of displeasure on his face I began to imagine it quite possible that he considered me a "thing like that" for coming to bother him at such a time; thereupon I hastened to set him at ease and told him that I was going to leave Luchen the following day. He did not show much warmth in urging me to stay. Thus we dragged through supper.

Winter days are short at best, and, with snow falling, night soon enveloped the village. Every one was busy by the lamplight, but outdoors it was quiet and still. Falling upon a thick mattress of snow, the flakes seemed to swish-swish, making one feel all the more lonely and depressed. Sitting alone under the yellow light of the vegetable oil lamp, I thought of the fate of the poor, forlorn woman who had been cast into the garbage dump like a discarded toy. Hitherto she had continued to remind people of her miserable existence in the garbage dump, much to the surprise and wonder of those who have reason to find life worth living. Now she had at last been swept away clean by the Unpredictable. Whether souls continue to exist or not I do not know, but I did know that at least one who had no reason to find life worth living was at last no longer living and that those who looked upon her as an eyesore no longer had to look at her. It was a good thing, whether looked at from her point of view or from that of others. As I listened to the swish-swishing of the snowflakes outside and pondered along this line of thought I began to take comfort and to feel better.

And I began to put together the fragments that I had

heard about her until her story became a fairly coherent whole.

Sister Hsiang-lin was not a native of Luchen. One year in the early part of winter they needed a new maid at Uncle Four's and the middlewoman, old Mrs. Wei, had brought her. She wore a black skirt, a blue, lined coat and light blue vest, and her hair was tied with white strings as a sign of mourning. She was about twenty-six years old, of a dark yellow complexion, with a faint suggestion of color in her cheeks. Old Mrs. Wei called her Sister Hsiang-lin, said that she was a neighbor of her mother's and that as her husband had recently died she had come out to seek employment. Uncle Four frowned and Aunt Four guessed the cause; he did not like the idea of widows. But the woman had regular features and large, strong hands and feet. She was quiet and docile and it appeared that she would make an industrious and faithful servant. Aunt Four kept her in spite of Uncle Four's frown. During the trial period she worked all day as though unhappy without employment. She was strong and could do everything that a man could do. On the third day they decided to keep her, at the monthly wage of 500 *cash*.

Everyone called her Sister Hsiang-lin; no one asked her surname, but since the middlewoman was from Weichiashan and said that she was a neighbor of her mother's, her name was probably Wei. She was not talkative and spoke only in answer to questions, and that rather briefly. Not until after some ten days did it gradually become known that she had at home a stern mother-in-law, a brother-in-law about ten years old and able to go out to gather fuel, and that her husband who had died in the spring was ten years younger than she and also made his living by cutting firewood. This was all that was known about her.

The days went by quickly and she showed no signs of losing her initial industry; she never complained about her fare or spared her strength. People all talked about the woman help in the house of His Honor Lu who was more capable and industrious than a man. At the year-end she did all the cleaning, sweeping, and killed the chickens and ducks and cooked them; it was actually not necessary to hire temporary help. She seemed happy too; her face grew fuller and traces of smiles appeared around the corners of her mouth.

But shortly after the New Year she returned one day, pale and agitated, from washing rice at the river; she said she had seen a man who looked like an elder cousin-in-law loitering in the distance on the opposite bank, and she feared he was watching her. Aunt Four questioned her but could get no more out of her. When he heard of this incident, Uncle Four knitted his brows and said, "I do not like it. I am afraid that she ran away from home."

As a matter of fact, she had come away without her mother-in-law's permission, and it was not long before this supposition proved to be true.

About ten days later, when the incident had been almost forgotten, old Mrs. Wei suddenly appeared with a woman about thirty years old, whom she introduced as Sister Hsiang-lin's mother-in-law. Though dressed like a woman from the hill villages, she was self composed and capable of speech. She apologized for her intrusion and said that she had come to take her daughter-in-law home to help with the spring chores, as only she and her young son were at home.

"What else can we do since her mother-in-law wants her back?" Uncle Four said.

Therefore, her wages, which amounted to 1,750 *cash* and of which she had not spent a penny, were handed over to the mother-in-law. The woman took Sister Hsiang-lin's clothes, expressed her thanks, and went away.

Sister Hsiang-lin was not present during this transaction and it did not occur to Aunt and Uncle Four to summon her. It was not until toward noon when she began to feel hungry that Aunt Four suddenly remembered that Sister Hsiang-lin had gone out to wash rice and wondered what had happened to her.

"Aiya! Where is the rice?" she exclaimed. "Did not Sister Hsiang-lin go out to wash the rice?"

She began searching for the washing basket, first in the kitchen, then in the courtyard, then in the bedroom, but there was no trace of it. Uncle Four looked outside the gate but did not see it either, and it was not until he went to the river that he saw the basket resting peacefully on the bank, a head of green vegetable beside it.

Then he learned from eyewitnesses what had happened. A covered boat had been moored in the river all morning, but no one paid any attention to it at the time. When Sister Hsiang-lin came out to wash rice, two men that looked like people from the hills, jumped out, seized her as she bent over her task and dragged her into the boat. Sister Hsiang-lin uttered a few cries but was soon silent, probably because she was gagged. Then two women embarked, one a stranger and the other old Mrs. Wei. Some thought that they did see Sister Hsiang-lin lying bound on the bottom of the boat.

"The rascals! But . . . ," Uncle Four said.

That day Aunt Four cooked the midday dinner herself, while her son Niu-erh tended the fire.

Old Mrs. Wei returned after the midday dinner.

"What do you mean by your outrageous behavior? And you have the audacity to come back to see us!" Aunt Four said vehemently over the dish-washing. "You brought her here yourself, and then you conspire with them to kidnap her, causing such a scandal. What will people say? Do you want to make a laughingstock of us?"

"Aiya, aiya! I was duped, really, and I have come back to explain. She came to me and asked me to find a place for her. How was I to know that her mother-in-law knew nothing of it? I beg your forgiveness. It was all my fault, old and weak woman that I am. I should have been more careful. Fortunately, your house has been noted for its generosity and I know you would not return measure for measure with people like us. I shall most certainly find you a good maid to atone for myself."

Thus the episode was closed and shortly afterwards forgotten.

Only Aunt Four, who had difficulty in finding a satisfactory servant, sometimes mentioned Sister Hsiang-lin, whose successors either were lazy or complained of their food, or both. "I wonder what has become of her," Aunt Four would say, hoping that she might come back again. By the beginning of the following year she gave up this hope.

Toward the end of the first month, however, old Mrs. Wei came to offer her New Year's greetings. She was slightly intoxicated with wine and said that she had been late in coming because she had visited her mother at Weichiashan for a few days. The conversation naturally turned to Sister Hsiang-lin.

"That one. She has entered her lucky years," old Mrs. Wei said with pleasure. "When her mother-in-law came to get her, she was already promised to Huo Lao-lui of Huo-chiatsun and so a few days after her return she was put into a wedding sedan and carried away."

"Aiya! what a mother-in-law!" Aunt Four said, surprised.

"Aiya! you talk exactly like a lady of a great family. Among us poor people in the hills this is nothing. She has a younger brother-in-law who had to get married. If they did not marry her off where were they to get the money for his wedding? Her mother-in-law was a capable and clever one. She knew how to go about things. She married her off into the hills. In the village, she would not have gotten much for Sister Hsiang-lin, but because there are not many who will marry into the hills, she got 80,000 *cash*. Now her second son is married. She spent only 50,000 and had a clear profit of over 10,000 after expenses. See what a good stroke of business that was?"

"But how could Sister Hsiang-lin ever consent to such a thing?"

"What is there to consent or not to consent? Any bride will make a scene; but all one has to do is bind her up, stuff her into the sedan, carry her to the groom's house, put the bridal hat on her, assist her through the ceremony, put her into the bridal chamber, shut the door—and leave the rest to the groom. But Sister Hsiang-lin was different and unusually difficult. People said it was probably because she had worked in the house of a scholar that she acted differently from the common people. *Tai-tai,* we have seen all sorts of them, these 'again' women; we have seen the kind that weep and cry, the kind that attempt suicide, and the kind that spoil the wedding ceremony by upsetting and breaking things. But Sister Hsiang-lin was worse than any of these. I was told that she bellowed and cursed all the way, so that she had lost her voice when she reached the Huo village. Dragging her out of the sedan, three men were not enough to hold her through the ceremony. Once they loosed their hold on her for a moment, and—*Amitofo*—she dashed her head against the corner of the wedding table, and gave herself a big gash. The blood flowed so freely that two handfuls of incense ash and a bandage could not stop it. She continued to curse after she had been dragged into the wedding chamber and shut in with her man. Aiya-ya, I never . . ." She shook her head, lowered her eyes and was silent for a moment.

"And later?" Aunt Four asked.

"It was said that she did not get up all the next day," she answered, raising her eyes.

"And after that?"

"Well, she got up eventually and by the end of the year she gave birth to a boy. Someone happened to visit the Huo village while I was at my mother's and said on his return that he had seen the mother and the child and that they were both healthy and plump. There is no mother-in-law above her and her man is strong and a willing worker. They have their own house. Ai-ai, she has entered her lucky years."

After that Aunt Four no longer mentioned Sister Hsiang-lin.

But in the fall of one year—it must have been two years after the news of Sister Hsiang-lin's good luck was brought by Mrs. Wei—she reappeared in the courtyard of Uncle Four's house. She put on the table a round basket in the form of a water chestnut and outside under the eaves she left her bundle of bedding. She wore, as on her first visit, white hairstrings, black skirt, blue, lined coat, light blue vest, and her skin was dark yellow as before, but without any trace of color in her cheeks. Instead, traces of tears could be observed around her eyes, which were not as alive as before. Old Mrs. Wei again accompanied her and made this recital to Aunt Four:

"This is truly what is called 'Heaven has unpredictable storms.' Her man was a strong and sturdy one. Who would ever have thought that he would die of influenza? He had gotten well, but he ate a bowl of cold rice and it came back again. Fortunately she had her son and she was capable, could cut firewood, pick tea, or raise silkworms. She was managing all right. Who would ever have thought that her child would be carried off by a wolf? Spring was nearing its end and yet a wolf appeared in the village. Who would have thought of such a thing? Now she is alone. Her elder brother-in-law took possession of her house and put her out. She is now at the end of her road and has no other way except to appeal to her old mistress. Now she has no entanglements and as *tai-tai* happens to be in need of a new maid I have brought her. I think as she is familiar with things here she would be much better than a strange hand."

"I was a fool, really," Sister Hsiang-lin raised her lusterless eyes and said. "I knew that the wild beasts came down to the village to seek food when they couldn't find anything in the hills during the snow season, but I did not know they would come down in the spring. I got up early and opened the door. I gave a basket of beans to our Ah Mao and told him to sit on the gate sill and peel them. He was an obedient child and did everything I told him. He went out and I went behind the house to cut wood and wash rice. After putting the rice in the pot, I wanted to put the beans over it to steam. I called Ah Mao but he did not answer. I went out and looked. I saw beans spilled all over the ground but could not see our Ah Mao. He never went out to play at the neighbors' but I went and looked for him. I did not find him. I was frightened and asked people to go out and search for him. In the afternoon they found one of his shoes in the bramble. They all said that there was no hope, that the wolf must have got him. They went into the bush and sure enough they found him lying in the grass, all his insides gone, his hand still holding on tightly to the handle of the basket . . ." She broke off sobbing.

Aunt Four hesitated at first, but her eyes reddened after hearing the story. Then she told Sister Hsiang-lin to take the basket and bundle to the maid's room. Old Mrs. Wei sighed with relief, and Sister Hsiang-lin seemed to feel better than when she arrived. As she was familiar with the house, she went and set her things in order without being directed, and thenceforward she again became a maidservant at Luchen.

And everybody called her Sister Hsiang-lin as before.

But this time her fortune had changed considerably. Two or three days later her employers realized that her hands were not as clever and efficient as formerly, her memory failed, her deathlike face never showed the shadow of a smile. Aunt Four could not conceal her displeasure. Uncle Four had frowned as usual when she came, but made no protest as he knew how difficult it was to find a satisfactory servant; he only cautioned Aunt Four, saying that though such people were a pitiable lot, yet she was after all a bane against morality, and that it was all right for her to help in ordinary tasks but she must not touch anything in connection with the ancestral sacrifices. These Aunt Four must prepare herself, else they would be unclean and the ancestors would not touch them.

Preparation of the ancestral sacrifices was the most important event in Uncle Four's house and Sister Hsiang-lin used to be busiest at such a time. Now she had nothing to do. When the table was placed in the center of the hall with a curtain in front of it, she started to arrange the wine cups and chopsticks as she used to do.

"Sister Hsiang-lin, please leave those things alone. I will arrange them," Aunt Four hastened to say.

She drew back her hands in embarrassment and then went to get the candlesticks.

"Sister Hsiang-lin, leave that alone. I'll get it," Aunt Four again said hastily. After hovering around for a little while, Sister Hsiang-lin withdrew in bewilderment. The only thing she was permitted to do that day was to tend the fire in the kitchen.

People in the village still called her Sister Hsiang-lin, but the tone of their voices was different; they still talked with her, but they were scornful of her. She did not seem to notice the change; she only stared vacantly and recited the story that she could not forget, night or day ——

"I was a fool, really . . ." Her tears would flow and her voice grow tremulous.

It was a very effective story; men would stop smiling and walk away in confusion; women not only seemed to forgive her and to banish the look of scorn on their faces, but shed tears with her. Some older women, not having heard her own recital, would come to her and listen to her until her voice broke, when they would let fall the tears that had been gradually accumulating in their eyes, heave some sighs and go away satisfied. She was their chief topic of conversation.

Sister Hsiang-lin continued to repeat her story and often attracted three or five listeners. But the story soon became familiar to everyone, and after a while even the kindest and most patient of old ladies ceased to shed any tears. Still later almost everyone in the village could recite her story, and was bored by it.

"I was really a fool, really," she would begin.

"Yes, you knew that wild beasts came down to the village to seek food only when they cannot find anything in the hills," people would thus stop her and walk away.

She would stand gaping and staring for a while and then walk away, a little embarrassed. Still, she tried to bring up the story of Ah Mao by some ruse—a basket, beans, or some other children. For instance, if she saw a child two or three years old, she would say, "Ai-ai, if our Ah Mao were alive he would be as big as that . . ."

The children were afraid of her and of the look in her eyes, and they would tug at their mothers' coats and urge them to go away. And thus Sister Hsiang-lin would be left alone to wander off by herself. Soon people caught on to her new trick; they would forestall her when there were children around by saying, "Sister Hsiang-lin, if your Ah Mao were alive, would he not be as big as that?"

She might not have realized that her sorrow, after having been carefully chewed and relished for so long, had now become insipid dregs, only fit to spit out; but she was able to sense the indifference and the sarcasm in the question and to realize that there was no need of her answering it.

The New Year festivities last a long time in Luchen and begin to occupy people after the twentieth of the last month of the year. At Uncle Four's house they had to hire a temporary man helper, but the work was too much for him and another woman was hired. But she, Liu-ma, was a devout vegetarian and would not kill the chickens and ducks; she only washed dishes. Sister Hsiang-lin had nothing to do but tend the fire. She sat and watched Liu-ma wash the dishes. A light snow was falling outside.

"Ai-ai, I was really a fool," Sister Hsiang-lin soliloquized after looking at the sky, sighing.

"Sister Hsiang-lin, there you go again," Liu-ma looked at her impatiently. "Let me ask you, did you not get your scar when you dashed your head against the table that time?"

"Mmm," she answered evasively.

"Let me ask you, why did you finally give in?"

"I?"

"Yes, you. I think you must have been willing. Otherwise . . ."

"Ah-ah, but you do not know how strong he was."

"I do not believe it. I do not believe that a strong woman like you could not resist him. You must have finally become willing though you now blame it on his strength."

"Ah-ah you . . . you should have tried to resist him yourself," she said with a smile.

Liu-ma laughed, her wrinkled face shriveling up like a peach stone; her tiny dry eyes shifted from the scar on Sister Hsiang-lin's forehead to the latter's eyes, discomforting her and causing her to gather up her smile and turn her eyes to look at the snowflakes.

"Sister Hsiang-lin, you have miscalculated badly," Liu-ma said mysteriously. "You should have resisted to the end, or dashed your head until you were dead. That would have been the thing to do. But now? You lived with your second man only two years and got for it a monstrous evil name. Just think, when you get to the lower world, those two ghost husbands will fight over you. Whom would they give you to? The Great King Yenlo could only have you sawed in two and divided between them . . ."

Sister Hsiang-lin was terrified: this was something that she had not heard about in the hills.

"I think you should atone for your crime while there is still time. Donate a doorsill to the T'u-ti temple as your effigy, so that you might be trampled upon by a thousand men's feet and straddled over by ten thousand men's legs as atonement for your great sin. Then you may escape the tortures in store for you."

Sister Hsiang-lin did not say anything then, but she must have been deeply affected. The next day she got up with black rings around her eyes. After breakfast she went to the T'u-ti temple on the western edge of the village to donate the doorsill. At first the keeper would not accept the gift, but her tears and entreaties finally prevailed and he accepted the offer at the price of 12,000 *cash*.

She had not spoken with anyone for a long time, for she had become an avoided object because of the tiresome story about her Ah Mao; nevertheless, after her conversation with Liu-ma—which seemed to have been broadcast immediately—people began to take a new interest in her and would try to coax her to talk. As to the subject, it was naturally a new one, centering upon the scar on her forehead.

"Sister Hsiang-lin, let me ask you, why did you finally give in?" one would say.

"Ai, too bad you broke your head for nothing," another would echo, looking at her scar.

From their faces and voices she gathered that they were making fun of her; she only stared vacantly and said nothing, later she did not even turn her head. She tightened her mouth and went about her duties—sweeping, washing vegetables and rice, running errands, bearing the scar of her shame. In about a year, she got all the wages that Aunt Four had kept for her, changed them into twelve Mexican dollars, asked for leave to go to the western edge of the village. She soon returned and told Aunt Four that she had donated her doorsill at the T'u-ti temple. She appeared to be in better spirits than she had been for a long time and her eyes showed signs of life.

She worked unusually hard at the ancestral sacrifices at the winter solstice. After watching Aunt Four fill the dishes with the sacrificial things and Ah Niu place the table in the center of the hall, she went confidently to get the wine cups and chopsticks.

"Don't you bother, Sister Hsiang-lin!" Aunt Four said in a panicky voice.

She withdrew her hands as if from a hot iron, her face black and pale like burnt coal. She did not try to get the candlesticks. She only stood as if lost, and did not go away until Uncle Four came in to light the incense sticks and dismissed her. This time the change in her was extraordinary. Not only were her eyes sunken the next day, but her wits seemed to have left her entirely. She became terribly afraid, not only of the night and dark corners, but also of people, including her own employers. She would sneak about, trembling like a mouse that had ventured out of its hole in daylight; or she would sit abstractedly like a wooden idol. In less than half a year, her hair became gray, her memory grew worse and worse, until she sometimes forgot to go out to wash rice in the river.

"What is the matter with Sister Hsiang-lin? We should not

have kept her in the first place," Aunt Four would say sometimes, in her hearing, as a warning to her.

But she continued in the same condition, and showed no signs of recovering her wits. They began to think of sending her away, to tell her to go back to old Mrs. Wei. When I was still living at Luchen they used to talk of sending her away, but they only talked about it; from what I saw on this visit, it was evident that they did finally carry out their threat. But whether she became a beggar immediately after leaving Uncle Four's house or whether she first went to old Mrs. Wei and then became a beggar, I could not say.

I was awakened by loud explosions of firecrackers close by. As I blinked at the yellow lamp flame about the size of a bean I heard the crackling of a string of firecrackers—the New Year's ceremony was on at Uncle Four's and I knew that it must be about the fifth watch. With half-shut eyes I heard dreamily the continued crackling in the distance; it seemed to form a thick cloud of festive sounds in the sky, mingling with the snowflakes and enveloping the entire village. In the arms of this festive sound, I felt carefree and comfortable, and the fears and melancholy I had felt all the previous day and the first part of the night were swept away by this atmosphere of joy and blessedness. I fancied that the gods and sages of heaven above and earth below, drunk and satiated with incense and sacrifices of wine and meat, were reeling unsteadily in the sky, ready to confer unlimited blessings upon the inhabitants of Luchen.

The Diary of a Madman

THE BROTHERS —— (I shall not mention their names) were good friends of mine in my old middle-school days but I had not seen them for many years and had gradually lost track of them. Recently I heard that one of them was seriously ill, and as I happened to be visiting my native heath, I went to call on them. I saw only one of them and he told me that it was his younger brother who had been ill. He thanked me for coming such a long way to inquire after his brother and said that the latter had recovered and had gone to a certain district to await appointment. He laughed as he showed me two volumes of diaries which his brother had kept during his illness, saying that I, an old friend of theirs, might as well have them and see for myself what manner of illness it was. I took the volumes home and after going over them decided that he must have suffered an attack of what is known as persecution phobia.

The writing was confused and incoherent and full of wild and extraordinary fancies. There were no dates, but from the lack of uniformity in the shade of ink and in the style of calligraphy, it was evident that the entries covered quite a period of time. Occasionally there were passages with some degree of coherence. I transcribe here some of these passages and present them for the study of the medical world. I have not changed anything in matters of fact and style but have altered all the personal names, though they happen to be those of villagers unknown to the outside world and it is of no consequence one way or another. As to the title, it is the author's own choice after his recovery.

April 2, 1918

1.

The moon is very beautiful tonight.

Since it was over thirty years ago that I saw it last, the sight of it makes me feel particularly good. Now I realize that for the last thirty years or more I have been living in ignorance and darkness. But I must be on my guard. Did not Chao's dog look at me with malignant eyes?

I have good reason to be afraid.

2.

There is no moonlight at all tonight and I know that this bodes ill. Even as I went out cautiously this morning I was struck by something strange about Chao Kuei-weng's behavior. He looked as if he were afraid of me, as if thinking of doing me harm. Seven or eight other men were whispering among themselves about me, though they tried to appear innocent. Everyone I met on the street acted the same way. One of the most vicious among them opened his mouth and grinned at me; I shivered from head to heels, for I realized that their plans were set and they were about ready to strike.

But I walked on unafraid. Then I came to a group of children, also talking about me, their eyes exactly like those of Chao Kuei-weng and their faces blue like steel. What grudge do they hold against me, I thought, that they should act like this? I could not refrain from shouting at them, "Now tell me!" But they ran away.

What enmity is there between Chao Kuei-weng and my-self, I thought, what enmity is there between me and the people on the street? I can remember only one thing. Twenty years ago I trampled the daily account book[1] of Mr. Hoary Tradition under my feet, a deed which he greatly resented. Although Chao Kuei-weng did not know Mr. Hoary Tradition, he must have heard of the incident and in his indignation must have turned the people on the street against me. But how about the children? They were not even born at the time; why should they stare at me today with such fearful eyes, as if afraid of me and thinking of doing me harm? This frightens and puzzles me and makes me sad.

I understand now! Their mothers and fathers must have told them!

3.

I cannot sleep at night. One must study a thing before one can understand it.

They—some of them—have been bambooed and put into cangues by the magistrate, some have been slapped in the face by the gentry, some have had their wives assaulted by the constables, and some have seen their parents hounded to death by creditors; but their faces were never so fearful and menacing then as they were yesterday.

The strangest thing of all was that the woman who was beating her son on the street yesterday should have had her eyes fixed on me when she cursed her son, saying, "Your father's ——, I won't feel right until I have taken a few bites at you!" I started violently and could not hide my fear. At

---

[1] An allusion to the Classics, which have been characterized by their critics as of no more value and no more edifying than the account book kept by shopkeepers.

this the ghoulish crowd, with blue faces and protruding tusks, burst into laughter.

Just then Chen Lao-wu caught up with me and forcibly dragged me home.

After I was dragged home, everyone pretended not to know me; their eyes were like those of everyone else. As soon as they got me into the study, they closed the door and chained it from the outside as if they were shutting up a chicken or a duck. The more I thought about this the more befuddled I became.

A few days ago a tenant from the Wolf Village came to complain of hard times and told my elder brother that a very wicked man in the village had been beaten to death by the villagers and that some of the men had taken out his heart and fried it in oil and had eaten it in the belief that this would give them more courage. When I put in a few words in protest against this savage practice, both the tenant and my brother gave me a hard look.

I suddenly realized that their eyes were the same as those of the people on the street.

When I think about this, I become cold from head to feet.

If they ate another human being, it is not at all inconceivable that they might eat me.

All signs point to this possibility: remember what the woman said about biting off a few pieces of her son's flesh, remember the fiendish glee of the crowd with blue faces and protruding tusks, remember the story told by the tenant the other day. I see venom in their words and knives behind their laughter; their teeth, white and menacing, are those of cannibals.

I did not think that I could be considered a wicked man, but since I trampled Mr. Hoary Tradition's book under my feet, I am no longer so sure. They seem to think so, though I cannot really fathom their thoughts. They have a way of branding anyone they don't like as a wicked man. I still remember how my elder brother, when he was teaching me composition, used to reward me with circles of approval when I criticized the good and to commend me on my cleverness and originality when I spoke a few words for the wicked. How can I guess just what is in their minds, especially when they want to eat human flesh?

One must study things before one can understand them. I thought I had read somewhere that man-eating was a common practice in ancient times, but I was not sure. I decided to look it up in my history. This history contained no dates, but over every page was scrawled the words "Benevolence and Righteousness." It was not until I had read half through the night (I could not sleep anyway) that I began to make out the words hidden between the lines and to discover that the book was nothing but a record of man-eating!

It was written in the book and hinted at by the tenant, and they all looked at me with such strange eyes—though they smiled all the time!

Since I am a man, they are probably thinking of eating me!

4.

I sat quietly for a while this morning. Chen Lao-wu brought in my meal, a bowl of vegetables and a bowl of steamed fish. The fish's eyes were hard and white, its mouth was open, as is the case with people who are thinking of eating human flesh. I ate a few pieces, but I could not tell whether the slippery stuff was fish or man, and I threw up everything.

I said, "Lao-wu, tell my brother that I feel stifled in here and want to go into the garden for a walk." Lao-wu went out without answering, but after a while he came back and opened the door.

I did not move, for I was sure that they would not abandon their evil course and I wanted to see just how they were going to manage me. I was right. My brother came in slowly with an old man, who, being afraid that I would see the wicked light in his eyes, looked down at the ground and stole glances at me over the edges of his spectacles. "You seem to look very well today," my brother said. I answered "Yes." My brother said, "We have asked Dr. Ho to come and take a look at you." I said, "All right!" but did I not know that this old man was in reality the executioner in disguise! He had only come to feel how fat I was under the pretext of feeling my pulse, so that he could share a piece of flesh as a reward. Not wishing to spoil their little game for the moment, I gave the old man my hands, which I had involuntarily tightened into fists, and waited to see what he was going to do. The old man sat there with his eyes closed and felt my hand and meditated for a long while. Then he opened his ghostly eyes and said, "Do not worry too much. You will be all right after resting quietly for a few days."

Do not worry too much and rest quietly! Of course! They will have more to eat after I grow fat with rest! What is "all right" about that as far as I am concerned? These people want to eat human flesh but they are so timid and afraid, so anxious to hide their designs, so unwilling to strike an open and direct blow. They make me laugh. And so, unable to restrain myself, I burst into laughter and the laughter did me good. I knew that there was in this laughter courage and righteousness. The old man and my brother both paled; they were cowed by my courage and righteousness.

But the more courage I had the more they would want to eat me in order to partake of my courage. The old man stepped outside the door and before they had walked very far, he whispered to my brother, "Must be eaten[2] without delay!" My brother nodded assent. And so you are in it too! This was a great discovery. Though it seems unthinkable, it is really quite possible that my own brother has been conspiring with the others to eat me.

So my brother is a man-eater!

And I am a man-eater's brother!

Though I may be eaten up by man-eaters, I shall nevertheless be the brother of a man-eating man!

5.

I have been trying to make a concession these last few days and grant that the old man was not an executioner in disguise but was really a doctor. Even then he may still be a man-eating man. For since it is clearly stated in the *Pen Ts'ao* something or other[3] written by Li Shih-chen, the father of his profession, that human flesh could be boiled and eaten, how could he deny that he does not eat human beings himself?

Neither do I unjustly suspect my own brother. When he was teaching me, he said with his own mouth that during times of famine people "exchanged their children to eat"; and once in discussing a certain wicked man he said that he not only deserved death, but also deserved to have his "flesh eaten and his skin slept upon." I was young then and my heart beat wildly for a long time. A few days ago when the

[2] *Ch'ih,* to eat, is used also in the sense of taking medicine.

[3] That is, the *Pen Ts'ao Kang Mu,* the Chinese *Materia Medica* as revised and enlarged by Li Shih-chen.

tenant of the Wolf Village came and told about that horrible affair, he did not appear to be shocked in the least, but repeatedly nodded his head with approval. From this one can see that he is still as inhuman as ever. Since one may exchange one's children to eat, one may exchange anyone and eat anybody. I used to listen to his high-sounding discourses attentively and to take them at their face value; but I now realize that when he was thus holding forth, not only was his heart filled with the desire to eat human flesh but his lips were actually greased with human fat!

6.

It is thickly dark. I do not know whether it is day or night. That dog of the Chao's is barking again.

As vicious as lions, as timid as rabbits, as cunning as foxes . . .

7.

I know their plot now; they will not and dare not kill me outright for fear of the consequences, but they will try to drive me to suicide by every trick they know. I need only recall the behavior of the men and women on the street to realize this. It would suit them best if I should take off my waistband, tie it to the beam and hang myself; they would then obtain their wish without being charged with murder. What rejoicing and ghoulish laughter there would be! Or they might frighten and torture me to death; they could still have a few bites apiece though I should be somewhat leaner.

They are only capable of eating dead men's flesh! I recall reading somewhere about a loathsome animal known as the hyena; its eyes and features are revolting to see, and it not only feeds on dead men's flesh but chews up and swallows even the biggest bones. It is fearful to think of. The hyena is a relative of the wolf and the wolf is kin to the dog. The other day Chao's dog eyed me several times, which proves that it is also in the plot.

The old man could not deceive me though he kept his eyes on the ground.

The most despicable of all is my elder brother. Why is it that though a human being himself, he has not the least fear of man-eating, but is, on the contrary, conspiring to eat me? Is it because he is used to it and does not realize that it is wrong, or is it because he has lost his conscience and would knowingly commit a wrong?

I shall begin with him in cursing man-eating men; I shall also begin with him in converting man-eating men from their wicked ways.

8.

But they must know these things already . . .

One day a man came to me. He was about twenty years old. His features were somewhat indistinct. He smiled and nodded to me, but his smile was not natural. I asked him, "Is it right to eat human beings?" He said, still smiling, "This is not a year of famine, how could such a thing occur?" I realized immediately that he was also of the same gang, that he also liked to eat human flesh. I became a hundred times bolder and insisted:

"But is it right?"

"What's the use of asking such a question? You certainly can say the strangest things . . . Nice weather we are having today."

The weather was nice and the moon very bright, but I insisted: "But is it right?"

He did not seem to like this and answered vaguely, "No . . ."

"Not right? Then why do they persist in it?"

"That is not true . . ."

"Not true? Why, only recently it happened in the Wolf Village, and it is written in all the books, red, blood-red!"

His countenance changed, blue like steel, and he said with a wild look in his eyes, "Maybe so, but this has always been so . . ."

"Does that make it right?"

"I don't want to argue with you about these things. You should not talk about them; it is wrong of you to do it!"

I jumped up and opened my eyes, only to find that the man had disappeared and that I was bathed in sweat. He was much younger than my brother but he was of the same gang. His father and mother must have corrupted him, and I am afraid that he has already corrupted his children; that is why even the children stare at me with such a wicked light in their eyes.

9.

Everyone wants to eat others but is afraid of being eaten himself, and so everyone looks at everyone else with such profound distrust and suspicion . . .

What a relief it would be if everyone banished such thoughts from his mind and went about his work and ate and slept with a carefree heart! It takes but little effort to step over this obstacle that bars the gateway to freedom, and yet they—parents and children, brothers and sisters, husbands and wives, teachers and pupils, friends and enemies and strangers—they all band together, encourage and restrain one another, and refuse to step over this one barrier even till death.

10.

Early in the morning I went to see my brother, who was standing outside the front hall gazing at the sky. I went up to him and with my back to the door said in an unusually calm and peaceful manner, "Brother, I have something to say to you."

"Please go ahead," he replied, turning around abruptly and nodding.

"I have only a few words but I find it difficult to say them. Brother, in the beginning all the savages probably ate a little human flesh. Later on, some of them gave up this practice because their hearts were different. They tried their best to improve themselves and they became human, real human beings, while others continued to eat human flesh. The case of these savages is similar to that of the insects, some of which became fish and birds and monkeys and eventually men, while others did not try to better themselves and remained insects. How shameful are the men who eat men compared with those who do not: their shame must be even greater than the shame that the insects feel toward the monkeys.

"It is true that it was a long, long time ago that Yi-ya steamed up his own son for Chieh and Chou[4] to eat; the trouble is that people have continued to eat one another from the creation of heaven and earth by P'an Ku to the son

[4] The legend alluded to here actually centers around King Wen. When he was served with his own son's flesh by the tyrant Chou, he pretended not to know the truth. Had he betrayed the intuition that was attributed to him as a great sage, Chou would have murdered him as a potential rival.

of Yi-ya, and from the son of Yi-ya to Hsu Hsi-lin[5] and from Hsu Hsi-lin to the man they caught in the Wolf Village. Only last year when a prisoner was executed in the city, a man with tuberculosis dipped a roll in the victim's blood and ate it.[6]

"Now they want to eat me. I can well understand that you cannot stop them all by yourself. But why must you join their conspiracy? What will men who eat men be incapable of! If they can eat me, they can eat you and eat one another. All that is needed to bring about peace and goodwill to all is a desire to better oneself, to take one step in the right direction. The world may have always been what it is, but that does not mean that we should not try to make it better than it has been. You say it is impossible? Brother, I believe that you are capable of saying that. You said it was impossible the other day when the tenant asked for a reduction of rent!"

At first he only smiled coldly, but his eyes gradually became fierce and cruel, and when I laid bare his secret his whole face became blue. The crowd that had been standing outside the gate—including Chao Kuei-weng and his dog—had gradually edged their way in. The features of some of them could not be made out; they were as if covered with gauze; others were still blue-faced and tusked, smiling gloatingly. I recognized them to be of the same gang, all of them men who ate other men, though their opinions about it differed: some felt that it had always been so and

[5] Revolutionary executed in 1907. His body was reported mutilated and his heart devoured by the bodyguards of the Manchu official whom he had assassinated.

[6] This incident forms the central theme in "Medicine," included in Snow's *Living China*.

that it was as it should be, while others knew that it was wrong, but wanted to eat just the same. The latter were more sensitive to my exposure of their plot, so on hearing what I said, they became furious, though they only smiled coldly.

At this point my brother suddenly assumed a fierce air and shouted loudly, "Get out, all of you! What is there to see about a madman?"

Then I discovered another of their clever schemes. They not only would not change their ways, but they had carefully laid their plot so as to stigmatize me as a madman. Then after they had eaten me, they would not only go free but might even be thanked for it. The people of the Wolf Village branded their victim as a wicked man, when they wanted to feast upon him. This was an old trick with them.

Chen Lao-wu also came in glowering with great indignation. But he could not stop me from speaking. I insisted on speaking to these people, and I said, "You must repent, repent from the bottom of your hearts! You must know that there will be no place in the world of the future for man-eating men. If you do not change, you will eat up one another. However fertile you may be, in the end men that are really human beings will annihilate you, as hunters annihilate the wolves! You will be just like the insects!"

The crowd was driven off by Chen Lao-wu. My brother disappeared I knew not where. Chen Lao-wu persuaded me to go back to my room. All was dark in the room. The cross-beam and the rafters shook over me; and after shaking for a while, they grew bigger and piled themselves upon me. They were so heavy that I could not stir. They, too, wanted me to die. I knew their weight was false, and so I wriggled out. I sweated all over. I said, "You must all change at once, change from the bottom of your hearts. You must know that the future has no place for man-eating men . . ."

11.

I know now that they ate my younger sister.

The sun did not come out and the door did not open. Every day two meals were brought to me.

As soon as I picked up the chopsticks, I would think of my brother; and I knew that he was solely responsible for the death of my sister. She was only five years old, and her adorable face is still vivid in my memory. Mother cried incessantly, but he persuaded her not to cry, probably because it made him uncomfortable since he himself had eaten her up. If he still felt the prick of his conscience . . .

Whether or not mother knew that sister was eaten up by brother was something that I shall never know.

Maybe mother knew but did not say anything because she also felt that it was as it should be. I recall that when I was four or five years old we were once sitting in the courtyard to keep cool. Brother said that when parents were sick, the children must, if they wanted to be filial, cut off a piece of their own flesh and boil it and offer it to them to eat.[7] Mother did not say that that would not do. If it was all right to eat a slice, it was all right to eat a whole human being. But the way she cried that day was most heartbreaking. It moves me still as I recall it now.

It is a very strange world indeed!

12.

I must not think about it any longer.

[7] There is a superstition that such an act of piety would move the gods and bring about the recovery of the parents.

Only today do I realize that this world in which I have moved about for half a lifetime has been for over four thousand years a man-eating world. Brother was at the time of sister's death in charge of the affairs of the family. It is not at all impossible that he had mixed her flesh in the food and gave us to eat of it without our knowledge.

It is not at all impossible that I had myself eaten a few slices of my sister's flesh! And now it has come to be my turn . . .

Although I have a tradition of four thousand years of man-eating, I did not know till now how difficult it is to find a true and innocent man.

13.

Maybe there are still some infants that have not yet eaten men.

Save, save the infants . . .

DATE DUE

1/20			
GAYLORD			PRINTED IN U.S.A.